# DODECAHEDRON

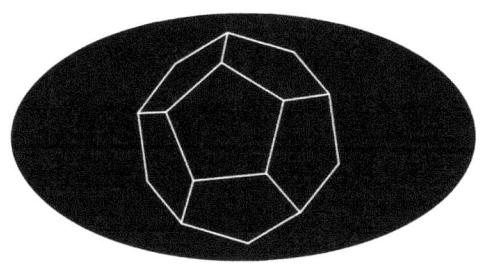

### THE STORY
### OF THE
### SECOND STONE

# Dodecahedron

Emmanuel C Lachlan

Copyright © Emmanuel C Lachlan 2023

All rights reserved. No part of this publication may be reproduced, stored in a retrieval system or transmitted in any form or by any means electronic, mechanical, audio, visual or otherwise, without prior permission of the copyright owner. Nor can it be circulated in any form of binding or cover other than that in which it is published and without similar conditions including this condition being imposed on the subsequent purchaser.

ISBN: 978-1-7391397-7-3

Written by Emmanuel C Lachlan and published by Emmanuel C Lachlan Publishing in association with Writersworld, this book is produced entirely in the UK, is available to order from most book shops in the United Kingdom, and is globally available via UK-based Internet book retailers.

Cover Design: Emmanuel C Lachlan and Jag Lall

Copy editor: Sue Croft

WRITERSWORLD
2 Bear Close, Woodstock,
Oxfordshire
OX20 1JX
United Kingdom
www.writersworld.co.uk

The text pages of this book are produced via an independent certification process that ensures the trees from which the paper is produced comes from well managed sources that exclude the risk of using illegally logged timber while leaving options to use post-consumer recycled paper as well.

An epic fantasy-adventure
for 14+

compiled by
Jun-Qi


Other books in the Ocellus series:

Ocellus: The Story of the Twelfth Stone

Mobius: The Story of the Eighth Stone

# CHAPTERS

| | |
|---|---|
| ONE: The Forbidden Section | 1 |
| TWO: Domes | 11 |
| THREE: Pyramids; Cones; and Cubes | 20 |
| FOUR: Alliances | 33 |
| FIVE: Spheres | 41 |
| SIX: Matching | 50 |
| SEVEN: Webs | 58 |
| EIGHT: Balls | 69 |
| NINE: Stealth and Psychology | 76 |
| TEN: Spirit of Avena | 85 |
| ELEVEN: Phial | 93 |
| TWELVE: Truth | 103 |
| THIRTEEN: Resolved | 116 |
| FOURTEEN: Clones | 125 |
| FIFTEEN: Scar | 135 |
| SIXTEEN: A Little Roll of Cloth | 148 |
| SEVENTEEN: Maze within a Maze | 162 |
| EIGHTEEN: Elbows, Legs and Foreheads | 175 |
| NINETEEN: Rumours | 188 |
| TWENTY: The Case | 201 |
| TWENTY-ONE: Elevators | 214 |
| TWENTY-TWO: The Next War | 229 |
| TWENTY-THREE: Way to Go | 241 |

# ONE: The Forbidden Section

'All rise for the judgement of the Court!'

Tanun didn't want to rise, but the enforcer pulled his handcuffed wrist up when he stood, forcing Tanun to stand up as well. He winced as the handcuff scraped the wet blood across the broken flesh around his wrist.

The Chief Elder, flanked by five Elders on either side, read from the tablet floating in front of her.

'The Court has reached a unanimous verdict. For the crime of illegally entering the forbidden section of the library by use of a mislaid access ring, Tanun is found guilty. Furthermore, he has shown no regret or remorse since his discovery and detention, and offered no apology for his crime. The penalty is well known and our unanimous agreement is to impose the maximum sentence. Tanun is therefore sentenced to death.'

'Silence in court!'

'We have, however, listened to the pleading of Tanun's defence counsel, and on account of Tanun's age of seventeen, we have reluctantly agreed to commute his death sentence to that of ... banishment.

'Silence in court!'

'Furthermore, the Elders have also unanimously agreed that henceforth, access to the library will be restricted to those over three hundred years of age. Sentencing of the person who mislaid the access ring will be made when Tanun is removed from the Court.'

As he was dragged away, Tanun spotted Chyke in the viewing gallery and caught his eye. How his younger brother had managed to sneak in was a puzzle, but then,

Chyke was always wangling people and things to his advantage.

The cell door hissed shut, and now the restraints had been removed, Tanun rubbed his wrists and ankles. The red had seeped through his grey boiler suit to form crimson rings at the end of each sleeve and leg. He lifted the domed lid away from the plate. Two food cubes. Water. Could have been worse, he supposed. He wondered how long he'd got. Did they throw you out in dark-time?

\* \* \*

'Right, Laddie. Hold out your wrists. We don't want any funny business, do we? Legs.'

Tanun wasn't sure how a seventeen-year-old in shackles could cause any funny business surrounded by seven enforcers, but he was careful to obey each command. He didn't want another beating.

'Let's go. Short walk for you. Here we are. This is your hatch. Hold still while I remove your restraints. Now your ankle tag. Word of advice, young man. You're better off facing the rungs as you go down. And don't jump, because if you break your ankle no one will come to help. Off you go.'

Tanun turned to face inwards, and with his left leg searched for the first rung. The pine scent in the air made him catch his breath and he had to concentrate on each rung as he stepped farther down.

'Hold up. Here's your rucksack.'

Tanun had to climb back up nine rungs, almost to the top of the hatch. He held the left sidebar and reached up with his right arm while an enforcer lowered the rucksack by a strap. He caught the strap and swung the rucksack around so he could get his right arm through, held the right sidebar and slipped his left arm through the other strap. The sound of the hatch closing made him look up, so he let go of the right sidebar and looked around. The dome filled nearly all his vision, but when he leant back he could see heathland far below, and what he took to be woodland in the distance. After he had climbed down a hundred rungs, he could see the end of two of the other five supporting legs of the dome, but in the woodland, something caught by the light of the two suns, which were still quite low, dazzled him momentarily. He dropped down faster and faster until he lost his step. He hung from the sidebars, his flailing feet seeking the rungs again.

After dropping the last three rungs into the three-metre dish that each leg of the dome rested in, he crawled over the rim and sat on the ground. While he got his breath back he tried to sort out his bearings. *Should have counted the rungs*, he told himself. *Must have been at least a thousand. So, this was it. Banishment. To certain death, they must have assumed. The scientists stressed that the environment was still poisonous outside the dome, and after all, no one had ever returned, had they?* Tanun looked across to where he thought the glint had been, and after humming and hawing, settled on making for the wood.

About a kilometre before he reached the trees, he again caught a glint of something and pushed through the bracken to see two metal rails. He stepped onto the nearest and imagined it ringing from an approaching train. The knowledge pods said railways had died out over eight thousand years ago, but Tanun had always found trains intriguing. Although there was no sign anyone else had come that way, he settled on following the remnants of the railway track into the wood.

Stumbling over rotten sleepers and twisted metal, he

thought back to the delicate paper books in the library, especially his favourite, *The Illustrated Book of Steam Trains*, and finding the mislaid access ring to the forbidden section on his sixteenth birthday – what a present that was. So, he'd thought. Sneaking in to discover the rows and rows of secret books, especially those of ancient philosophers like Epstein, Lambert, and Deuchamp. He'd been enthralled by their reasoning, arguments, and rhetoric. And he'd understood why the Elders had deemed them subversive and locked them away.

The track emerged from the wood, and as it started to climb, Tanun recalled the last three days. There he was, in the forbidden section, lost in Deuchamp's eloquence, until he'd looked up to see seven Enforcers. Seven! For an unarmed seventeen-year-old. Dragged to an isolation cell. The protocols, the process, and the pretence of justice. And the so-called trial. Tanun kicked a rock. He hadn't even been allowed to speak until the end. And when he had, the Elders, outraged at his logical dismantling of their established order, had made their decision quickly and unanimously. He knew he shouldn't have laughed when they announced that henceforth access to the library would be restricted to those over three-hundred years old. At least he'd caught his brother's eye before being dragged away.

He rounded the curve of a hill to see the track disappearing into a narrow tunnel. He reckoned dark-time would be soon, so made camp near the entrance, pulled the inflatable tent from the rucksack and opened the packet of food-cubes. While he nibbled at one, he stared up at the white dots. *They must be stars. I read about them in the remains of that large book with four white letters on the cover.* He crawled into his tent and wrapped the insucover around himself. When sleep came, though, a nightmare tormented him. He was lying on the railway track as a train steamed towards him, its whistle screaming ever louder and higher.

At light-time he hesitated at the tunnel entrance. There was nothing for it, he convinced himself, so he held the lantern out in front and forced himself into the black, although he kept looking back at the shrinking oval of light. He kept to the middle as best he could until the lamp faded and blackness smothered him. After stumbling along for an hour in absolute darkness and a silence that was absolute apart from his steps, a noise made him stop. The rails had started ringing. Tanun felt sure, though, there was something else and turned his head left and right to listen. He smiled. A whistle screaming louder and higher. He flung himself against the wall and slithered down to the rocks, stones, and sleepers. And waited.

No train came. What was happening? The black must have been playing tricks. Imagination on overload. How long could this tunnel be? As he pushed himself up, his right palm pressed against something smooth – unlike any other rock or stone in the tunnel. He ran his hand back and forth over the glassy smoothness and curled his fingers around the oval. He held it against his cheek. 'You're a friend. I'm gonna keep you,' he told it. 'A memento of this never-ending tunnel.' He set off again, looking for any sign of light and listening for any hint of sound.

A pinprick of light rose in the distance. Evolved into a star. An oval. Tanun started running, but the rocks and broken sleepers made him stumble and he had to tread slowly. As he tested each step, he rubbed his wrists, itching from the dried blood. When he stumbled into the light he had to shield his eyes. He turned to look back into the black. 'If there's another one, I don't think I'll do a tunnel again. Need to rest.' He walked a little farther along the cutting until he found a patch of smooth blue grass. He flung his rucksack down and stretched out to study the glassy-black, oval-shaped stone. Even in the pitch black of the tunnel he could tell the stone was unlike any of the others. They had all been rough and uneven with sharp edges. Tanun turned the stone in his hand and saw a pattern on the other face. 'What's that? Is that meant to be a dodecahedron? Why carve a pattern on a stone? And if you did, why would you leave it in a tunnel?'

'A tunnel is a good place to leave a stone – if you want to hide it, that is.'

Tanun started, and scrambling to his feet saw a very tall man in a green cloak walking from the tunnel entrance. When the man was about three metres away he seated himself on a rock. 'Please, sit back down, Tanun. Do not be alarmed. I wish you no harm.'

'Were you in there all the time? And how do you know my name?'

'No, I was not in the tunnel any of the time. I thought letting you see me at a distance would startle you a little less. My name is Cassièl. I am not from the domes.'

'No, I guess not. No one is that tall. Or wears a green cloak. Not that I've seen, anyway. You said 'domes', by the way. Do you live out here? The environment is poisonous.'

'I do not live out here, either. And just so you know, the environment has not been poisonous for thousands of years. Your years.'

'My years?'

'Your planet's year. Lemtor is but one of trillions of inhabited planets and almost all orbit their star – or stars in your case, at a different rate from any other.'

'Were those stars I saw? At dark-time?'

'Yes. You are very advanced in some things, Tanun, yet retarded in others because of living in such a controlled society within a so-called protective dome. Or more accurately, sphere.'

'No one thinks about living in the dome. Because we always have, I suppose. And mentioning outside, you know, beyond the dome, is frowned upon.'

'That is how the Elders control society.'

'Tell me about it! You're right. Actually, the dome is a sphere ... on stilts. Wonder why we call it a dome. Anyhow ... Cassièl ... if you're not from the dome, and you don't live out here, where do you live? And you still haven't told me how you know my name. Who are you?'

'Are you ready to learn some stuff you will not find in the knowledge pods, or even the old books?'

Tanun nodded.

'I mentioned Lemtor is just one of trillions of planets, and Lemtor's stars are part of a collection of stars called a galaxy.'

'Yeah, I know about them.'

'Good. Your galaxy is called Unserni. And there are trillions of galaxies in this universe, which is called Qydar. But – and this is the more important bit – there are many universes, each with their own rules governing matter and energy and life. Some are what you would call physical universes, like this one. However, the majority are entirely spiritual universes with no physicality. I am from one of those spiritual universes. My universe is called Amnia. Amnia was the first.'

'If you're spiritual with no physicality, how come I can see you?'

'Amnians can manifest as physical Essentia – that is

our name for any life-form. To make it a bit easier for you, what you see is an avatar. Tanun, did you know your brother was following you?'

'What?'

'Chyke is just inside the tunnel. He has been watching us.'

'Oh, no. How? How did he get outside?'

'I will let him tell you. Call him over.'

'Chyke? I know you're there. Come on out. Come and join us. This is Cassièl and he's Ok.'

Chyke poked his head out, looked back once into the tunnel, turned, and shuffled towards them.

When he was a few metres away, Tanun said, 'What were you thinking? And how the hell did you get out? Sorry, this is Cassièl. Sit down.'

'Great welcome, I must say. I followed the enforcers and saw which hatch they used for you.'

'But we can't open them.'

'Enforcers can. I stole an access ring.'

'Oh, great.'

'You used one!'

'Yeah, and look where it got me.'

'It got you,' Cassièl reminded him, 'out of your dome and away from that repressive society!'

'What does he know?'

'Cassièl knows a lot, Chyke. More than you can imagine. And our names.'

'If you say so.'

'It's true. Anyway, Cassièl, look, it's great to meet you and everything, but why are you here talking to me, and how am I – we – going to survive outside the dome? I've only enough food cubes for two more dark-times. And now Chyke's here.'

'Oh, thanks. After I risked everything to follow you.'

'I didn't ask you to! Thinking about it, though, I'm glad you're here now.'

'See?'

'Listen, boys, there is a lot I need to tell you. And it concerns that stone.'

'What, this?' Tanun held out his palm with the glassy-black stone he'd picked up in the tunnel.

'Yes. It is not just a stone. The stone has special properties. But before all that, walk with me to the next woodland. In there you will find plenty of food to live on if you know where to look. And fresh water. You are fortunate. Your rucksack has some useful survival gear. Tent, knives, rope, bandages. That is at least a small plus for your Elders. Beyond the wood is another dome.'

'Another dome? No, can't be. Really?'

'Another dome. Really. There are millions of domes. You were just not told about them. Relax, the Governors there are rather different from your Elders, and I know they will welcome you both.'

'How do you know all this?' said Chyke.

'Tanun can fill you in. Beneficial, you being together.'

'The systems will have detected Chyke is missing,' said Tanun.

'They will.'

'And?'

'What are they going to do? After all, they will not leave their dome to look for him, will they?'

'No, they never would. They speak of the outside like it's the end of the world.'

'Well, it nearly was, once.'

'But you said that was thousands of years ago!'

'Yes. And as I said, the outside has been safe for a long

time, but many inside the domes do not want to relinquish control.'

'Can't get my head around there being millions of domes. What about this one you mentioned? The other side of the wood?'

'Much, much bigger, and the people are friendlier. The Governors there, and other domes in their alliance, have been trying to reach a consensus to persuade the rest to open up the domes. Liberate the people. To no avail, so far. Some domes support the alliance. The majority don't.'

'Seems I was unlucky in being born in my particular dome.'

'And me,' said Chyke. 'I hate the Elders. We can't do anything without permission. Every moment is controlled.'

'That is all about to change. Come on. Up you get, both of you. The wood.'

Chyke stood up, but hesitated to follow his brother. 'Can we trust him, Tanun?'

'I don't know why I do, but I do.'

'You are right to be wary, Chyke,' said Cassièl. 'When we get to the wood, I will prove to you I am genuine.'

'How?'

'You will see.'

# TWO: Domes

Although Chyke kept looking up to Cassièl as they moved farther into the wood, it was Tanun who couldn't contain himself any longer.

'Come on, Cassièl. You were going to prove you're genuine.'

'Yes, I was. This is as good a place as any to camp for the night. Take off your rucksack.'

When Tanun's rucksack hit the ground, the tent slithered out and inflated. The lantern, which had extinguished in the tunnel, rose to hang on a branch and light the area. Sticks assembled into a cone which burst into flame, and a pot floated above with no sign of support. Seeds and leaves from the woodland trees flowed into the pot. Fruits fell gently from smaller trees and bushes and gathered into a pile by the side of the tent, and a flagon of elderflower water appeared next to Chyke.

'In the tent you will find there are two insucovers. Dark-time will be cold after the dome. Now, the stew needs a while so gather round the fire and we can talk.'

Tanun looked to Chyke, who was gazing from the fire to the tent, to the lantern, and to the fruits and the flagon.

'How did you do that?' he said.

'Not permitted, really, but we are in an unusual situation,' replied Cassièl. 'You missed some of my explanation to Tanun, so he can fill you in on that. I will fill you in further while the stew cooks – incidentally it will be quite bland – meaning the flavours will not taste strong because your bodies are used to food cubes. Nothing wrong with those, but your insides are not familiar with real food straight from nature. Ok. After the last religion war, around five thousand years ago, those that survived used their technological know-how to create the domes, and retreated inside- '

'What's that smell, Cassièl?' interrupted Tanun. 'Making me so hungry.'

'The stew. Vegetable stew.'

'Not heard of ... stew.'

'I think you are both in for a pleasant surprise. Anyway, to continue, the environment was severely damaged and took nearly three thousand years to recover. So when it did, for approximately the last two thousand years almost everyone, certainly in this area, could have ventured from the domes and re-established living outside. When people assume power, though, they are very often reluctant to give it up. By keeping millions of you confined, those with the power could control society. And you. That is why knowledge is restricted and why the Elders have a forbidden section in your library ... ah, the stew is ready.'

'This is amazing,' said Chyke. 'Never had anything like this. It tastes and smells incredible. Is there any left?'

'Enough for you both. Tanun?'

'Great, thanks, Cassièl. To think all this is possible and we've been deliberately kept in ignorance.'

'You will find that applies to many things. Glad my cooking is to your liking. Now, to the stone.'

Tanun showed Chyke the stone. 'I found this in the tunnel. In the complete black. I was pushing myself up from the ground when my hand felt this smooth oval. Actually, Cassièl, how did you know I'd even found it?'

Chyke peered closer to the stone. 'What's that?'

'An engraving. A dodecahedron, I think. Cassièl says the stone's special.'

'Yes, it is a dodecahedron and yes, the stone is most definitely special. I have searched for that stone for trillions of years. But when I found it, here on Lemtor in the tunnel, I could not pick it up. Retrieve it is the proper term. Yet I have to take the stone back to my universe.'

'You're not eating any stew,' said Chyke.

'No. As I explained to Tanun, I am an avatar, a spirit manifesting in physical form. To make it easier for you.'

'Oh yeah, Cassièl told me,' said Tanun. 'Tell you more later.'

'What's so special about the stone and why do you need it?' said Chyke.

'There are thirteen of these stones altogether. This one is the second. They form the Master Circle. This Master Circle generates all energy, matter, and life. Everywhere. All universes, galaxies, stars, and planets.'

'What? That little thing?'

'The thirteen little things.'

'If it's so important, why was it in the tunnel?'

'It was in the tunnel, Chyke, because evil creatures hid it there. The most evil creatures you can imagine in your worst dark-time nightmare. They are shapeshifters and I can assure you, you do not want to meet one.'

'I'm convinced.'

'Trillions of years ago, these ... creatures ... stole all thirteen and hid each on a different planet. They hid the Dodecahedron stone on Lemtor.'

Chyke scraped the last of the stew from his bowl and made sure he'd licked the spoon clean. 'Great stuff with the tent and the stew, but all that's a bit hard to believe.'

'Of course it is. So the best thing is for me to show you my universe. I think you would be convinced, then.'

'Yeah, I would. Show away.'

'Tanun needs to hold out the stone on his left palm. You, Chyke, need to put your left forefinger on the middle of the engraving.'

'O ... kay ....'

Tanun held out the stone on his palm and Cassièl nodded to Chyke to lower his forefinger.

'Your hair, Tanun!' said Chyke

Silver rays shone up from the boys' heads into the dark-time sky.

'Yours too!'

'Right, boys. I will now lower my forefinger onto Chyke's and we will transpose to Amnia, my universe. I promise no harm will come to you.'

Some minutes later Chyke looked at Tanun and then at Cassièl. 'Was something meant to happen?'

'Something was meant to happen, Chyke. This is most unusual. Tanun? Please, could I have the stone for a moment?'

Tanun extended his arm towards Cassièl with the stone on his palm, but when Cassièl reached to take it, he could not remove it.

'Perhaps you're not as powerful as you say you are,' said Chyke. 'Or the stone is weirder than you said it was.'

'Both, probably. I am sorry about that, you two. Keep it safe, Tanun. Keep it with you, always. I need to consider the implications. Tell you what. It's very late and we have quite a trek tomorrow to the next dome, so get yourselves ready for sleep. I will make breakfast for you at light-time.'

'But what are *you* going to do?' asked Chyke.

'Think.'

'All dark-time?'

'All dark-time. Sleep well. You will be quite safe in the tent.'

'Come on, Chyke. Best do as Cassièl says.'

'Just cos you're older, doesn't mean you can boss me around, you know.'

'Oh, I think it does. Anyway, my little brother, you're here by invitation, don't forget.'

'Great. How long are you going to use that on me?'

'Aww, let's see ... about a million years.'

At light-time, Cassièl did not wake the boys. Instead, he waited for Tanun to emerge, bleary-eyed, from the tent.

'Why didn't you wake us? Have you just sat out here all the time?'

'You both needed the sleep. And I did not just sit. In fact, I did not sit at all. I talked to other Amnians about the problem with the stone.'

'Oh, were others here?'

'No. For us, Tanun, physical distance is irrelevant. We can think to each other wherever we are.'

'Cool. Useful. In the dome we use the nodes and they connect to every other node in the dome.'

'That's a good system. Now, I've made what you would consider a very unusual breakfast. When you are packed and ready, you can try this porridge.'

'Not heard of that. Cassièl, whenever I tried to study history, or the environment outside the dome, the knowledge pods always said, "Refer to Elders".'

'Because they did not want you to know that sort of stuff. Like I said, knowledge is power.'

'Sorry, I'm a bit worried now. I've no experience of outside. No one has. Everything was provided for us.'

'As long as you obeyed the rules.'

'As long as you obeyed the rules,' echoed Tanun.

'You have done well, Tanun. Natural for you to feel like that. Anyone would in your situation. When we get to the other dome, though, you will have the best of both worlds. Security of the dome *and* the right to venture outside. I suggest you go outside as often as you can to acclimatize. And make sure Chyke does as well.'

'What about me?' Chyke had crawled out of the tent and was focusing on the pot above the fire.

'When you are ready, Chyke, I have a special breakfast for you.'

Chyke dug his spoon into his bowl. 'This is really great, too. What is it again?'

'Porridge. Made from oats. They're a cereal crop and very common. Oats occur across many planets and you'll see them growing because there are a lot of oat fields between this wood and the next dome.'

'To think we just have food cubes!'

'Had.'

Chyke sent Cassièl a look full of questions and took a deep breath. 'I've been thinking. I'd like to go back. I'm not sure I've done the right thing leaving the dome. Wanted to see Tanun and that blocked out any thoughts about afterwards. Somehow thought we would both go back.'

'They will not let you back, Chyke,' said Cassièl. 'To them, that would create chaos. You would have proved the outside was safe. Cause a breakdown of their established order.'

Tanun looked up from his porridge and asked if Cassièl knew what he'd said at his trial.

'Yes, that was brave of you, Tanun, and well argued. Although they will know by now, I suspect they did not notice Chyke was missing for a long while because they would not have considered he might have escaped. In any case, they will now deem Chyke's absence a plus because they would have had to place him under close monitoring, being the brother of a disrupter. I believe you and Chyke have a chance of a better life away from your old dome and with the new.'

'Will they just let us in?' said Tanun. 'At the other dome?'

'Probably. They take in lots of people from other domes. The domes do not exist in isolation. Most have joined one of the alliances. The Governors at the next dome will see you two as strengthening their case for liberalisation. Much, much more important than any of that, though, is the matter of the stone. Dodecahedron.'

'Oh, yeah,' said Chyke. 'Is it broken?'

'No, I do not believe so. Impossible to break, or damage a Nucleus. That is their proper term. There is, however, a problem. A problem that puts you two at great risk.'

'Great. We've left our dome and can't go back, and now you say there's another problem?'

'More than one, I suspect. We must set off. We can talk on the way.'

Tanun and Chyke packed the tent and lamp into the rucksack, and when Tanun looked behind after they had set off, he could see no evidence anyone had made camp. The wood grew denser and darker, and after an hour Cassièl said it might rain. He had to explain what rain was, how it formed and fell, and how it was a vital resource for vegetation and crops.

'Ok, I need to tell you more about the stone – and about Amnia and Amnians.' Just as Cassièl said this, a blinding flash of lightning illuminated the forest ahead of them. 'Wait. There will be a bang.'

Tanun and Chyke stared up at the tops of the trees. When it came, the bang lifted both of them off their feet.

'What the crud was that?' said Chyke.

'The flash was lightning. Electricity generated in the sky and travelling to the ground. Usually. The bang was the air expanding from the heat of the lightning. Nothing to worry about. Unless the lightning hits you. Or a tree nearby explodes. Or falls on you.'

'Ok, I get it.' Chyke held out his palm. 'Is this the rain?'

'This is the rain. There will be lots. We must keep going.'

Trudging behind Cassièl, the boys became more and more bedraggled, dishevelled, and disheartened as the bullets of rain found their way through the canopy of branches. Tanun continually shook his wrists and ankles because his boiler suit kept clinging to his wounds, and Chyke moaned he was wet through and his boiler suit was really uncomfortable. 'Why did it have to rain on us?' he moaned. 'The old dome wasn't so bad after all.'

After another half an hour, Cassièl said they were nearly at the edge. 'Good job the storm has passed. Walking though fields is not a good idea with lightning.'

The trees had thinned, and the green sky was bleeding through the canopy. 'There it is. You can see the dome through the trees.'

'Wow. That's gigantic,' said Chyke. 'How far is it?'

'About an hour through the oat fields. Should be there before dark-time. You should dry out now the suns are shining.'

Cassièl led the boys into a field of ripe oats, but they had to follow him by sound because the stalks reached past their heads. Cassièl plucked some ears and showed the boys how to slide the oats from their casing. 'Very good for you. Better cooked, though. The porridge you had was made from oats.'

'Incredible,' said Tanun. 'The first one hundred levels

of our dome are for food manufacture and waste disposal. Can't believe food grows out here.'

'At this dome, they grow most of their food outside.'

Tanun kept staring up at the geodesic sphere as it filled nearly all his forward vision, and he thought back to his descent from the dome. As his feet had searched for each rung, he'd puzzled how the people that long ago had developed the technology to construct such a thing, and how well it had endured, apparently for thousands of years. Back then, he surmised, people must have been pretty advanced to have made the domes during the religion wars, but then he remembered the railways, and trains.

'Ok, boys. They probably already know we are here. Watched us approaching through the fields, I expect.'

As the three of them stood by one of the dishes in which each leg rested, the boys strained to take in its size and the height of the legs. Tanun wondered what the inside would be like, but Chyke was staring at the converging rungs, pondering how anyone could possibly climb that many.

# THREE: Pyramids, Cones, and Cubes

'Cassièl. Welcome.'

Tanun and Chyke looked around because the voice seemed to have come from everywhere.

'I see you have you brought us the two boys. Excellent. They look as if they are in need of some clean clothes and hot food. Use the steps on the nearest leg. Tell them to be careful.'

'What, all the way up there?' said Chyke, still struggling to see to the top of the leg. 'That's way higher than the legs on our dome.'

'Three thousand, nine hundred and ninety-nine rungs,' said Cassièl. 'Take your time. Rest when you need. I will follow you up.'

Chyke looked at Tanun, who was now eyeing the steps from the top to the bottom and to the top again. 'We can do it, Chyke. You go first. Stop when you need to rest ... and don't fall on me.'

Chyke set off at a pace, Tanun scrambling after him, but both slowed after ninety rungs and stopped to rest at one-hundred and twenty-three.

'This is so much higher than ours!' Chyke called. 'What's that blowing?'

'That's the wind. Air moving about. Make sure you hold on.'

'Smells. Nice, actually.'

'I think the smell's from the trees. This dome must be twice the size. Let's count fifty and then rest. Do it in bursts.'

'Good idea. My legs are killing me, so this is gonna take

forever. Is Cassièl following us?

Tanun held the bar on each side and leant back. 'No. I can just see him. He's watching us from down there.'

After three hours, while they were leaning against the rungs for another rest, Tanun said, 'I reckon one more burst should do it. We're ever so high, Chyke.'

'Don't tell me! The wind's whistling too. I can't grip the bars any tighter.'

Tanun straightened his arms to lean back and looked around. 'Look, left and behind, Chyke. There's another dome!'

'Can't look, can't look. Got to stay close to the rungs. Focus on the next rung. Just focus on the next rung.'

'We're nearly there. One more go should do it. Come on.'

As Chyke's head reached the last rung, a hatch cover in the dome slid open and he looked up to see two hands reaching for him. One more rung. One more rung. As his head approached the opening, the hands grabbed his wrists and pulled him through. Tanun increased his pace and hands pulled him through the hatch too. Both boys crumpled to the floor.

Cassièl was waiting for them. 'Well climbed.'

'We didn't expect to see you so soon, Cassièl,' said the dark-skinned man who had lifted the boys into the hatch room.

'No. Events have overtaken us. This is Tanun. Up you get.' Cassièl helped Tanun stand up. 'Seventeen. The banished one.'

'I guessed so, from his wrists and ankles. Well done doing the climb with those.'

And this is Chyke, fifteen, his younger brother.' Cassièl helped Chyke to stand. 'Sneaked out to follow him. Rather brave. And resourceful too, from what I have heard so far.'

'Good for you, Chyke. I hope your brother appreciated your effort!'

Although the boys were furiously rubbing their calves, neither could help laughing at the remark.

'You are honoured, boys,' said Cassièl. 'This is Lento-Fin, the Governor-General. Although I strongly suspect he's here more because of what Tanun has in his pocket than wanting to welcome two dirty wretches.'

'Ha-ha, thank you, Cassièl. Not true at all. Welcome to you both. I trust you will find us rather different from the Elders in your dome. Everyone here is encouraged to go outside, although not all wish to.'

*No, thought Tanun, I shouldn't think they would with that many rungs.*

'We do have rules, of course, but they can wait. Cassièl, shall we take them to their den and they can clean up and put on fresh clothes?'

'Yes. Then we must talk. We have much to discuss.'

Lento-Fin beckoned the boys out of the hatch room and indicated they should follow him along the curved corridor. After a few minutes they reached a line of elevators. 'In here. We're going up many levels.'

As the elevator rose, the boys' legs buckled from the force.

**Level 230** announced the elevator.

'This is your level. Along here. You will share 230-125. Small, but clean. The door opens and shuts when it recognises your retina. Give it a try.'

Tanun turned to face the door. Whoosh. The door slid sideways in an instant.

'But how did it already know?' said Tanun.

'I like it,' said Chyke.

'Everything you need in there,' said Lento-Fin. 'Bunk beds. Bathroom and shower. Put your dirty clothes in the correct chute. Cassièl will collect you later. Off you go and get cleaned up.'

Tanun and Chyke stepped through and the door whooshed shut behind. Tanun scanned the low ceiling and the room with its vaguely curved outer wall and window. He thought of his room back in his dome on level 103, located somewhere towards the middle. No window there. He wasn't sure there were any windows anywhere in the old dome.

'Look at this window, Chyke. Really high.'

They stood side by side by the full-height window in silence, trying to take in all that had happened, and stared down across the golden fields.

'The suns are low,' said Tanun. 'Soon be dark-time outside. Anyhow, after the last few days this is loads better. Great room, great window, natural light, and an Elder – sorry, Governor – who spoke nicely.'

'Dunno, yet. That stone might cause a lot of trouble. Cassièl said it would. He said we're at great risk, remember? Don't get how that can be. And we've only met one person and he's the top Governor.'

'Yeah, but Cassièl's Ok and Lento-Fin was friendly. It'll be all right, Chyke.'

'Those shapeshifters who stole the stones. They don't sound much fun. And they're searching for yours.'

'Need to find out more about that. Feels safe in here, though.'

'Let's hope it is. How will we ever find our way around? It's massive.'

'Must be maps. Let's get cleaned up. Can't wait to get out of these clothes. You go first.''

'Wow!' Chyke shouted, 'Look at this, Tanun.'

Chyke was standing in a clear closed cylinder with water blasting down. Two fluffy vertical brushes revolved around him. When the water stopped, the brushes retracted and the integral door slid around the cylinder. 'That's amazing,' he said as he stepped out. 'You can be clean in less than a minute. Go on, your go.'

Tanun put the stone on the bottom bunk and peeled off his damp boiler suit which clung and rubbed his wrists and ankles. As soon as he had stepped into the cylinder, the door slid around, the water jetted down, and the brushes began whirring. He wasn't sure where the cleangel came from, but within two seconds he was enveloped in suds and bubbles. Just as abruptly, the water stopped and the door slid open. Chyke threw him a towel and pointed to a chute. Tanun pushed his dirty clothes in and pulled out a light-grey boiler suit, and socks, pants, and boots from another chute, checking them for size. He sat down on the bottom bunk next to Chyke and put the stone in his pocket. 'How come everything's the right size?'

'They couldn't have been expecting us, could they?' said Chyke. 'Hey — look at your wrists and ankles — they're loads better. Must have been hell wearing those shackles.'

'Yeah, was. Skin's still sore but the shower's helped.'

'What was your cell like?'

'Small. About a quarter of this. Bench, basin, and toilet. You know, whenever I asked the knowledge pods to tell me more about the outside, or the religion wars, I got a restricted message every time: "Refer to Elders".'

'You're always trying to find out more. Causes trouble.'

'Says he who stole an access ring and escaped!'

'To find you. Anyway, bound to be pods here. Let's ask.'

'Yup. Hungry?'

'Starving. Hurry up, Cassièl.'

The whoosh made Tanun and Chyke both turn. In the doorway stood a girl with cropped fair hair, dressed in a camouflage boiler suit. Must be sixteen, Tanun reckoned. Possibly a bit older.

'Greetings. I am Joor-Jen. Please follow me. We are to go to the meeting hall.'

The boys half-walked, half-ran to keep up with her as she marched along the corridor. When she stopped, an elevator door in the wall slid sideways and she waved her arm to encourage them in.

'Level 1240. That's the meeting room, by the way.'

'This dome is so much bigger than ours,' said Chyke.

'There are bigger domes than this.'

**Level 300**

'Really like to see those. How old are you?'

'Seventeen. Same as your brother. You are fifteen.'

'Do you know everything about us?'

'Nearly.' Joor-Jen smiled.

'Where's Cassièl?' said Tanun.

**Level 500**

'Cassièl is talking with Lento-Fin and asked if I would mind collecting you. I didn't. You see, I rather like collecting boys.'

Tanun shook his head at Chyke, who had screwed up his face.

'How exactly do you go about collecting them?' asked Chyke. 'Boys?'

'That would give away too many secrets. And I can assure you, I never give away secrets. I am Tanun's apostle, so we shall see a lot of each other.'

'Apostle?' Tanun moved back a step from her.

**Level 700**

'I am to look after you and protect you from danger. And help you adapt.'

Tanun blew out his cheeks. 'Sounds a bit, I dunno, sinister.'

'An apostle is assigned to every newcomer. Sometimes two apostles, depending. Nothing to worry about.'

**Level 900**

'There's plenty to worry about. First, I was banished, which is how I came to find a stupid stone. Then Cassièl – he's an alien, by the way – appears and says horrible creatures are after it. Then we trekked forever to another dome.'

'There are millions of domes.'

'I know that. Cassièl said. And now we're off to a meeting.'

'Yeah, I agree, brother. When will someone tell us what's going on?'

'Sorry. It is not for me to tell you, Chyke, but you'll soon meet your apostles. Seems you two were kept away from much knowledge so you've a lot of catching up to do. By the way, we all know Cassièl's an alien. Albeit, a friendly shapeshifter.'

**Level 1100**

'Everyone was kept away from knowledge, not just us,' said Tanun. 'How many newcomers do you get?'

'Newcomers from other domes arrive all the time. Some have been banished, like you. Some have escaped. Some had heard of our policy of liberalisation, but some come to cause trouble. Disrupters. Spies. Terrorists.'

'Well, we're not spies or terrorists.'

'You are a disrupter, though, Tanun.'

**Level 1200**

'Only for reading forbidden books.'

'And for keeping a lost access ring instead of handing it in.'

'How do you know that?'

'Talk spreads fast. All the domes have spies. Because we are open, we have to assess any newcomer for safety. And decide how they will contribute to the welfare of the dome. Your assessments will be soon.'

'The more I learn, the less I feel I know.'

'You will soon learn more.'

'This is crazy,' said Chyke. 'At least we could move around our dome on our own.'

'Where your ankle-tag permitted.'

'Yeah, well, course. Don't you have a tag?'

'We don't have ankle tags here.'

'Well, that's something.'

'Yours will be removed at your assessment.'

'Good. Perhaps I could get to like this place.'

'We have a DD ... in our neck.'

'DD?' Chyke made a face at Joor-Jen.

'Digital device. Small. Don't know it's there.'

'Oh. Whether you want to or not?'

'There is no whether.'

Chyke blew out his cheeks like his brother and turned to him. 'What d'you reckon?'

'Still prefer this. We've got to settle in, that's all. Adapt, as Joor-Jen said. Quite glad you're here, you little git.'

'I thought I was glad.'

### Level 1240

'Here we are. Not far now.'

Tanun and Chyke followed Joor-Jen into the meeting room where she led them to a long table on the left at a right angle to the door. Lento-Fin and Cassièl were sitting halfway along the table, deep in conversation.

'Tanun – here.' Joor-Jen pointed. 'You, Chyke, here.'

'Yes, Ma'am.'

Joor-Jen sat down on Tanun's left, next to Cassièl, while Chyke sat one space farther to Tanun's right and looked down the length of the room at the tables left and right, at right angles to his. Hundreds of people were talking, gesticulating, drinking, and often glancing at what he now took to be the top table. Two children about his age appeared from behind and sat down on either side.

'Hello, Chyke,' said the girl on his left, staring at his neck, 'I'm Peeso-Lun and this is Bento-Tor, my twin brother. We're your apostles.'

'I get two? Why? When are we going to eat?'

'Soon,' said Bento-Tor, who was also staring at his neck. 'You must be starved, walking all that way from 1279-41130.'

'Ravenous. Cassièl over there made us something called a stew and something else called … er … porridge. Both amazing. Not like the food cubes we had in our dome. Um, you just said 1279-41130. Is that our dome?'

'Everyone has to learn the dome IDs. Didn't you? Most have been mapped and identified – as far as the mountains, anyway.'

'We were told ours was the only one.'

'Only dome? That's ridiculous.'

'So, what's this one?'

Bento-Tor shook his head at Peeso-Lun and smiled. 'This is 1279-41618.'

While Chyke, Peeso-Lun, and Bento-Tor were conversing at the far end of the room, two doors opened and servers came in pushing a procession of trolleys behind everyone seated at the tables. Chyke followed the first trolley to the right side of the top table. A plate from the trolley was placed in front of him. 'Wow. Smells great, but what are they?' He checked to see if everyone had the same and stared from the orange pyramids on his plate to the mauve cubes next to the green cones. A generous squiggle of blue linked the three piles. The smell made him more ravenous, but he found the colours and shapes intimidating. He looked at Peeso-Lun.

'You and Tanun must be important. We only get these vegetables on special days, and we don't normally eat in the meeting room either. Go on, Chyke. While they're hot.'

Chyke prodded the pyramids, cubes, and cones before stabbing one of each onto his fork, and although he'd not had anything like them before, he had to admit to himself they tasted great, and in between talking with Peeso-Lun and Bento-Tor he finished every scrap on his plate, including the blue sauce. Stew, porridge, coloured shapes. He shook his head and wondered what could be next.

'So, Chyke,' said Bento-Tor, 'tell us about your dome. How did you sneak out to follow Tanun? So dangerous. And brave. And illegal.'

'How d'you know I did that? Joor-Jen knew as well. Everyone seems to know about us. Doesn't matter, I suppose. Well, although we're always arguing and fighting, it was so wrong, you know, banishing him. Tanun hadn't done any harm and I couldn't bear life in the dome without him, so I decided to escape and catch up with him. I hid all dark-time in a corridor near his cell, and at light-time followed the enforcers to the hatch.'

'Didn't they see you?' Bento-Tor raised his eyebrows.

'I'm good at sneaking. Anyway, they were preoccupied with Tanun.'

'But how did you open the hatch?'

'I stole an access ring from an enforcer.'

'Fantastic. How?'

'Wasn't easy. Waited until she'd dozed off in dark-time and with a fork I'd bent into a sort of hook, I lifted the ring from her breast pocket. Took a few goes. Trouble was, the ring wouldn't open Tanun's hatch. I panicked that I'd never find the right hatch, but I ran along to the next one and luckily, the ring worked. The enforcers must work in zones. Look. I've kept it.'

'Wow. You'd better give that to Joor-Jen. At the moment, she's the senior apostle here.'

'Suppose so. I don't need it anymore. You know, I had absolutely no idea what outside would be like. None of us did. We were told the outside's still poisonous. Didn't know how long I'd survive, or even whether I'd find my brother. I just knew it was worth the risk. Funny, I thought eleven hundred rungs was a lot.'

'Eleven hundred? Is that all?' Bento-Tor shook his head. 'Definitely one of the smaller domes. Early version. Chyke, some areas outside are still poisonous, although it's Ok around here for a few hundred domes. What about your food and your knowledge engineering?'

'Food's easy. We each got four food-cubes a day. They appeared in our portal in our room, with the water. Up until we're twenty we have to go to the knowledge pods for twelve hours a day. Tanun said the knowledge pods were censored and we learnt only what the Elders allowed us. Same with the library. Not sure how he knew that. He was always challenging the rules and demanding to know the reasoning for something.'

'Funny, cos he seems so quiet. I'd have thought you were the rebellious one.'

'Tanun is quieter. Steely quiet. He often beats me when we fight. Not because he's older and bigger. Because he's so focused. I'm learning how to divert him, though. Anyway, what about your food and your knowledge pods?'

'As soon as we're five,' said Bento-Tor, 'we have to study the knowledge pods from light-time to food-time. After food, we have to help on the farms again until dark-time. Each session is about a third. We have to do that until we're sixteen.'

'What happens then?'

'Matching. Each boy is allocated to a girl. Neither has to study anymore if they don't want to. They must work on the farms, though. We all do.'

'How weird. What's the point of that? And what if you don't like who you're matched with?'

'The point, Chyke, obviously, is to reproduce. The Governors believe we must grow the population to stand any chance of creating a new world outside the domes. If you don't like your pairing, you just have to make the best of it.'

'Yuck. You've got to be joking. Doesn't bear thinking about. I'd rather go back to my dome.'

'Ha-ha. Chyke, honestly – you can't go back there now, can you?'

'Can't I?'

'Think about it. How would you get there? Do you know the way back? And how would you alert them when you got there? If you did, they wouldn't let you in, anyway, would they? Anyhow, you're required here. Didn't Joor-Jen tell you? There's talk of our dome being attacked by some of the other domes. Most of the domes are in an alliance and two big alliances disagree with our alliance's policy of liberalisation and believe we are a bad influence. They want to invade our domes and take us over. Make us part of their restrictive alliance.'

'Oh, no. One minute I'm sneaking out to find my brother, and the next I'm going to be involved in a war. I thought Lemtor had the final war ... five thousand years ago.'

'There is no such thing as the final war, Chyke. Only the next war.'

'Deep, Bento-Tor. If you're such a thinker, can you tell me exactly why any of this involves Tanun and me?'

# FOUR: Alliances

Lento-Fin stood and addressed the room, which had fallen silent. 'Thank you, everyone. Cassièl is again our guest and he will speak shortly, but first, please welcome two young newcomers from 1279-41130. Stand up, Tanun. And his younger brother, Chyke. Stand up, Chyke. Tanun was banished for reading books in the forbidden section – I know, I know – and Chyke here made the brave decision to escape the dome and follow his brother. A noble act, considering they both believed the environment was poisonous outside their dome – which they also believed was the only one!'

Laughter, mingled with some cheers, rolled towards the top table.

'You can sit down, boys. We are grateful they will join our defence teams. More of that in a moment, as Cassièl will now bring you up to date on the situation concerning the Dodecahedron stone and the alliances across Lemtor.'

'Thank you, Lento-Fin. As I mentioned on my previous visits, after the KimMorii had hidden the Dodecahedron stone here on Lemtor, they did not just disappear. After fomenting the religion wars ten thousand years ago, they shared the technology to enable the construction of the domes – or rather, spheres, and they watched and they waited.'

*So that's how the domes were developed*, thought Tanun, remembering back to his descent.

'Being shapeshifters they are masters of disguise and have insinuated themselves into the hierarchy of many domes and inculcated dissent because this suited their purpose. Their presence was mainly to watch over the stone. However, the KimMorii are always looking to take over planets and exploit their resources. The inhabitants are usually then deployed as slaves ... for as long as they survive. In the Percutio Alliance, the KimMorii influence is much stronger than in the Dicio Alliance.'

Tanun shook his head. To think a few dark-times ago he didn't even know there were other domes, let alone alliances.

'The good news is, I have located the Dodecahedron stone ... in an ancient railway tunnel. The bad news is, I cannot retrieve it. I could not pick up the stone.'

The room dissolved into murmurings and mutterings until Cassièl held up his hand.

'I do not understand why, and I am devoting much thought to the problem. Fortunately, though, young Tanun here, after he was banished, was following a railway track which went through the tunnel, and in there he discovered the Dodecahedron stone. In the pitch black. Well done, Tanun.' Cassièl nodded to him. 'And he had the good sense to keep it. Unfortunately, although he was willing to give me the stone, I could not take it from him, just as I could not pick it up in the tunnel. The thing is, the KimMorii will know Dodecahedron has been discovered and moved, but they are not yet smart enough to know by whom and to where. That, my friends, is merely a matter of what you call time.'

*Just great*, Tanun thought. *The KimMorii will eventually track me down. What if they got inside this dome?*

'So, you must prepare,' Cassièl continued. 'The KimMorii enjoy seeing civil strife and as you know, are already encouraging the other alliances to attack your liberal alliance. All the while they will be frantically trying to locate Dodecahedron.' Cassièl moved back from the table and stood behind Tanun with his hands on Tanun's shoulders. 'If they succeed and take Dodecahedron from Tanun by force, he will die.'

Tanun looked across to see Chyke giving him a panicked look.

'We have learnt that if any one of the thirteen stones is taken from the possessor without permission, the possessor is nearly always dispersed. The taker is often mortally injured as well, but of course, neither concerns the KimMorii. Because of the problem with the stone, I cannot relieve Tanun and you of the burden. However, Chyke? I do recommend you relieve yourself of *your* burden and give your stolen access ring to Joor-Jen.'

The laughter did not help Chyke's reddening face as he passed the access ring to Joor-Jen, who ostentatiously unbuttoned the left breast pocket of her boiler suit and dropped in the ring.

'The KimMorii would likely move Dodecahedron away from Lemtor, but they will not cease in their plans to plunder your planet's resources and make all Lemtorn slaves. While I investigate how Tanun can safely and successfully give me Dodecahedron, you should prepare for the civil war that is brewing. I am sorry that I cannot help you in that matter, other than providing advice.'

*Why not?* Tanun frowned. *Why can't he help us? He's so clever at everything and surely this alliance is in the right, and the other alliances are in the wrong?*

'I ask that you train Tanun and Chyke. Help them achieve Special Forces grade, so if the worst happens and you are invaded, they will stand a better chance.'

'Thank you, Cassièl,' said Lento-Fin. 'We value your presence and your guidance. Joor-Jen, together with

Peeso-Lun and Bento-Tor, have been assigned to Tanun and Chyke. Their training will start next light-time. All captains please double-check our defences and alert the other domes in our alliance. Tanun and Chyke? We have more to discuss but you both look exhausted. Joor-Jen, would you please take them back to their den? And until they start their training, please be gentle with them.'

Tanun and Chyke stared blankly at each other while the room erupted in laughter.

'Will we train all light-time?' asked Tanun as they walked with Joor-Jen to an elevator.

'A third. Afterwards we'll get food and then you'll have your assessments. Your DD will be fitted and Chyke's ankle-tag will be removed.

After their door had whooshed open, Joor-Jen leant towards Chyke and kissed him on his forehead. She kissed Tanun on the lips and held him in an embrace before breaking away. 'I'll collect you both at light-time. Sleep well.'

'Phew,' said Tanun, 'wasn't expecting that.'

'Hoping, though.'

'Don't be ridiculous.'

'You're blushing! Look, I've loads to tell you, but I can't keep my eyes open. Can I have the top?'

'Sure. I don't care.'

Chyke climbed up to the top bunk and didn't hear Tanun say sleep well.

While Tanun thought back to Joor-Jen's kiss, he rubbed his wrists and ankles and wondered if another shower would help them heal faster. *Worth a go*, he told himself. He pulled off his boiler suit and put the stone on his bunk. Before he made for the shower, he stood at the window and stared into the black. In the dark of the room, he could see lights twinkling far in the distance and assumed they must be from another dome.

When he'd showered, he was so tired he didn't put on a clean boilersuit but crashed straight onto his bunk.

* * *

'Up, now, Chyke. Shower.'

Chyke opened his eyes – and stared into Joor-Jen's.

'Great. Can't we lock our door?'

'Retinas, remember? You have until I reach one hundred to be ready to leave. One, two, three–'

'Ok, Ok, I get it. Why doesn't Tanun need to shower?'

'By the looks of his wrists and ankles, he showered after I brought you back.'

Chyke climbed down the ladder moaning about his stiff legs, and disappeared into the bathroom.

'Wake up, Tanun. We have to go.'

Tanun opened his eyes, sat up straight and banged his head on the top bunk.

'Don't be embarrassed.'

Tanun leapt out of his bunk and grabbed clean clothes from the chute on the other wall. As he hopped around, he said, 'Honestly, Joor-Jen, you nearly gave me a heart attack. I've never, you know, been undressed in front of a girl before.'

'You're behind the times, Tanun. Chyke will update you, but at sixteen, each boy is matched to a girl.'

'Matched? What for? Hurry up, Chyke. I'm ready.'

Chyke emerged from the bathroom, but froze when he saw Joor-Jen's back as she talked with Tanun. 'Tanun, chuck us some clean clothes.'

When Chyke had dressed he said, 'At least Peeso-Lun and Bento-Tor weren't here.'

'Yeah,' said Tanun, 'and at least you crashed out with your clothes on. I didn't have any and there was Joor-Jen staring at me when I woke up.' He looked at Joor-Jen. 'No offence.'

'I assure you, Tanun,' Joor-Jen smiled, 'I am not in the least offended. Let's go.'

Tanun and Chyke followed Joor-Jen to a hatch where she told them Peeso-Lun and Bento-Tor were waiting at the bottom of the rungs.

'As I said before, we have a third allocated for training, although that includes getting down and up again. Then your assessments and DDs. Sleep for the last third. Peeso-Lun and Bento-Tor will collect you next light-time. You might want to make sure you're dressed, Tanun.'

'I certainly shall.'

'Will it hurt?' said Chyke. 'The DD?'

'Not for too long. Better to have it done when you're born. Down you go. You first, Chyke. Then Tanun. I'll be two rungs above you.'

Tanun and Chyke soon worked out they could hold the side bars and slide down, at least until the friction created too much heat on their hands, and their descent took a quarter of the time their ascent had taken the previous light-time. Chyke told Tanun about the matching and how you didn't get any choice in who you were matched with. Tanun shook his head and told his brother, who was also shaking his head, he didn't like the sound of that at all.

The boys jumped the last four rungs to see a smiling Peeso-Lun and Bento-Tor a few metres away from the dish of the leg, with a variety of straps across their shoulders from which hung devices neither Tanun nor Chyke had seen before.

'Hey, Tanun. Hey Chyke. This is going to be great.'

As Joor-Jen jumped the last six rungs, Peeso-Lun said, 'We're all ready, Joor-Jen. Shall we move to the edge of the oat-field?'

While they walked, Joor-Jen told Tanun and Chyke they would focus on close combat skills that session and next time move on to weapons.

*  *  *

'Sorry about the black eye, Tanun,' said Joor-Jen as they climbed the rungs. 'I didn't want to make your wrists and ankles worse, so I concentrated on body and head blows.'

'What about my nosebleed?' muttered Chyke.

'That too.'

Peeso-Lun had started climbing first, followed by Bento-Tor. Chyke followed him, and then Tanun with Joor-Jen last.

'My legs are still stiff from the last climb,' said Chyke. 'This is so much harder.'

'You'll get used to it,' Bento-Tor shouted down. 'We have.'

'Next time, Tanun,' said Joor-Jen, 'you must show more aggression. More like Chyke.'

'I will. But I got you with that sasae-tsurikomi-ashi throw.'

'You did. That was truly excellent. Need more like that next session.'

'When did you start training?'

'We start at three. Can't believe you didn't do any combat training in your dome.'

'The Elders wouldn't risk that. Give us too much power ... we must be half-way by now?'

'Just over. Arrogant of them to assume no one from outside would attack them.'

'Arrogance sums them up.'

'When we get to the hatch, Chyke will go with Peeso-Lun and Bento-Tor. They will show him the knowledge pods and get food. When his DD has been fitted, he'll go back to your den.'

'Ok. And me?'

'We'll get food and look at the knowledge pods together. I can stay with you while you have your DD fitted, if you'd like.'

'Yeah, that'll be good.'

'I'll take you back to your den. You'll need to rest until light-time.'

'Doesn't sound much fun. This DD.'

'As I said, easier when you're younger. You'll be fine.'

# FIVE: Spheres

Cassièl addressed the Amnian Forum and explained the difficulty in retrieving Dodecahedron. 'I could not pick it up in the railway tunnel, and later, neither could I take the stone from Tanun, despite him offering it freely to me.'

'We are grateful you have located the first Nucleus,' said Anselm. 'However, the problem with retrieval is puzzling. While we consider this issue, is Tanun a trustworthy child?'

'He is. And so is Chyke, his younger brother. They are both rather destabilised at present because they have just discovered there are millions of domes on Lemtor and that the outside environment is mostly safe. They are very adaptable, though.'

'Tanun is on the cusp of adulthood,' said Septies, 'and I wonder if a child would be more successful in retrieving the Nucleus? We have speculated about this because children appear to have an affinity with Principium. Perhaps we should have anticipated the first Nucleus we found presenting us with challenges.'

'We should,' said Cassièl. 'Nevertheless, that is a worthy suggestion. I could transpose Ennti to Lemtor and see if she is able to retrieve it.'

'We should explore this,' said Anselm, 'bearing in mind that her safety and the safety of any Amnian child is paramount.'

'I shall arrange extra protection when we have agreed the details,' said Ellye.

'Excellent,' said Anselm. 'We all feel calmer with your attention on the matter. Cassièl? How soon do you propose to take Ennti to attempt to retrieve Dodecahedron?'

'Very soon. The situation on Lemtor is unstable and civil war between the dome alliances is imminent. And we anticipate that the KimMorii will react aggressively to finding out that Dodecahedron has been discovered. Despite all that, I believe Tanun can cope with the concept of another alien, albeit a child, visiting to relieve him of the burden.'

'Very well,' said Anselm. 'Keep Ellye apprised so she may oversee the mission.'

'I will, ForumPrinceps.'

'We will reconvene after Cassièl's investigations. The Forum is closed.'

* * *

While Peeso-Lun and Bento-Tor led Chyke away to the refectory, Tanun waved at him and called out he'd catch him later. By the look on Chyke's face, Tanun wasn't sure Chyke was too happy about being separated. Tanun smiled to himself at Chyke's directness and straight-talking until life threw him a swerve and he went all timid and quiet.

'You two are so close,' said Joor-Jen, observing Tanun. 'You compete at everything, yet each needs the other to define themselves.'

'Does that really come across? I'd never thought of that before.'

'You wouldn't. You're in the play.'

'Too deep.'

'While Chyke's getting food, let's go to the knowledge pods. Ready for an experience?'

The door didn't whoosh as Joor-Jen led Tanun into the silent darkened room which Tanun reckoned must have spanned a whole level of the dome. Grey. Looking around, the colour everywhere was pale grey. Floor, ceiling, desks, and chairs. He traced the perimeter as far as he could. No windows to disturb the colour balance. Just about every desk and screen was in use by a child. Their boiler suits, unexpectedly colourful, leapt out from their grey surroundings, but not one head turned away from a screen as they passed.

Joor-Jen weaved between the desks and pointed to a chair at an unoccupied desk. 'Right. This is the knowledge room. We're not meant to talk, but a bit of whispering should be Ok.'

Tanun stared at the thin vertical clear screen which took up most of the desk. 'This is so different from ours. Ours is primitive compared to this. We have a much smaller screen and loads fewer desks. How many in here?'

'Desks?'

'Yeah.'

'A bit under half a million.'

'Amazing. So quiet.'

'You offend only once. What do you want to look at? Something that was blocked?'

'Guess so. Loads of things. Um, the religion wars.'

'Good one. Pod, access the religion wars. Timeline.'

Pod: **Active. Yes, Joor-Jen? Do you want me to recite? If so, you must wear earpieces.**

'Sure. Here, Tanun. Put these on.'

'Fantastic. In our old dome we had to read everything on the screen. There was no narration. This is brilliant.'

While Tanun and Joor-Jen watched the thin clear screen display moving pictures on the subject, they listened to the narration.

**Section: Religion Wars**

Subsection: Timeline

Timeline T1

T1 begins:

The series of wars known as the religion wars began towards the end of the seventeen-thousands.

There is no exact date on record, however, the first major skirmish using Bosun missiles, which resulted in the loss of more than three million people within the first hour, is generally accepted to have occurred on the four-hundred-and fiftieth light-time of seventeen-thousand-eight-hundred and thirty-one.

Tanun leaned closer to Joor-Jen as they watched the pictures on the screen and listened to the narrative.

Although the Southern Religion Alliance (SRA) never claimed responsibility, there is general agreement this alliance fired the first Bosun missiles at a civilian target.

'Pod, pause. What is it, Tanun?'

'When I was trying to find out about this, a link took me to Bosun missiles, but for an instant, before the "Refer to Elders" message came up, I saw a link from Bosun missiles to KimMorii. Had no idea what that meant.'

'Pod, continue,' instructed Joor-Jen.

Timeline T2

T2 begins

Throughout the ten-thousand-year war, there were frequent attempts at negotiation and more than three hundred and fifty thousand ceasefires agreed, but no permanent accommodation was ever reached and most ceasefires were used by all sides, to improve logistics and move armoury to favoured positions.

Timeline T3

T3 begins:

Around twenty-seven-thousand-eight-hundred, with the SRA gaining territory, together with more and more worshippers (willing and coerced), the Eastern and Northern Religious Alliance (ENRA) launched what they believed would be a winning counteroffensive and deployed genome disrupters.

Timeline T4

T4 begins:

There were many unforeseen consequences from this action, not least of which was the rendering of the majority of plant-life and many animal species infertile and the generation of seven-hundred and seventy-million cubic kilometres of hydrocyanic gas.

Timeline T5

T5 begins:

However, towards the end of the religion wars, for about the last two-thousand years, the alliances had been developing protective geodesic spheres in which people could live if the outside environment became intolerable.

Tanun's left shoulder was pressing against Joor-Jen's right, and his left leg was partially across her legs while they concentrated on the screen. He didn't know which cleangel she used, but made a mental note to ask her if there were different ones because hers was the best ever.

Timeline T6

T6 begins:

Professor Dome achieved great insight into how these spheres could be constructed of suitably light yet strong materials and made tolerable for occupation by thousands, often up to millions of people.

His concept of protecting the spheres by mounting them on tall stilts or legs, with rungs, terminating in dishes, serving the purpose of strengthening the legs as well as deterring unauthorized access, was widely adopted.

Timeline T7

T7 begins

In recognition of Dome's work, the spheres have since been generally known colloquially as, and referred to as, domes.

Subsection Timeline ends.

Joor-Jen. Would you like me to send the data to your DD?"

'No. Not this time.'

Pod. Dormant

For a long while, Tanun and Joor-Jen looked in silence at the empty screen until he moved his legs and took his hand from hers so he could take off his earpieces.

'Thanks, Joor-Jen. I guess you knew all that?'

'Mostly. We start with learning about the religion wars, I suppose because they define how we come to be living in protective domes with a depleted population.'

'At least the mystery as to why the spheres are called domes is sorted.'

'Yes. Later sections do not present Professor Dome in a good light.'

'Oh. He should be considered a hero, shouldn't he?'

'People believe he must have had help from somewhere to have conceived the engineering and the special materials required.'

'Does it matter?'

'If the help came from the KimMorii, it probably does.'

'Oh, crap. Was he a co-operator then?'

'That's what people believe. To some, that still makes him a hero. To others, he's a rogue. A very evil one at that.'

'There's so much I want to ask the pods. How the people from the domes formed alliances, what food is produced, how big the railway network was – what's the population now and what was it before?'

'Knowledge is infinite, Tanun. You could spend your whole life in here and never reach a millionth.'

'I know. But because we – I – missed out on so much, I want to catch up.'

'We'll come here as often as we can, but you have your training and we have our work on the farms.'

'I'd forgotten about that.'

'Time for food and your DD. We can head out that way.'

\* \* \*

After Joor-Jen and Tanun had taken food in the refectory, she took Tanun down to medical level 297. Tanun whispered in her ear he was nervous, so she told him the assessments were painless and would be over quickly. The whole process was fairly automated, apart from the psych-eval at the end. She assured him she would be waiting outside to take him for his DD fitting.

'This is it.' She kissed him on his cheek. 'In you go.'

'Hello Tanun. I am medic Bee-Sun. Through here, please. We need some scans so you will need to lie on that bed. Without your clothes. After we've scanned your eyes, we'll place a protector over them while we do the brain and body scan.'

Tanun stared at the bed, which looked as if it slid into the cylinder at its head. *Can I run? Where to? Would the doors open? Too late anyway. I'm probably on a hundred screens already.*

'No need to be nervous, Tanun. We see thousands of people. Put your clothes on that chair and lie on the bed face up.'

Keeping his eyes nearly closed, because, like a child, if he couldn't see others he hoped others wouldn't be able to see him, he hung his clothes on the chair and climbed onto the bed.

'Right. Nothing to worry about, but eyes first. Stare straight upwards.'

A pair of small spheres whirred down and stopped a centimetre from his eyes.

'Excellent. I'm going to place this protector over your eyes and you will feel the bed move into the scanner. Keep as still as you can and it will be over quicker.'

*What can I think of to take my mind off all this? All I can think about is how embarrassing this is. My body must be on all those screens. What if I get an erection? Better not think about that. Autosuggestion and all that. How long is it going to take? What are they testing? Hurry up. Hurry up. I've really had enough.*

'Excellent, Tanun. All done. When you're ready, please get dressed and medic Yan-See will take you to the next room and ask you some questions.'

'Please sit down there, Tanun,' said Yan-See. 'I am going to ask you one hundred and one questions – quite quickly. We have found the best way is to answer quickly as well, without thinking too much about the answer. Is that clear? Is there anything you want to ask me?'

'Will I get to see the results of everything?'

'Of course you will. We will send them to your DD. Ready for me to start?'

'Sure.'

\* \* \*

'Hey, Tanun. Not so bad?'

'Not if you like laying naked on a bed, Joor-Jen.'

'You seem to.'

'Thanks.'

'Two rooms along. I can come in with you.'

'I don't need to undress again, do I?'

'Not unless you want to. Just your top. Here we are. Let's go in.'

'Hello, Tanun. I am senior medic Kel-Lin. Please try to relax. The more tense your muscles are, the more discomfort you'll experience.'

Tanun looked around the room with its bed on wheels, a fearsome-looking metal frame at one end, instruments in metal dishes and huge lights at the end of flexible hoses. He rubbed his nose from the sharp disinfectant smell.

'When you're ready, take off your top and lie on the bed face-down with your head over that end. If you'd like Joor-Jen to hold your hand, that's no problem.'

'Please.'

'I'm going to raise the bed so your neck is level with my eyes. Joor-Jen, the other side, please.'

Tanun reached for her hand, and when their fingers interlocked, he felt his neck relax.

'We fit a rigid frame over your head and shoulders to hold you still during the implant. Lowering it now. Tightening it now. Well done. Now, an injection in your neck to numb the muscle. Sharp stab. Well done, Tanun.'

He couldn't move his upper body. The metal frame held his head, neck, and shoulder tightly in position. All he could do was stare at the floor. When he tried to recoil from the pain, the frame didn't flex.

'Sorry, Tanun. The first insertion didn't take. I have to try another.'

He gripped Joor-Jen's fingers. *Lucky I can't move – I'd probably dislocate something.*

'I'm going to give you another jab to help with the pain. Third-time lucky.'

He wanted to. With all his might, he wanted to. But he wasn't going to cry out and let a stupid DD win.

'All done, Tanun. One of my best patients. Please keep the dressing on for six dark-times. Showering won't trouble it.'

Tanun sat on the chair and as he pulled his top over his head, his hand lingered over the large dressing on his neck.

'Are you taking him back, Joor-Jen? Good. He needs to sleep until light-time. Nice to have met you, Tanun.'

In the elevator, Tanun admitted to Joor-Jen he wasn't feeling that great. She told him it was pretty normal to feel rough afterwards. 'The older you are, the worse it tends to be.'

The door to 230-125 whooshed sideways. 'I'll see you to your bed,' said Joor-Jen. 'Don't forget, Peeso-Lun and Bento-Tor will be collecting you at light-time.'

Tanun flopped onto his bunk. 'I'd forgotten.'

'Chyke's out of it as well, by the looks of it.'

'Know the feeling. Thanks, Joor-Jen.'

Joor-Jen knelt and kissed him quickly on his lips. Sleep well.'

# SIX: Matching

Tanun was lying on his bunk listening to a knowledge pod narration on his DD about food production outside the dome when Joor-Jen whooshed in. 'Hi, Joor-Jen.'

'Where's Chyke?'

'With Peeso-Lun. Said they were going to study weaponry through the religion wars.'

'Big subject. Lento-Fin has asked me to tell you Cassièl will be visiting again to try to relieve you of Dodecahedron.'

'Waste of time. We know he can't.'

'This visit will be different. He's bringing a child. His child.'

Tanun sat up on his bunk. 'Cassièl? Children?'

'Why not?'

'Just that, well, never thought of him like that.'

'Like what?'

'He just seems ... detached. Not of this world.'

'Well, he isn't.'

'Suppose that's it. How old?'

'Don't know. I imagine their years are a bit different from ours.'

'Imagine so. When's this going to happen? Where?'

'Here. Now. On your own. Best way.'

Tanun blew out his cheeks. *At least I'll be rid of Dodecahedron. Remembering to take it everywhere with me is such a drag. And while it's here, those KimMorii creatures could cause trouble. The sooner I'm rid of the stone, the sooner we can all be left alone.* 'Thanks for the info, Joor-Jen. Do I just hang around and wait?'

'That's what Lento-Fin said. Were you going anywhere?'

'Very funny.'

Joor-Jen stared down at Tanun and with a clipped voice said, 'Shall we get food afterwards? Something to discuss, and you can tell me all about it.'

'Good idea. Is something wrong?'

'Not wrong. Um, not wrong. Let's wait until Cassièl's visited.'

'Let's not. I can tell something's not right. Tell me.'

'Don't get mad,' Joor-Jen breathed out. 'You know boys and girls are matched up? At sixteen?'

'I know.'

'Chyke's sixteen.'

'And?'

'The pods have run a matching. They do this every ninety dark-times.'

Tanun stared into Joor-Jen's eyes. *What is she going to say? I know Chyke and Peeso-Lun have got close. Inevitable, I guess.*

'The matching says Chyke ... and me, are an optimum pairing.'

Tanun swallowed as bile rose in his throat. *I must have misheard. Must have been daydreaming again. Tormenting thoughts have got in ... I wonder why Joor-Jen is still standing there?*

'Aren't you going to say something?'

Joor-Jen's voice brought him back into the room. 'Like ... that's great, Joor-Jen? Like ... I'm so happy for you both? Like ... fantastic, you're made for each other?'

'I ... I ... look, I thought ...' Tanun shook his head. 'Look, that's just a system. Doesn't do feelings.'

'Do you do feelings, Tanun?'

'What's that supposed to mean? Don't you know my feelings for you?'

'How am I supposed to know? You never show any feelings. No warmth, care.'

Tanun put his head in his hands. 'You're an apostle. I guessed you were spoken for. Had special privileges.'

'That's transactional, Tanun. Analytical. Where are your feelings?' Joor-Jen bent down towards him. 'Wouldn't they override any analysis? Anyhow, Chyke knows as well. Says we ought to start practising as soon as possible. Funny, I asked him if he was worried about how you'd react.'

'That's good of you.'

'He got it wrong, though. Said you'd be pleased and would probably carry on studying.'

Tanun leaped up from his bunk and stood face-to-face with Joor-Jen. 'You are not getting matched with my brother. I'll do whatever I have to, to stop that happening.'

'And what right do you think you have?'

'I'm his brother! And-' Tanun sniffed as his eyes filled with tears, 'I couldn't bear it. I may not show it, Joor-Jen, but I think about you every moment. I want to be with you all the time and I hate it when we're not together.' Tanun reached out and pulled her to him.

Joor-Jen resisted slightly, then relented and said, 'Tanun, you haven't said anything, or showed the slightest feelings before. Now that I have a match, you've somehow motivated yourself enough to prevent Chyke and me getting together. How can I believe you? Trust you? How do I know your feelings are genuine and not just sour circs?'

Tanun pulled her tighter. 'It's not Chyke. Not because of him. I want the best for him, whatever that is. It's ... it's

... I couldn't bear us being apart. I can't lose you, Joor-Jen. I have to show you and yet I don't know how. That's the problem. I thought you were out of reach. Thought you would laugh at me. I just assumed you had someone. After all, you're eighteen. Didn't want to put you in a difficult situation.'

Joor-Jen put her arm around Tanun. 'Let's sit on your bunk. Don't cry. I had no idea this is how you felt. I knew you were special. Under your matter-of-fact attitude, you're deep. I could see that. I knew, I just knew. You challenged your Elders in your trial! And when you had your DD fitted, most people screamed. You didn't. You took it. Even though it took three insertions. And in training, you've taken more blows, more falls than anyone ever. Why, why, why didn't you show me how you felt?'

Tanun turned from looking at the floor to Joor-Jen. 'Sorry, Joor-Jen. I couldn't have dealt with the rejection. Thought I'd just have to suck it up.'

Joor-Jen studied his red eyes and leant into him until their lips met.

'I need to go,' she said, pulling away. 'Cassièl will be here any moment. I won't forget what you said, Tanun. I saw your real self. You should show it more often, you know? I liked it. Look, I'll tell Chyke. I'll explain ... just because the system has matched us, doesn't make it compulsory. There. Sorted. Good luck with Cassièl.'

'See you. And thank you.'

'You didn't need to say that.'

Tanun went to the bathroom and splashed his face and head with water. After drying himself he sat on his bunk, trying to recapture her smell. When three knocks on his door startled him, he wasn't sure how long he'd been sitting there. Nobody had ever knocked.

'Greetings, Tanun. Please, may we enter?'

'Sure.'

'Hello, Tanun,' said Cassièl. 'I hope you are feeling better now. I understand Joor-Jen pre-warned you. This is Ennti. My daughter.'

'Hello, Tanun. I am pleased to meet you.'

Tanun smiled at a slight girl about half Cassièl's height, wearing a red cloak.

She held out her hand to him.

As Tanun shook her hand, she said, 'I have learnt about you and your brother. You have been brave, challenging your Elders and keeping the Nucleus safe for us. My father wants to see if I can retrieve Dodecahedron and relieve you of the burden.'

'I'm very pleased to meet you, Ennti. I must admit, I hadn't considered Cassièl might have children.'

'Empirically, he does. I think in your terms, I am approximately nine years, but of course in mine that is more like three million of your years. Father?'

'Right, Ennti. As we've discussed, Tanun will hold out Dodecahedron on his left palm, and we will see if you can take it from him.'

Tanun rummaged under his pillow and placed Dodecahedron on his left palm. He extended his arm towards Ennti. 'Ennti,' he said, looking into her eyes, 'please take Dodecahedron.'

Ennti looked to Cassièl. 'Now, Father?'

Cassièl nodded. Tanun closed his eyes. Ennti reached for the stone. But she could not lift it from Tanun's palm.

Tanun looked at the stone and then at Ennti. Ennti looked to her father. Cassièl looked at Tanun.

'I am so sorry, Tanun. Despite this I am still convinced there will be a way. I am also convinced the solution involves children in some way or other. Might be siblings, brothers, sisters. Could be twins. Meanwhile, as I have said before, please keep the stone safe and always keep it with you. Never leave it on its own. When I have pondered the problem further, I shall return. Come on, Ennti. We should not really be here.'

'Please, Father. Please could I talk with Tanun a little longer? I have learnt so much about physical beings, but that is not as great as actually being in the presence of one.'

'Feeling like a specimen, Tanun?' said Cassièl.

Tanun laughed. 'Yeah, a bit. Don't mind though. Ennti. How do you learn things? I mean, we have the knowledge pods, but we're physical, as you said.'

'Oh, we have lessons. By thought. And nearly all of us like reading. We have a large bibliotheca.'

Tanun shook his head. 'I'm amazed how similar it all is. Except for communicating by thought.'

'And our timelines are different. And there are approximately 9,547,632 children – is that your term? – children? – at each lesson. And–

'I think Tanun gets your point, Ennti. Before we go, is there anything you would like to ask him?'

'Tanun. You are very nice. Because you are so nice, I hope you have a girlfriend.'

Tanun laughed, but felt the heat rising in his face and felt it must have shown. 'I think I do, Ennti. And I hope when you are older you will have a nice boyfriend.'

'I will. I wish we could meet again and compare them, but I fear our timelines will prevent that.'

'And our timeline has run out,' said Cassièl. 'Come on, Ennti. Thank you for everything, Tanun.'

'No problem, Cassièl. Bye, Ennti.'

'Goodbye, Tanun. I enjoyed meeting you.'

* * *

Peeso-Lun and Bento-Tor led Tanun and Chyke from their den to the hatch. This light-time, they'd explained, they'd be working far from the dome in the vegetable fields, as was required of everyone.

'We'll be about an hour away, so we'll still be able to see the dome,' said Bento-Tor. 'We have to harvest two types of vegetable. Telcs and circs. Telcs are long and green one end and white the other. Circs are round and yellow. Both are root crops and require digging out. Each of us must fill the two bags from our rucksacks.'

With the two suns high in the benevolent green sky and a soft breeze carrying a spicy scent from the woods beyond the oat fields, Tanun pulled the top of his boilersuit down and let the warmth and smells and tickling breeze wander over him.

Everyone worked along the rows in a staggered formation, laying the vegetables on the raised mounds to dry before packing. Chyke worked opposite Tanun, slightly to his left. After about an hour and a half, Chyke called across, 'Hey, Tanun. Did Joor-Jen tell you?'

'Tell me what?'

'We've been matched.' Chyke sent Tanun a victorious smile. 'The system has matched Joor-Jen and me.'

Tanun stopped digging, leant on his fork and stared at his brother. 'The system might have matched you, but that doesn't mean anything. Joor-Jen's an apostle. She can choose.'

'Yes. And she's chosen me. We've talked about it.'

Tanun lifted his fork and shoved it back into the ground. 'When? Because the other dark-time, in our den,

Joor-Jen promised she'd chosen me. So, you're out of date, brother.'

'You're bluffing. When did she see you?'

'I said. You and Peeso-Lun were at the pods again. Getting on Ok with her, are you?'

'What if I am? What's it to you?'

'Nothing to me. I hope you'll be very happy together. Because you won't be with Joor-Jen.'

'You're just a git. I'll put Joor-Jen right, you'll see. She promised.'

'Seems promises are cheap. Stay away from her. She's mine.'

'You're deluded, that's what you are. You've never shown her any feelings.'

'Back off right now, Chyke. My feelings are my own. I don't need you monitoring them.'

'You've lost, Tanun. Admit it.'

'Give it a rest. Or I'll have to make you.'

'Oh, big brother, playing the- '

The wail of a siren climbed, climbed, climbed to a crescendo and descended, then climbed, climbed and descended again, over and over. Spades, forks, picks, and hoes fell to the ground as everyone clamped their hands over their ears and looked to the sky. When it came, the impact made many fly backwards like little figurines pulled by a string in their back. Earth and debris rained down for several minutes.

# SEVEN: Webs

With his arms trapped, and buried upright almost to his neck, Tanun screwed up his face to try to ease the pain of the siren. Tried to move his arms. Made some space. Kicked with his legs and trod earth. Slid and grabbed, grabbed and slid, over and over until he fell panting onto the scorched earth. As he spat blood and bits, he screamed at the top of his voice, 'I WISH THAT SIREN WOULD SHUT UP!'

Chyke rolled to a stop at the bottom of the crater. His spade tumbled on top of him. He too pressed his hands over his ears to reduce the wailing siren and tried to get his bearings. *What just happened? Must have been an explosion. Where is everybody?* After turning onto his hands and knees he scrambled up the side of the crater, frequently sliding down again on smouldering rocks and stones, until he eventually flopped breathless over the edge.

'Up you get.' Tanun offered his muddy bloody hand and pulled Chyke upright. 'Must have been a missile. Didn't hit the dome. Let's see if we can find others.'

Staggering a little, they walked in a wider and wider circle until Chyke pointed at an arm sticking up from the ground a few metres away. Tanun dug the earth away with his hands to reveal a head. He wiped away the muck from the face to see Bento-Tor.

'Thanks,' he said, spitting blood and teeth. 'Yuck.'

'I'm going to dig around you,' said Chyke. 'So keep still. I don't want to hit you with the spade. Tanun will pull you out when I've got rid of some earth.'

After Chyke had dug away piles of earth and stones,

Tanun gripped both wrists and dragged Bento-Tor up from the sliding soil.

'Thanks, thanks, thanks. I owe you. Mouth's killing me. Where's Peeso-Lun?'

'Dunno,' said Tanun. 'You're the first we found. We'd better make for the dome. I wish they'd stop that siren.'

Bento-Tor pulled away from Tanun's grip. 'Gotta find Peeso-Lun. She must be here.'

'I get that, but listen, we don't know where to look. Everything's been turned over. Would take us loads of light-times.'

'And another missile might hit us any moment,' said Chyke.

'You three. To the dome. Now!' A marshal appeared and pointed with a look that didn't negotiate.

Bento-Tor straightened. 'I want to find Peeso-Lun.'

'Get yourself to the dome. If anyone's alive, the rescue teams will find them. Go. Now.'

Bento-Tor turned to Tanun. 'I can't just leave her.'

'Come on.' He gripped Bento-Tor's upper arm and pulled him forward. 'The rescue teams will find her. I reckon we're in for a beating if we don't move. For all we know, she's already climbing the rungs.'

Tanun, Chyke, and Bento-Tor made their way through the landscape of craters, smashed vegetables, and metal of all shapes and sizes long buried from the religion wars, giant, elongated triangles of metal, long hollow cylinders three or four metres in length, hinged slats of metal, twisted and tortured into grotesque statues and hats and helmets with eye-pieces and ear-covers. As they passed mounds of scattered telcs and circs, each of them retched at the sight of a leg, or arm, or head, resting incongruously among the vegetables. Nearer the dome, thousands of people were queueing to make their way up the leg. Some seemed unaffected in any way, but others were staggering, leaning on another, being carried, unrecognisable from blood or torn flesh. As the siren faded, the moans and the screams rose to take its place. Down the other five legs flowed streams of search and rescue teams. Marshals were funnelling the well and the wounded to the ascent leg, and Tanun, Chyke, and Bento-Tor shuffled along in the queue until they reached the dish at the bottom of the leg.

'You three don't look so bad,' said a marshal.

'Teeth, that's all,' said Bento-Tor. 'Actually, I was buried and these guys saved me.'

'Good on you, boys. Names?'

'Bento-Tor.'

'You're military.'

'Yeah.'

'You?'

'Tanun.'

'Chyke. Newcomers.'

'Missiles don't discriminate. Up you go, then. Go to medical. Get checked out.'

*** 

Tanun opened his eyes to see Cassièl and Lento-Fin staring down at him. The moment of confusion dissolved into the memory of the blast, digging out Bento-Tor, and the bodies and bits scattered like litter across the tortured landscape. And the climb.

'Where am I?'

'On the medical level,' said Lento-Fin. 'You're fine, but you were in shock. Chyke's Ok, too, and we've fixed Bento-Tor's teeth. Well done for rescuing him. Tanun, I'm sorry, but Peeso-Lun caught a lot of the blast. The teams have found most of her.'

'Crap. Poor Bento-Tor. I told him she was probably climbing the rungs. What an idiot.'

'Not at all,' said Cassièl. 'You said the right thing to get him back to the dome. There was nothing he could have done. I expect you saved him a blow from a marshal.'

'What happened?'

'The Percutio Alliance launched a missile at our dome – and other domes in our alliance,' said Lento-Fin. 'Our defences deflected the missile from its target into the fields. Still a significant loss of life, but less so than if the missile had struck the dome.'

'That's a hell of a decision.'

'War, Tanun, war. You can go back to your den now and rest. Joor-Jen is waiting outside. She'll take you.'

Oh. His face burned from the memory of their last encounter. And Chyke. The argument in the field – how trivial that was now. Although the situation was still awkward.

'Neither Lento-Fin nor I can help you in that regard,' said Cassièl, aware of Tanun's thoughts. 'You three will just have to figure it out.'

'A word of advice,' said Lento-Fin. 'Joor-Jen was brought here as an orphan. Her parents were convicted of sedition and were executed. Her guardian escaped from the dome and made her way here with a baby – Joor-Jen. The penalty for that would also be death.'

'Wow. I always felt she had a backstory, but nothing like that. She doesn't open up much.'

'No. Joor-Jen has had to forge her identity and fight to establish herself as a bona fide member of this dome. As you have learnt, she's become a formidable fighter, and yet her emotional journey, understandably, has been difficult. Joor-Jen does not always know what Joor-Jen wants. Interpreting Joor-Jen's intentions and the webs she spins are often beyond her, let alone the rest of us.'

'Thanks, Lento-Fin. I've experienced some of that. I just hope Chyke doesn't get caught in one of her webs.'

'First, you have to know there's a web.'

When Tanun and Joor-Jen arrived back at his den, she gave him a long kiss in the doorway and said she would collect him and Chyke at light-time to go to the briefing on the missile and the consultation about the alliance's response.

Tanun checked the top bunk. Chyke was quite still, facing the wall with the cover pulled almost over his head. Tanun sat on his bunk, counting his bruises. He knew they'd been incredibly lucky, but couldn't understand how he, Chyke, and Bento-Tor had survived, yet Peeso-Lun hadn't. Where was the logic in who survived and who didn't? But there was no logic in war. War. How could it be happening? After thousands of years? He buried his head in his hands, but after a while felt calmer and decided a shower would help.

He stayed in the shower for longer than usual, going over the argument he'd had with Chyke just before the missile. Afterwards, he remembered to put on a clean boiler suit before crashing onto his bunk.

*  *  *

Bento-Tor strode from the door to the bunk beds. 'You're awake. Where's Chyke?'

'What?' Tanun stood up and stared at the top bunk. An empty top bunk. 'What the hell's he playing at?'

Bento-Tor moved Chyke's bed cover. 'Blood. Might be

from the blast. Was he here when you got back last dark-time?'

'Yeah. Asleep. Don't know who brought him.'

'I did.'

'Joor-Jen brought me back,' Tanun said. 'I felt pretty rough so I had a shower. Can't say I looked at his bunk afterwards. What a git. I bet he's with Joor-Jen.'

'He isn't. She's with Lento-Fin. They're preparing for the big meeting. I've got a really bad feeling about this, Tanun.'

'How do you mean?' But when Tanun turned to look at Bento-Tor, he saw his bloodshot eyes. 'Sorry, sorry, Bento-Tor. I'm at fault. I should have said about Peeso-Lun. I'm so sorry. So sorry. There's no justice. No logic.' Bento-Tor fell against Tanun and they wrapped their arms around each other. 'Listen. I'm going to look after you. I know you're Chyke's apostle. Well, I guess you still are, but that doesn't mean I'm not here for you. Any time you need.'

Bento-Tor wiped his eyes. 'Thanks, Tanun. I won't forget.' He pulled away and stared at the window. 'We did everything together. Can't believe she won't walk in the door or sit in the refectory and explain something the knowledge pods said. Beat me again in close-combat. What a sister.'

'It'll be like that for a long time, but it'll get better. I meant it, you know, when I said I'll be here for you. Are you Ok now to tell me what you meant? Your bad feeling?'

'Don't want to say, really. Chyke wouldn't be the first. Every dome in every alliance has spies, infiltrators. People working against. Tanun, I think Chyke's been kidnapped.'

Tanun fought the nausea rising in his throat and pulled Bento-Tor down so they could both sit on his bunk. 'But how? How could they get in?'

'They were probably already here. Come on, we must tell Joor-Jen.'

* * *

Lento-Fin and Joor-Jen were deep in conversation at the top table when Bento-Tor and Tanun entered the meeting room. Tanun followed Bento-Tor and they stood and waited for the conversation to pause. People were rushing here and there preparing the tables for the meeting. Tanun looked along the thin vertical clear screens which formed a continuous line down the table on the left, along the table facing the top table, and back up along the table on the right.

'Hello, Bento-Tor,' said Lento-Fin. 'And hello, Tanun. Feeling Ok?'

Before Tanun could reply that although he felt Ok from the DD he did not feel Ok about Chyke, Bento-Tor spoke.

'Chyke's been kidnapped.'

Joor-Jen stood up and stared at Tanun. 'You sure? How do you know that?'

'Because Bento-Tor said so!' said Tanun. 'I saw Chyke on his bunk when I got back. I thought he had come to you. But ... there was blood on his sheet. He was there last darktime. Gone this light-time.'

'I suspect Bento-Tor is right,' said Lento-Fin. 'Joor-Jen – get the investigators onto this and check who's also missing. That might give us a clue. Bento-Tor and you, Tanun, will have to help the investigators by answering some questions.'

'What questions?' said Tanun. 'Chyke's missing. Isn't that obvious?'

'Questions like, "Are you one hundred percent sure it was Chyke you saw on his bunk? Was he facing you? Did you see his face? It was dark-time. You were groggy. Perhaps it was an imposter. A dummy. A dead body".'

'Lento-Fin's quite right, Tanun,' said Bento-Tor. 'Professional investigators know how to look at a situation from every angle. Verify assumptions.'

'Suppose so. Sorry. Bit stressed.'

Joor-Jen took Tanun and Bento-Tor down to level 298 and told them this would be where the investigators would do their questioning. After locating room 103, she kissed Tanun on the lips and left him and Bento-Tor waiting together outside the room, saying she had to go to the meeting.

'Do you get the feeling we're the accused?' said Tanun.

'No, not really, Tanun. All the investigations I've known are like this. Dedicated investigators are very clever at establishing facts and timelines. For example, I saw Chyke was missing, you didn't. Even though you were on the bunk underneath.'

'I know I didn't. Was a bit groggy.'

'Don't beat yourself up about it.'

'Bento-Tor. Please come with me,' said a tall man. 'Tanun. Wait there.'

Bento-Tor sat down at the grey desk and looked through the transparent screen at the man.

'Now, Bento-Tor. I am investigator Sin-Tun.' As Sin-Tun spoke, his words appeared on the screen and scrolled upwards. 'Neither you nor Tanun is under suspicion, but this is a very serious event so we want to understand exactly what happened and when. I am very sorry for your loss, this is the last thing you need, but if you are clear and accurate, you will be out of here more quickly. Start with you and Chyke reaching his den.'

'Ok. We were both on the medical level, but I

recovered more quickly than Chyke, despite my teeth, so I went and found him. When the medics said he could go back to his den, they let me take him. When we got there, he said he had to sleep, so I actually helped him up to his top bunk.'

'So, he didn't shower or take off his clothes?'

'No. Chyke likes to sleep in his boiler suit and shower at light-time.'

'Which way did he lie?'

'Er, facing away, I think. Yes, that's it. I remember he pulled his cover almost over his head and seemed to go to sleep immediately.'

'What did you do next?'

'After I'd said sleep well, I remember wondering how long Tanun would be. I've since learnt he was very late back because he'd been talking with Lento-Fin. I couldn't face going back to my den on my own, so I went to the refectory.'

'What did you do there?'

'Drank. Hot drinks, cold drinks, green drinks, blue drinks. Something to do. Dark-time seemed endless. Always does when you're awake.'

'What happened next?'

'Joor-Jen came and sat with me. Something happened. I couldn't hold it in anymore and I broke down. I still couldn't believe Peeso-Lun wouldn't be around. Joor-Jen was brilliant. She either didn't say anything, or when she did she said exactly the right thing. When I'd got myself together, she said Xen-Lin wanted to see me, and after that, work was what I needed and would do me good. Displacement activity, she said, whatever that means. Told me to go and collect Tanun and Chyke for the briefing before I went to Xen-Lin.'

'Did you go straight to Tanun and Chyke's den?'

'Yes, I did.'

'Are you sure about that, Bento-Tor?'

'Um. Well, no, not exactly. It's difficult. Sorry, didn't want to admit it. I went to a wet room and bawled my eyes out. Then I went to their den. I didn't see Xen-Lin, in case you're wondering.'

'Who noticed Chyke was missing?'

'I did. Tanun was awake, lying on his bunk.'

'What did you say? What did he say?'

'I said, "Where's Chyke?". Tanun said something, can't remember what, and stood up. He was annoyed. He thought Chyke had gone to Joor-Jen.'

'Many thanks, Bento-Tor. Appreciate your honesty, especially given how you are feeling after your loss. Would you like to keep your den, or would moving in with Tanun help, perhaps?'

'Oh. Well, actually, I know I'm due for matching, but I'm really good friends with Xen-Lin. Could he move in with me? We've wanted to for a while.'

'I see. That should not be a problem. I will update the system and arrange for his things to be moved to your den. Would you mind waiting outside while I talk to Tanun? You could take him back to his den when we've finished.'

'Tanun, I am investigator Sin-Tun. I want you to understand, neither you nor Bento-Tor is under suspicion, but this is a very serious event so we want to understand exactly what happened and when. I appreciate your brother is missing, so this is very stressful, and the last thing you need, but if you are clear and accurate you will be out of here more quickly. Start when you and Joor-Jen reached your den.'

'To be honest, everything's a bit of a blur. I was feeling

rough in the elevator. I don't remember walking along the corridor, but I do remember the door sliding open.'

'And?'

'I was desperate to get to my bed. I sat on it for a while, counting my bruises.'

'Are you sure that's all, Tanun? Think carefully.'

'I'm sure that's all. Oh, I know. I checked on Chyke before sitting on my bunk.'

'How did you check?'

'Just looked up at him. He was quite still, with his cover almost over his head.'

'So, you don't actually know for certain who you saw was actually Chyke?'

'Er, he was facing away, and I didn't see his face, if that's what you mean, but the shape and size seemed right. And how he sleeps curled up.'

'What did you do next?'

'I had a shower. I was still covered in earth and blood and everything. Actually, I was in there longer than normal. When the shower stopped, I started it again.'

'Afterwards?'

'Put on a clean boiler suit and crashed out.'

'Did you check on Chyke again?'

'Er, no. I'd only been a few minutes.'

'Thank you, Tanun. Bento-Tor will take you back.'

# EIGHT: Balls

Hood pulled off. Tape pulled off.

'Argh!'

Four KimMorii enforcers. Female on the left. Knelt. Fitted ankle tag. Stood up. Slapped him across the face.

'Argh.'

'Release him from his chair.'

Male on the right, 'Any funny business, sunshine, and next time you'll be strapped so tight to that chair your balls will burst. Sleep well.'

Chyke didn't move from his chair for a long while after the door had whooshed shut. When he stood up, he rubbed his wrists and ankles, but the collar of his boiler suit scratched a wound on his neck as he fell onto the hard coverless bench. *Look. Chair's not even a chair. Just a frame. Lighter, I suppose. I shouldn't have struggled. Git with the knife nicked me as he pressed the tape over my mouth.* He looked around. *Cell's like Tanun said. I guess I must be back in the old dome, but why? Why would they care that I'd escaped? One less mouth to feed. What are they going to do with me? I suppose that depends on why they kidnapped me.*

The cell turned in an instant into total darkness.

* * *

Sin-Tun explained to Lento-Fin and the nine Governors that Chyke had indeed been kidnapped and was taken while Tanun was in the shower. Very professionally executed, he said. The team had comprised two Special Forces from Chyke's old dome plus two infiltrators from this dome, Can-Bor and Lyn-Kre. Lento-Fin asked how long these two had been working for the enemy and Sin-

Tun suggested at least ten years. He said both Tanun and Bento-Tor had been honest, except Tanun had missed out the kiss with Joor-Jen in the doorway, and Bento-Tor had missed out seeing Xen-Lin briefly. Lento-Fin said he would have done the same at their age, but thank goodness for the knowledge pods which recorded everything. Sin-Tun said he had set up another investigation into why the infiltrators had not been detected, which drew agreement from everyone. Lento-Fin asked what motive there could be to kidnap Chyke, but not Tanun, and Sin-Tun explained this must mean the KimMorii and the Elders from Tanun and Chyke's dome thought he had the stone.

Lento-Fin said that regardless, they must not abandon Chyke and should devise a plan to rescue him.

'That will be fraught with peril,' said a Governor. 'Apart from the difficulty of gaining access, it would mean activating at least two of our sleepers in 1279-41130.'

'But as well as rescuing Chyke, we might gain useful intelligence while doing so.'

'If the mission should go awry, Chyke would be killed,' said another Governor.

'Then it must not,' said Lento-Fin.

The meeting room had filled during the discussion in anticipation of the planned briefing, and an aide to Lento-Fin said, 'Everyone is ready. We should start on time.'

'Yes, thank you, we should.'

He stood to address the assembled Governors, administrators, medics, soldiers, and Special Forces. Joor-Jen arrived with Tanun and stood to the side of the top table.

'Thank you for attending this briefing. As you know, the Percutio Alliance launched missiles at our dome and thirty-one others in our alliance. We suffered the fewest fatalities, with only four-hundred and twenty-one, and seventeen hundred and thirty-two injured. However, we believe this is only the beginning. And to compound this tragedy, the next dark-time, a newcomer, young Chyke, was kidnapped from his den, helped by infiltrators here.'

Mumbling and cries of shock rose until Lento-Fin raised his hand.

'Naturally, investigations into both these events are in process, and in response, two missions are planned. The first will attempt to disable the weaponry at the nearest Percutio Alliance dome, which is where we believe the missile that nearly hit us originated. This will, of course, be a covert operation where stealth will be more important than brute force. The second mission will be to rescue Chyke. Our intelligence suggests he has been taken back to his original dome, and although we can only guess at the reason, that hardly matters. This will probably be the more difficult mission, so our top Special Forces, Joor-Jen, Bento-Tor, and Xen-Lin will lead it, plus two further SFs.'

Tanun stepped forward to protest that he should be on the mission to rescue Chyke, but Joor-Jen held him back with her arm.

'Wait. And listen. There's a reason.'

'And myself, with Tanun, and four SFs, will execute the disabling mission. Let's set to, rescuing Chyke and defending our alliance and what we believe in.'

When the briefing had ended, Joor-Jen told Tanun that before his mission he was to have another session of advanced training with her and Xen-Lin and they would shortly descend to the oat fields. Tanun challenged why they had to go outside and Joor-Jen said because if there were another missile, they would stand more chance outside than in the dome.

After descending, Tanun went through his close-combat skills with each of them, including defending against a knife, an axe, and a chain. Before they finished, Joor-Jen introduced a selection of different spears and a bow with seven arrows. Tanun mocked that would be reverting to savagery and no-way would those ancient weapons be used.

Joor-Jen said anything was possible with the enemy and he should be trained not only in their use, but more importantly, their avoidance in battle. When the session ended, she presented him with a shoulder holster and a pulse gun. 'This is a 10/10. Good for 10k distance and ten thousand discharges. Hence its name. Silent, but that's deceptive. Don't get hit by one. The pulses paralyse all your voluntary movements. Exaggerates all your involuntary. Until your heart gives up. Not a pretty sight. Or experience.'

'I still wish I was coming with you. I know I'll be with Lento-Fin, but thinking about you two and Chyke all the time will be torture.'

'Your torture doesn't compare to what Chyke might be experiencing. I've done rescues before. I'm good at them. And so has Bento-Tor and Xen-Lin.'

'There's so much I don't know about you.'

'Time for target practice. Our SFs have set some high targets across the fields towards the woods. Let's go.'

On the climb back up, Tanun asked Joor-Jen and Xen-Lin about their previous rescues and Joor-Jen told him about a rescue of thirteen-year-old girl twins who had been banished from their dome for using telepathy between themselves. Joor-Jen said one of the patrols had found them wandering around far from their dome and brought them here.

'So, after banishing them, why would they kidnap them?' said Tanun.

'As far as we could tell, the Elders of their dome decided they should weaponize their telepathy. Probably told to and encouraged by the KimMorii.'

'And you were successful?'

'We rescued the twins,' said Xen-Lin

'And?'

'They're safe in another liberal alliance dome. Many battles. Lots killed on both sides. Whole thing was pretty bloody.'

'Thanks, Xen-Lin. When was this?'

'Seven-hundred and eighty-seven light-times ago.'

'Amazing. You were so young.'

'We both were. In this dome you have to grow up quickly.'

'I'm learning that.'

After Xen-Lin had closed the hatch, he told Tanun it was great to meet him and said he was off to find Bento-Tor. Joor-Jen suggested she and Tanun went to the refectory and the knowledge pods.

'Xen-Lin doesn't say much,' said Tanun.

'Hard to believe for an apostle ... and an SF, but he's quite shy,' said Joor-Jen.

'Obviously friends with Bento-Tor.'

'They're very close.'

'Good. Given Bento-Tor's grief.'

Once Joor-Jen and Tanun had settled at a desk in the knowledge room, Tanun said, 'I want to understand more about the structure of the domes and all the stuff that must be going on that we don't see.'

'Right. Let's think. Pod. Access dome construction and infrastructure.'

Pod Active. Yes, Joor-Jen. Do you want me to recite? If so, you must wear earpieces.

'Sure.'

While Tanun and Joor-Jen studied the moving pictures on the screen, they listened to the narration.

Section: Dome construction

Subsection: E1 Engineering

Subsection E1 begins

Using dome 1279-41618 as a template, the dome has a radius of 2,500 metres. As part of its internal bracing, there are 1250 levels, with a separation of four metres.

There are six external supporting legs arranged hexagonally, each of which terminates in a dish of 2.5 metres radius.

Each leg consists of 3,999 rungs with a handrail on either side. This construction acts to strengthen the structure against downward forces as well as discouraging unauthorised access.

'Pod, pause. Yes, Tanun. What is it?'

'Incredible engineering, which everyone seems to take for granted. I certainly did.'

'But that's just one of the differences between a child's perception of the world and an adult's.'

'Embarrassing.'

'Pod, continue.'

Subsection E2 begins

Internally, most levels have a peripheral corridor off which 30 radial corridors converge towards the centre. Internal elevators are located halfway along these radial corridors.

E2 ends

Subsection E3 begins

The first 250 levels are allocated to food production and waste recycling. Although the majority of food production is outside, some food is produced internally and both locations utilize the nitrogen and other elements from waste recycling.

Levels above 250 are generally given over to medical levels, personal living space — known as dens — communal living spaces, including the refectories, wet rooms, and meeting rooms.

For the last two thousand years, outside air has been drawn in through a hatch at the bottom of the dome and circulated via pull fans at the top of the dome.

Prior to this method, the air was processed through scrubbers conceived and designed by Professor Dome. All fabrication has ventilation holes to enable efficient circulation of air.

Subsection E3 ends

'Stop.'

Yes, Joor-Jen. Would you like me to send the data to your and Tanun's DDs?

'No. Not this time.'

Pod dormant

Just as Tanun and Joor-Jen reached his den, Bento-Tor and Xen-Lin walked past, carrying loads of towels from the wet room. They waved before disappearing into Bento-Tor's den.

'Are they sharing?' said Tanun, as he and Joor-Jen entered his den.

'They weren't, but they are now.'

'That's why he didn't want to move in with me when I asked. Are they – you know?'

'Yes. Have a problem with that?'

'No. Not at all. Just that ... being apostles and SFs ... '

'How's their sexuality got anything to do with that?'

'You're right. It hasn't.'

'Just so you know, Bento-Tor's obsessed with personal hygiene, the more so before he goes on a mission. One of his coping mechanisms.'

'And what are yours?'

Joor-Jen put her hands behind Tanun's head and pulled him towards her. Neither wanted to be the first to break, but after a long while, Joor-Jen did.

'I need more coping mechanisms,' smiled Tanun.

'Better not. Mission's at early light-time and all that.'

'You shouldn't have got me in a state, then.'

'Sorry. Another time. Promise.'

# NINE: Stealth and Psychology

The door whooshed open and the cell lit up as an enforcer brought in a tray. 'You've got a visitor. Best answer her questions. She's the type who gets upset if you don't. Onto the chair.'

Chyke got up from his bench and sat on the chair frame.

'No need to secure you. Not this time, anyhow. Remember, Tanun. For your own sake, be polite.'

The door whooshed shut.

'Tanun?' Chyke puzzled.'

Whoosh.

**'How generous of them.'**

Chyke stared at the tall figure in a black cloak and deep hood. The cloak hung in folds which ended in eight sharp points just above the floor. He tried, but couldn't see a face inside the black depths of the hood.

**'The Elders have kindly handed you over to me. A gesture of loyalty. I like that, but of course, they mistakenly believed you to be Tanun. I know, however, you're his brother, aren't you? His younger brother. Just one of my many powers, Chyke. No matter. There is much I can learn from you, isn't there?'**

'I don't know, is there? Who the hell are you? Or ... what the hell are you? So they snatched the wrong guy. Marvellous. Can't see what I can tell you. Great cloak, by the way.'

**'Chyke, Chyke, we mustn't get off on the wrong hand, must we? I am XorX. A KimMorii. We are shapeshifters. You might not have heard of me, or us, given your limited experience of life, but as we take over Lemtor you will get to know me ... and us ... very well. Now, because I am of a generous disposition I shall leave you to think about the answers to some questions I have. I have many more. Thousands, in fact, but let us start with these. And next visit,**

I shall expect the answers, so listen carefully, Chyke.'

Chyke closed his eyes.

'Question one. What was the real reason you followed Tanun? I do not believe you sneaked out of your dome just because Tanun was your brother. Question two. Did you, or Tanun, find anything unusual on your journey? An artefact, perhaps, or a stone? Question three. Has Cassièl been visiting 1279-41618? Think carefully, Chyke. I know the answers to these questions. I hope your answers match mine. For your sake.'

After XorX had left, Chyke stayed on the chair frame staring at the door for a long time. Hunger forced him to reach over for the tray, which he took back to his bench. *So, they were after Tanun. Probably because of the stone. Why the crud did Tanun have to find that stupid Dodecahedron stone?*

While he ate the food cube, he realised he'd have to concoct some answers for the KimMorii. What a git she was. And what a silly name. And cloak.

*Why did I follow Tanun? Because he was my brother, that's why. Trouble is, I don't think the stupid KimMorii can understand that. Did we find anything unusual? What? Being outside for the first time in our lives? Everything was unusual. Was Cassièl visiting the new dome? Who the hell is Cassièl? Never heard of her. Keep practising the answers,* he told himself, over and over and over. *Keep practising the answers. Make them automatic.*

* * *

At the bottom of the rungs, Lento-Fin addressed Tanun and the four SFs. 'We are making for a Percutio Alliance dome. It's about eighty kilometres so should take us three dark-times. The dome we're targeting contains the weaponry that launched the missile at us and the other domes. This is a covert operation. We must be well on the way back before the explosions. Questions?'

'Guess you all know,' said Tanun, 'but how are we going to get into the dome to set the explosives? And out again.'

'Good question, Tanun. Nearly all domes have a hatch at the bottom for air intake and discharging waste and so on. Varies with the size of dome – the hatch is high off the ground, but we have grappling rockets. That's our way in. After the first dark-time we'll be in enemy alliance territory so use all your training to detect any threat before anything happens.'

The four SFs punched each other's fists and Tanun wondered if they would ever include him in their rituals.

'Tanun?' Lento-Fin brought his attention back. '10/10 ready?'

Tanun felt for the weapon in its shoulder holster and checked its safety lock. 'Set and ready.'

*** * * ***

Joor-Jen, Bento-Tor, Xen-Lin and two SFs stood at the open hatch.

'Clean enough for you, Bento-Tor?' said Joor-Jen.

He smiled and nodded at her.

'Right. When we get to the bottom, we'll set off north-west. Although we could do the journey in two dark-times, I want us fresh, so we'll take three. Stealth and secrecy is our method. The two SFs punched each other's fists again.

'Right. Weapons check.'

'We checked at the top,' said one of the SFs.

'Weapons check.'

'Yes, Joor-Jen.'

'Xen-Lin?'

He lifted his shoulder straps slightly.

'Bento-Tor?'

He checked his 10/10, the curved knife on his belt, shook the roll of carbon rope around his shoulder and patted his stomach. Nodded at her.

'Let's get to the first wood.'

* * *

Tanun walked mostly with Lento-Fin while the fours SFs reconnoitred in a diamond shape around them.

'I hope you don't mind my asking, Lento-Fin, but you're the chief Governor. Should you really be on this mission? Any mission? Shouldn't you be organising things back in the dome?'

'I don't mind you asking, Tanun. That's a good point. We're fortunate in our dome. We have a good Council and everyone knows their role. I shouldn't say this, but I get bored with the administrative stuff. What we're doing now is what I grew up with. Sabotage. Running havoc. And if you ask the SFs, they'll tell you I'm the best saboteur there is. This one's important. Got to take them out before—'

The four SFs waved everyone down. Tanun crashed to the ground and lay as flat as he could. Heard a whine. Louder. Couldn't tell the direction. A rush of air lifted him a few centimetres. After he'd flumped down, he turned his head to see a missile glide past less than five metres above them.

'Think that's it for now,' said an SF. 'Headed for 1279-41623.'

Tanun got to his feet and brushed himself down. Checked his 10/10. 'What does that mean, Lento-Fin?'

'I think it means ... civil war has started.'

'How can a war start after all these years?'

'It never really stopped. Even when everyone was confined to the domes, there were still terrorists. Missiles.

Kidnappings. Poisonings.'

'Will we never learn?'

'Never's a long time and I won't live to see it, though I hope you do. Everyone, let's find some cover and make camp for the night.'

\* \* \*

The cell lit up. Six enforcers dragged him from his bench. A stranglehold while they stripped him. Pushed him onto the chair frame. Arms strapped tight to the uprights, legs to the front legs. Immobile. Alone again.

Whoosh. Whoosh

'My apologies, Chyke. Did I forget to mention you would be strapped to the chair? Naked? You see, in my experience, I find those being questioned answer more truthfully in that condition.'

Chyke flexed against the restraints. No slack.

'So, Chyke. Have you been thinking hard about my questions?'

With a thought, XorX spun the chair frame one-hundred-and-eighty degrees so Chyke was facing away from her and the door. She moved closer and pressed against the chair. Stroked Chyke's shoulders with her black-gloved hands.

Chyke grimaced.

Slid her hands down to his chest and up. 'I hope so.'

Chyke's grimace turned to a look of disgust.

XorX stepped back and spun the chair again so Chyke was facing her.

'What was the real reason you sneaked out to follow your brother?'

Chyke looked up into the hood, challenging. 'The real reason is that he's my brother. Although we fight, I love him. Don't suppose you'd understand that.'

'Ah, love. You poor physical beings. Such a burden. And did you find anything unusual on your journey? Did you, or Tanun perhaps, find a glassy-black, oval-shaped stone?'

'Define unusual. We'd lived in a dome all of our lives. Told the outside was poisonous. Everything was strange. I don't believe Tanun found anything. Not that he'd tell me, anyway, being his younger brother.'

'**Chyke.**' XorX flourished a solid black cylinder. 'Look at this. Make sure you have a good look.'

Chyke studied the object. *Must be – what? 40 cm long? And 3 cm diameter? One end tapered to a point.*

'**This little friend, Chyke, is fully charged. Very powerful, I can assure you. Depending on how it's used, some cry out. Some scream. Others vomit. Many ... pass out. With prolonged use some die, twitching within their restraints.**' XorX let her threats sink in, moved closer to Chyke and pressed the cylinder point against his lower stomach. '**So think very carefully before you answer the next question. Has Cassièl been visiting 1279-41618?**'

'Who the hell's Cassièl? Never heard of her. All we've met in our new dome is Lento-Fin, Joor-Jen, and Bento-Tor.' Chyke stared straight up into the hood but saw only darkness. And waited.

'**I believe you, I believe you. But this isn't the end of my questioning. Just the beginning. There is so much more I need to know. So much more I will know. I shall return.**'

Whoosh.

\* \* \*

'Is that it? It's even bigger.' Tanun stared at the dome from the woods about a kilometre distant.

'These are the more typical size,' said Lento-Fin. 'Your old dome and ours were the earlier ones when the technology was still developing.'

Lento-Fin said they would observe until well into dark-time to determine any patterns of people arriving or leaving. When he deemed the moment suitable, he and Tanun would run until they were underneath the dome where they would fire the grabbing rockets up to the hatch entrance.

'Time to paint your hands, face, and forehead, Tanun. No rush.'

'Good. You run two metres behind me. Follow my swerves. We shouldn't stop until we're right beneath the dome. Let's go.'

Tanun ran, crouching behind Lento-Fin. The ground was slippery from dew and keeping up with Lento-Fin's pace was more difficult than he'd expected. Although a straight line seemed the quickest, Lento-Fin swerved left and right and Tanun nearly slipped over three or four times in his wake. He blew out his cheeks as they raced past a dish and leg of the dome.

'Great stuff. We'll give it a few moments just to be sure. I don't think we've been detected but they're clever. They'll wait to give us a false sense of confidence.'

'So much more to all this than just hitting them with a 10/10, or breaking someone's neck.'

'Psychology is 99.9% of it. The other part, the encounter, point one.'

Crouched together under the massive dome, waiting until Lento-Fin felt they were secure, Tanun thought back to why he hadn't checked on Chyke when he'd come out of the shower. *If I'd alerted everyone then, they might have caught the kidnappers before they escaped. The argument over Joor-Jen seems so stupid now. What I wouldn't give for a fight with my brother. And where is Cassièl? He seems to appear and disappear whenever he wants. Still, now isn't the time to tackle Lento-Fin about him, but I definitely will on the way back.*

'Time for the grappling rockets. Two should do it. You fire one the same time as me. Make sure you hit the hatch.'

Lento-Fin uncoiled two lengths of carbon rope from his shoulder. Lifted two cones from his rucksack and fixed the rope to the pointed end of each.

'That should be enough. We'll have to jump up to grab the rope. Lift your feet off the ground when we do. We want to avoid any earthing of the dome through our bodies. That would give you a kick, I can tell you. Right. Take off your launcher and watch me. See how the end clips on to the barrel? Good. Let me just check it. Ok. Let's kneel. Hold the launcher like this. You're a quick learner, Tanun. I'll count down from five. Press the button on zero. Steady aim at the hatch door. Afterwards, absolute silence, so I can listen for any response. All set?'

Tanun nodded.

'Five-four-three-two-one-zero!'

The recoil nearly knocked Tanun over, but he steadied himself with his right hand. Two carbon ropes hung down to about two metres above the ground. He went to speak to Lento-Fin but saw, just in time, even in the darkness he was concentrating on any unusual noises while staring at the ropes swaying in the breeze.

'That was great targeting, Tanun. Think we got away with it. Let's pull the ropes together and see if we can open the hatch. Take off all the gear you won't need for the climb.'

When he'd taken off his field supplies and emergency rations and all the paraphernalia necessary for combat in the field, Lento-Fin nodded at him. They jumped together and grabbed the ropes, which moved down to almost ground level.

'Drop.'

Tanun let go and dropped the few centimetres to the ground, swaying left to avoid the rope touching him.

'Sorry, should have told you that might happen, but look, the hatch is open. Let's listen for a bit.'

Tanun knelt again, not because he was tired, but because at that moment the enormity of the entire mission consumed him. He was reading books in the library not long ago and now he was about to climb a rope and place signal disrupters.

'Perfectly normal, Tanun. Stay there for as long as you need. Everyone, and I mean everyone, has experienced what you just have. And it doesn't go away. You just learn to deal with it. The guys back there – me – Joor-Jen – Bento-Tor – every SF.'

'Bento-Tor?'

'You bet.'

'Feel Ok now. Don't know what happened.'

'I do. You're doing great. Now, when you're inside, look for a grey alarm box. Probably to your left, but could be anywhere. It opens from the bottom. Unscrew the lower wire clamp. Don't cut it. That will set the alarm off. Clear?'

Tanun nodded.

Lento-Fin handed him four small bulbous discs. 'These are the signal disrupters. When you're inside the hatch, place each as far from another as possible. Peel the back. They'll stick to anything. Down the rope. I'll be here.'

Tanun put the discs in his shoulder bag, tightened his boots and pulled on his gloves.

'Knife?'

'Check.'

'10/10?'

'Check.'

'Four disrupters?'

'Check.'

'Start when you're ready. Stealth. Don't get caught.'

# TEN: Spirit of Avena

Joor-Jen knew that sound. The familiar whine followed by the rush of air. She crawled to the tent flaps, trying not to wake Bento-Tor and Xen-Lin. The two SFs were standing by their tent, conferring. 'Missiles, Joor-Jen. Quite a lot. A coordinated attack. More than a random attack.'

*At least we are heading into a safer area*, she thought, *heading towards 1279-41130. Until the Liberal Alliance launches a counterattack, that is.* 'Bento-Tor. Xen-Lin. Up now. We have to go.'

'Ok. Missiles?' said Bento-Tor.

'Missiles. It's started.'

'I need to go into the woods.'

'So do I.'

'We all do. You two go first.'

When all the gear was packed, the five of them set off towards Chyke's old dome. Joor-Jen had told them that when they reached the woods about two kilometres from the dome, they would reconnoitre for movements.

'Agreed?'

'Agreed,' said Bento-Tor as they tracked through the trees.

'Let's hope the need doesn't arise,' said Joor-Jen.

'I feel more uneasy about this mission than any of the others,' said Bento-Tor.

'I do too. The stakes are always high, but they feel the highest this time. Not just because of Chyke. You're to be matched soon, aren't you?'

'Yeah. I've asked to be excluded.'

'Your decision. You've got to get over Peeso-Lun.'

'It's not that. Not only that.'

'Whatever you do, Bento-Tor, I'll support you.'

'I've asked if Xen-Lin can move in with me.'

'I know. If you're sure that's what you both want.'

Every so often as they tracked through the woods, a missile brushed the tops of the trees, although none of them ducked or cowered. When they reached the edge of the wood, Joor-Jen waved them to a stop.

'There it is. Tanun and Chyke's old dome. One of the earlier ones. We are still quite a distance from there but it's the only cover we have. Soon be dark-time so we'll make camp here and observe for a while. Bento-Tor, Xen-Lin, you,' Joor-Jen pointed at an SF, 'and I will climb. 'You,' she pointed at the other SF, 'will keep watch at the bottom. Let's hope our two infiltrators have managed to unlock the hatch.'

Two SFs moved a kilometre apart to observe anyone arriving or leaving the dome. While Joor-Jen, Bento-Tor, and Xen-Lin ate their energy biscuits, they went over the plan for when they were inside. The SF would stay at the hatch while she, Bento-Tor, and Xen-Lin sneaked along the corridors to locate the cells. When they were within about four metres, Chyke's DD would register on the Xen-Lin's detector and they could determine which cell he was in. Joor-Jen emphasised they didn't know what sort of state Chyke might be in and they might have to carry him.

'We can do that,' said Bento-Tor. 'I so want to get him out of there. I daren't imagine what they've done to him.'

'We know from prisoners we've rescued what they're capable of,' said Joor-Jen.

'I want to blast the gits into the sky,' said Xen-Lin.

'Stealth and psychology. That's our M O.'

'I know, I know.'

When the two SFs returned, they reported everything was quiet. Only two enforcers had descended and they had made their way into the woods three kilometres north.

'Let's swerve-run to the dome and get under a leg,' said Joor-Jen. 'A line. Me, SF, Bento-Tor, Xen-Lin, SF. Let's go – now!'

'That went well,' said Bento-Tor as they sheltered under the dome.

'Hope that's a sign,' said Xen-Lin.

'When I say, we'll start the climb,' said Joor-Jen. 'Easy, this one. Only a thousand. Ready?'

All three nodded.

'Silence on the rungs.'

When Joor-Jen reached the top, she hissed down to Bento-Tor three rungs below, 'I hope it's unlocked.'

She attached four suckers to the hatch, threaded the carbon rope through them then slung the slack down to Bento-Tor who weaved the rope around the rungs to form a pulley.

'Pull – slowly.'

As Bento-Tor pulled the rope pulley through the rungs, the hatch eased away and up from the dome.

'Slow. Slow. That's enough. Secure the rope.'

Joor-Jen climbed into the hatch room and offered a hand to Bento-Tor and Xen-Lin. 'No sign we've been detected.' She took the access ring from its recess and gave it to Bento-Tor.

'The detector reckons the cells are that way.' Xen-Lin pointed.

The SF stayed at the hatch as agreed, and Bento-Tor and Xen-Lin followed Joor-Jen along the corridor. Xen-Lin read flashing dots off the screen.

'One of these.' He pointed. 'That one.'

Joor-Jen stood with her back against the door and her 10/10 ready in both hands. 'The access ring, Bento-Tor.'

He pressed the ring into the recess and the door slid open. Joor-Jen stepped inside. And fell unconscious as the door closed in front of Bento-Tor and Xen-Lin. They ran back the way they'd come, but darts piercing their calves made them stumble and weave and fall against the corridor walls until the anaesthetic brought them both crashing down.

*　*　*

Tanun jumped to grab the rope and shinned up, using his sole and instep as he'd been taught, and didn't stop until he was just three metres from the top. The sweat had made his gloves slip and he swore he'd never complain about rungs again. Suspended in the dark, gripping with his hands and feet and swaying in the breeze, he looked down to Lento-Fin. As he did so, Dodecahedron jumped into his vision. Somehow, knowing it was in his breast pocket gave him the confidence to finish the climb.

He told the stone he was glad he'd kept it with him, just as Cassièl had instructed him, but this set off a train of questions again. *Where is Cassièl? Why hasn't he solved the problem of not being able to retrieve Dodecahedron? Why can't he rescue Chyke? Why isn't he helping the Liberal Alliance?* Tanun's frustration swelled to anger, which motivated him to pull himself over the hatch door where he fell panting on the floor of the dome. His camouflaged boiler suit felt damp and his hands smarted while he lay amongst the tangle of pipes, ducts, motors, and pumps. *Hardly any room to move, let alone stand up. And so hot. How do they maintain all the equipment? Can't get to anything properly. With all this throbbing, whirring, hisses, and clunks, it will be difficult to hear if anyone comes in.*

After surveying the complex maze two or three times, he formed a plan. *First off, over there, I can see a clean grey surface. Means crawling under a big pipe but better to get the difficult ones done first.* He shuffled along on his stomach under the pipe and felt the heat from it on his back and buttocks. He peeled off the backing of a disc and pressed it to the side of a motor. As he twisted around he saw another machine, probably a pump, and after peeling off the backing with his teeth he stretched out to stick the disc onto the casing. Easing back to his original position, he chose a narrower pipe to his left and stuck the final disc on the floor of the dome near the hatch. With all four disrupters deployed he sat bowed under the pipework, removed his gloves, wiped his hands on his sleeves, and used his scarf to dry his face and forehead.

The descent wasn't so tough, except his muscles kept cramping and a couple of times his feet flew away from the rope, leaving him dangling and supported only by his arms.

'Well done, Tanun. Great job. We'll move back to the wood while the others do their stuff. Have a load of biscuits because you'll have to go to the dome again. Don't worry, you won't have to climb. Need you to set these explosives against the legs when all the disrupters are in place.'

Tanun gorged on the energy biscuits but all the while fretted how his muscles would cope with another run. *Thank goodness I won't be expected to climb again. Funny that the descent was actually more tricky. And to think, not long ago I've never given any thought to all the infrastructure and processes needed to run a dome with millions of people. All that interested me was the library and the ancient philosophers. And that Joor-Jen keeps leading me on and then stopping. Are all girls like that?*

When Lento-Fin and the four SFs had planted their

signal disrupters inside the dome, they huddled together while Lento-Fin explained to Tanun how he should place the explosives. 'Not in the dish. About five rungs up and in the middle of the rung. Here, take this.' Lento-Fin passed Tanun a malleable length of explosive and explained to Tanun he should wind it round the rung and when it was secure, insert the charge. He passed Tanun a metal clip with two probes and said he should implant the probes as deeply as possible in the explosive. 'Reasonably safe until the charge is inserted. When you've planted all six, get back here as fast as you can. We won't fire the charges until you're back with us. Remember, swerve-run. Don't be tempted to run in a straight line.'

'We'll be watching,' said an SF. 'Should anyone appear, we'll zap them easily from here. Keep calm. Keep your wits about you.'

Tanun nodded, and as Lento-Fin passed him the six explosives, he slid them into his shoulder bag and hung the charges from his belt. Lento-Fin and the SFs slapped his back. 'When you're ready.'

While the three of them watched Tanun weave a path to the dome, an SF asked Lento-Fin if Tanun was up to it. He was very young, he said, and very inexperienced.

'So was Peeso-Lun and Bento-Tor. Not to mention Joor-Jen. If his generation is to carry on the fight for liberalisation, he's got to learn fast.'

Tanun's calf muscles cramped. Sweat ran down his neck into his scarf. The charges clinked as he swerved and the shoulder bag swung back and forth across his back. Five hundred metres. Keep swerving. Four hundred. Two hundred. Keep going, keep swerving. Fifty. Tanun slid feet first under the dome then twisted round to lie flat on his stomach behind a dish. He looked to the wood but in the dark could see only a black smudge. After waiting for his heart to calm, he wiped the sweat, tightened his boots and took off his gloves in the hope they'd dry a little. Talked to himself for courage. *I'll start with the farthest. Work my way here for the last one.* He crouch-crept to the far side and lifted out the first explosive. Wound it around the fifth rung and checked it was secure before unclipping a charge. He wasn't sure exactly where it should go, so settled on pressing the probes into the upper coils. One down, five to go.

After he'd had pressed the sixth charge into the soft, flesh-like material, he double-checked in his bag to confirm all the explosives and all the charges were gone. Now he had the run back to the woods. Click. His heightened senses heard it. Definitely behind. How far? A KimMorii enforcer dropped from high out of sight on the leg in front of him. Tanun fell and rolled to his right. Fired five in quick succession. Another enforcer launched at him from behind, knife targeted at his neck. Tanun rolled again, stood up and fired ten into the enforcer's back.

After seventy-five metres he remembered to swerve. So easy in a panic to forget all your training and just run in a blind panic. 'Keep swerving,' he chanted. The sweat on his neck made him pull his scarf free to wipe it away, but it wasn't sweat. The knife must have nicked him. How could a little nick cause so much blood?

He fell to his knees and Lento-Fin helped him to sit against a tree. He peeled back his jacket and studied the wound.

'Lucky. Only a nick. A centimetre to the left and you'd still be under the dome. Well done.' Lento-Fin peeled off a bandage and pressed it hard against the wound.

'Argh.'

'Sorry. Had to make a compression.'

Lento-Fin unscrewed a flask and held it to Tanun's lips. 'You won't have had anything like this. Take a good mouthful.'

When Tanun had stopped coughing, he sent Lento-Fin a quizzical look.

'Avena spirit. Made from oats. After boiling, distil the liquor. You're a lucky boy. This one's twenty years old. There are others I wouldn't use to clean the floor. Sit there and get yourself together. We need to fire the explosives. As soon as we have, we've got to get away from here. Up for it, Tanun?'

'I'm up for it.'

Lento-Fin sent the two SFs left and right to observe. From behind a tree, a few metres in front of Tanun, he took a flat metal square from his breast pocket, looked towards the dome and back and pressed the square seven times. He looked over at Tanun. Five-four-three-two-one-zero. They all saw the flashes before the rumbling and the shockwave reached them a second or so later.

'Up you get.' Lento-Fin pulled Tanun up. 'Let's go. Stay with me.'

# ELEVEN: Phial

'Chyke, my beautiful, beautiful boy. Seems you are quite popular. You appear to have a value I have not yet appreciated.'

Chyke reckoned this was the twenty-third visit from XorX. Keeping count gave him some sort of purpose and context. Without company, without books, without a routine, he'd devised a series of coping mechanisms for solitary confinement. Counted the dark-times. Counted the trays. Counted the visits. Told himself to keep reciting them.

'Foolish, misguided people from 1279-41618 attempted to rescue you. Failed to rescue you, of course. With our help, this dome is now quite secure. Did they not realise this attempt would just increase your punishment? So next visit, I promise, you will experience my little friend. Some say the pain can be quite exquisite. Others apparently are not convinced. And as a treat, I will let your failed rescuers hear you. And if you are very good, I will let you hear them. Perhaps you will be able to tell who they are from their screams. Ha-ha.'

\* \* \*

Xen-Lin opened his eyes. Taste of blood. Left knee throbbed. *Must have been drugged. These straps are tight as anything. Can't move. Shit, crap, shit. Guess they've got Bento-Tor as well.* 'Relying on you, B-T,' he muttered.

\* \* \*

Joor-Jen opened her eyes. She strained against the straps, but they had been pulled so tight she couldn't flex a muscle. Thoughts raced in and out. *Must have been drugged. Briefings about the mission. How could they have been discovered? Must have been idle chat. Has to have been a spy. The only thing possible is an SF. One, or more likely both of them.* She closed her eyes in frustration. *Is Bento-*

Tor close? Is Xen-Lin? Shook her head. *I can't bear to think of them as well as Chyke being tortured. What a total craphole.* Because she'd been unconscious, she didn't even know where they were in the dome or whether all the cells were in the same area. *How long will it be before my interrogation starts? Will they start with me, or the boys? Will I hear their screams? Will they hear mine?*

\* \* \*

The four enforcers threw Bento-Tor onto the bench. As he came to, he realised his left eye had almost closed from the swelling. His shoulders and elbows ached from the armlocks. Thoughts formed. *Must have been drugged.*

'Boy, are you in for some fun,' sniggered the lead enforcer. 'You might be young but they don't take kindly to anyone encroaching on our territory. You'll learn that again and again and again. Before the most painful drawn-out death, that is. You'll wish you hadn't been cloned.'

After the enforcers had left, Bento-Tor waited to see if anyone else would enter before sliding off his bench onto his hands and knees. His shoulders made him wince. The little coughs began quietly, but one after the other, grew more intense. The coughs became gags, harder and harder, until he put his right hand over his mouth and leant forward, his head and hand almost touching the floor. Making a gulping sound from the final heave, his tongue pushed a phial from his mouth and he let it fall into his hand. 'Euch.' After wiping the finger-sized phial with his scarf, he unscrewed the little tube, which fell into equal halves. He tipped the two needles onto his left palm, placed one on the chair frame and put the other back in the phial, which he pressed into the warmth of his left underarm. Back on his bench, he grabbed the needle from the chair and weaved it through the skin on his left palm. Discreet, but accessible. Now, all he could do was wait.

\* \* \*

Whoosh.

'Joor-Jen. Welcome. I have been eager to meet you.'

Joor-Jen stared up at the black cloak and gloves, but didn't look into the hood. A *KimMorii*. *What are they doing in this dome? The Elders must be supporting them. What the hell are the KimMorii giving them in return?* She looked down at the floor.

'I am XorX. I want to talk about Chyke. Ah, I see you know him. Chyke now knows me very well. He's been so cooperative, answering my questions. Perhaps because of the encouragement I've given him. There's more, so much more I need to ask him, but really, that pales into insignificance when I think what you can reveal to me. An enemy, after all.'

Joor-Jen looked up into the hood this time, but saw only black.

'You don't have to speak. Certainly not now. In fact, better you listen. When I deem the moment right, I will come back. With a host of questions, and you will be on that chair frame. And just as Chyke has experienced, you'll be naked. As I explained to him, I have found people answer more truthfully in that condition. And have a good look at this.'

Joor-Jen considered the black cylinder XorX waved in front of her face.

'This is my little friend. Packs quite a kick. Quite a kick. Chyke can confirm that. And next visit, I promise you'll get to know my friend ... intimately.'

Whoosh.

\* \* \*

'Xen-Lin. Welcome. We are flattered so many of you have chosen to join us. You are young for an SF. What special skills do you have? No matter. When I eventually allow you to die, I shall know them all.'

Xen-Lin's face and neck glowed red from his struggle against the straps.

'Are the straps too tight? They'll be tighter when you're naked. You see, while I am encouraging you to answer my questions, the muscle spasms can be quite intense, so you must be secured for your own safety. I need to visit another guest now, but when I return, Xen-Lin, I want you to answer one question. Why was it so important to rescue Chyke? I feel there is something I have not yet learnt about him. Will you help me establish what it is? I would so appreciate that.'

\* \* \*

Bento-Tor looked up when the door whooshed.

'Onto the chair, sunshine,' said the enforcer, 'ready for your visitor.'

Bento-Tor took his time to move from the bench to the chair frame. Just the one, he thought. Might not get a better chance. He lowered himself onto the frame. 'Not very comfortable, is it? Do you have something better?'

The enforcer moved towards him. 'Why, you little—'

Bento-Tor pushed the needle in and along the enforcer's jugular until it disappeared. Held the enforcer as he fell to quieten the fall, and took the belt, knife, and 10/10.

Whoosh. He took the access ring from its recess, looked at the row of cells until the corridor curved away. *Which cells? Which cells? Can only check them one by one,* he convinced himself. *Empty...empty...dead...dying.* Joor-Jen! He cut the straps. 'No weapons, only these.'

'Your eye.'

'It's Ok. Arms are worse.'

'You're amazing. I hoped and hoped but the situation felt bad.'

'It is bad. Let's get the others.'

They moved along the row of cells, all the time

listening for footsteps. Inside most cells, the occupant was dead. Or nearly.

'He's got to be here,' said Bento-Tor.

'He wasn't in the one Xen-Lin said.'

'They must have blockers here.'

'This one. Ready?'

Bento-Tor pressed the access ring into the recess and the door slid open. He ran in and cut Xen-Lin's straps.

'Thanks,' said Xen-Lin. 'Swallowed two teeth, but my left knee's the problem.'

'We'll get you out,' said Bento-Tor. 'Carry you if we have to. Got to find Chyke.'

The three of them worked their way along the cells. Many opened with no problem, but others stayed shut.

'Only seven left,' said Joor-Jen. 'Please let him be here.'

Bento-Tor inserted the access ring. When each door opened, if the person wasn't Chyke, Xen-Lin took the ring to the next cell. If Chyke wasn't there, Bento-Tor took the ring to the next cell and so on. They alternated like that until the last cell. Bento-Tor looked at Xen-Lin who looked at Joor-Jen who looked at Bento-Tor.

'Do it,' said Joor-Jen.

Whoosh.

The three of them stared at Chyke curled on his bench. Chyke lifted his head and stared through them.

'We have to go,' said Joor-Jen. 'Out of time. Bento-Tor and Xen-Lin, check the corridor each way.'

While they were checking the corridor, Joor-Jen pulled Chyke up from his bench.

'Joor-Jen,' he croaked. He flung his arms around her and she flung her arms around him. Their mouths met. When he pressed into her, she pulled away.

'I've missed you.'

'Chyke? Something's wrong, isn't it? I can tell, I can tell. What is it? Don't talk. We're up to our necks in crap, but we'll get you out. Wait here a moment.'

Joor-Jen went outside to find Bento-Tor and Xen-Lin and heard the door slide shut behind her. Dumbstruck for a moment, she took out the access ring and reinserted it. The door ignored her. She pounded on the door with her fists. The door ignored her. She leant her forehead against it, and heedless of revealing her presence, screamed, 'I love you, Chyke. I'm coming back for you, I'm coming back for you, Chyke, I promise.'

Bento-Tor came running round the curve of the corridor from the left, shouting, 'Run. Run.'

When she'd caught up with him, he passed her the 10/10, saying she was a better shot. He waved the enforcer's knife in front of his face at her. Around the next curve. Faster. Faster. They caught up with Xen-Lin and skidded to a stop. Their SF was in front of the hatch room, a 10/10 in each hand, crouching and firing at the enforcers, who were closing in. When he saw Joor-Jen and the boys, he stood up and ran towards the enemy enforcers, firing erratically. They turned to concentration their fire on him, allowing Bento-Tor, Xen-Lin, and Joor-Jen in turn to run into the hatch room, jump out and grab the rungs as they fell. Bento-To cried out as the sudden pull from his momentum stressed his already strained elbows and shoulders.

Three enforcers appeared at the hatch, firing down at them. Joor-Jen, two rungs above Xen-Lin, fired towards the open hatch while the three of them slid down the handrails as fast as they could. Their SF on the ground was standing to the right of the leg firing continuously up at the hatch. Joor-Jen saw an enforcer take aim and flung herself against the rungs. The pulses missed her, but hit Xen-Lin's right shoulder. He swung away from the rungs, hanging only by his left arm and screwed up his face from the agony in his muscles. 'I can't hold on, I can't hold on!'

Joor-Jen held the 10/10 in her mouth, wedged her feet behind the rungs, and hung upside down to reach for his left wrist. 'Up one rung,' she mumbled, 'step up one rung. Come on, Xen-Lin. For me.'

'I can't. My knee.'

'You can. Kill the pain. You can. Kill the pain. That's it.' She closed her fingers around his wrist. 'Got you.' She pulled him up towards her, but pulses fired from the ground hit his thighs and buttocks and he hung limp in her grasp. His wrist slipped from her fingers, the weight of his swinging body and sweaty wrist proving too much for her grip.

'No!'

Hanging upside down against the rungs, she watched Xen-Lin tumble past Bento-Tor and bounce against the rungs all the way to the bottom.

'Xen-Lin!' Bento Tor cried, and slid down as fast as his burning hands allowed.

After righting herself, Joor-Jen grabbed the rails and began sliding down, her hands burning too. Pulses whizzed past, and because of the pain she had to step the rest of the way, rung by rung.

'There's one down here,' shouted Bento-Tor to their SF, but saw him spin round and fall dead into the dish.

Joor-Jen and Bento-Tor knelt by Xen-Lin's mangled body, which had come to rest two metres from the dish.

His tears dropping over him, Bento-Tor closed Xen-Lin's eyes. 'What a warrior', he said. 'Taught me so much.' He lowered his head onto Xen-Lin's chest. *Peeso-Lun, Xen-*

*Lin. Too much pain – too much to bear.*

Joor-Jen was rubbing Bento-Tor's soaking back when he sensed a presence behind. He leapt up, swung round and slashed the enforcer's throat with his own knife. With a side-thrust he kicked the lifeless body as it fell. 'That's for Xen-Lin, you git.'

Joor-Jen kissed Xen-Lin's forehead and wiped her tears from his face. 'Sorry. I couldn't hold him.'

'He was hit from down here as well. Nothing you could have done. What are we going to do with the bodies?'

'We've got to go. They'll be after us. Let's burn Xen-Lin. Stop the gits getting him. Want to do it?'

Bento-Tor poured liquid from a flask over Xen-Lin's body. Clicked a small wheel at the top of a metal cube.

Joor-Jen and Bento-Tor didn't stop running until dark-time by when they had nearly reached the railway tunnel.'

\* \* \*

After an hour, Lento-Fin signalled they could stop and rest. He emphasised no fire, but tents should be Ok.

'I think it best we sleep in the open, Lento-Fin,' said an SF.

Lento-Fin looked to the sky and the missiles streaking overhead. 'Yes, it is. Tanun? Fear not. You'll take last watch so you can sleep awhile.'

'Thank you,' he puffed. 'What I don't understand is, if the disrupters have signals to stop their weapons, why did we have to blow up the dome?'

Lento-Fin glanced at the two SFs and smiled bleakly. 'Because, Tanun,' he said, turning back to him, 'most of the weapons would survive a dome collapse. Once they'd decoded the disrupters, the weapons could still have been used against us. And ... destroying an enemy dome sends the right sort of signal that we are well equipped, well-trained, and well-motivated to retaliate. Defence is all about appearing strong. Stealth and psychology. That's our M O.'

'M O?'

'Modus operandi. Method of operation. You're the one for the knowledge pods. Ok, everyone. We all deserve a drink after that. Moderate, though. We must be alert. You two have your own. Tanun, ready for another glug?'

'Only if it doesn't make me cough so much.'

While they were laughing, Tanun took a mouthful from Lento-Fin's flask and held the spirit in his mouth so it trickled drop by drop down his throat. 'Think I've worked out how to deal with it.'

'Get some sleep. I'll wake you for your shift.'

Tanun couldn't tell if the noises were in the woods or in his nightmares. He thrashed around until a nightmare about falling from high on a dome leg caused him so sit up in a start. Lento-Fin was asleep to his right, two SFs to his left. Where were the other two?

Movement. Over there. Several metres. He reached for his knife and 10/10. He couldn't even whisper to the others without being heard. He slid out of his sleeping bag and concentrated on sound and movement. Shuffled to his knees. Stood up. A KimMorii enforcer crashed through the branches at him and Tanun fired seven. Another from the right. No time to fire. Grabbed a wrist. A sasetsuri-komi-ashi throw sent the enforcer over his head. Lento-Fin plunged the knife into the enemy's mouth. Another enforcer. Because he was on the ground, Tanun slashed the enforcer's Achilles tendons. Lento-Fin fired ten as he fell screaming into silence.

The two SFs that had been asleep had rolled away into the wood. They returned, dragging an enforcer by his head towards Lento-Fin. Lento-Fin crouched down. 'How many?' The enforcer spat. One of the SFs tightened the carbon noose by uncrossing his hands slightly. 'I'll ask once more. How many?' The SF pulled tighter. 'Four,' the enforcer rasped. In a lightning movement, the SF uncrossed his hands and the head thumped to the ground. The SFs confirmed there were no more.

Lento-Fin turned to Tanun, 'You're a hero, Tanun.' 'That's a great sacrifice-fall you do. The issue with sacrifice falls, though, is they put you at a disadvantage if you don't execute them properly.'

'But I did.'

'You did,' Lento-Fin agreed and slapped his shoulder.'

'Good job we weren't in the tents, guys. And I reckon Tanun's on the way to being an SF. Even though he reads philosophy!'

Light-time was creeping up so they purloined all the weapons and field supplies. Lento-Fin said he thought those parts of the way back that were in the open would be relatively safe for travelling in light-time. Tanun asked if there would be retaliatory strikes after their sabotage and Lento-Fin assured him there would.

# TWELVE: Truth

The drizzle increased as Joor-Jen approached the leg of the dome and sat down. She held her head in her hands and screamed as the tiredness, the frustration, and the grief poured out. Bento-Tor knelt beside her and put this arm across her shoulders.

Without looking up, Joor-Jen said, 'You're amazing, Bento-Tor. You've more tricks than a card-sharp. Incredible to have escaped from your cell. Was it your old trick?'

'Yup.'

She turned to him and stroked his cheek. 'I know what loss feels like and I want to help you in any way I can.'

'Thanks, Joor-Jen. I just feel numb. Xen-Lin was special. Need to keep busy.'

'No problem there. We lost our SFs. Wasn't they who betrayed us. Must have been our infiltrators. They'd been turned somehow. How many more have? That's the problem. Lento-Fin and the Council will want some intelligence-gathering to determine the extent of damage.'

'They will, and I'll be up for that. Anything's better than moping around in the dome. Come on, let's do the climb.'

Bento-Tor went first, but as Joor-Jen climbed a few rungs below him, the monotony of the steps allowed her to go over the rescue. *Chyke. Still stuck in that cell. No wonder he was quiet. Suffered already. Now he'll be tortured to death, thanks to us. Holding him close in that cell, I felt my desire for him erupt. The matching's been right, after all. So why do I feel I'm trapped in a web between Tanun and Chyke? When I'm with Chyke the answer's obvious. He's the* one. For definite. But when I'm with Tanun, the answer's likewise obvious. He's the one. For definite. Opposites. Equals. Feels like we're all trapped in a web.*

She kicked a rung. She had to tell Tanun that Chyke was still a prisoner. With Chyke being no threat, she could be straight with him and tell him her true feelings for Chyke. *The sooner he knows, the sooner he can come to terms with the fact. Perhaps he will accept the reality and ask to be included in the next matching? Yes, that's the way forward. Let's get up there. A steady pace is always quicker. Think of hours and hours in a wet room. Think of the refectory. Has Tanun made it back? Don't think about it.*

At the hatch, two SFs helped her and Bento-Tor into the dome. The SFs scanned them with detectors to check for any implants, bugs, and comms devices.

'Have to check – those are the rules.'

'I'd be annoyed and disappointed if you hadn't. Can't wait to get to a wet room.'

'Well, if you need any help in there ...'

'Too kind, but I'll manage.'

Joor-Jen sensed their leery looks following her until she and Bento-Tor had disappeared around the curve of the corridor.

Inside her den, she off-loaded her belts, straps, the knife and 10/10, and boots and socks. Keeping her boiler suit on, she grabbed clean clothes and trudged along to the nearest wet room, stripped off and stood forever under the hot jets. The whirling brushes stroked away the exhaustion, the grief, and the Tanun and Chyke web. Until she stepped out to grab a towel, when they rushed right back in. She picked up her pile of dirties, went back to her den, sat on the floor and debated whether to find Tanun. *I'm too tired, and I'll have to work out what to say first.*

*Anyway, I don't even know if he's back from his mission. Or even alive.* She leapt up. The refectory was the answer. Not because she was hungry, although she was, but because she could pretend everything was normal. Chyke hadn't been kidnapped. Xen-Lin and two SFs were still alive. And Tanun was safely back.

* * *

In the drizzle, the dome hove into sight beyond the oat fields, and Tanun yearned to be inside. Chyke, Chyke. As soon as he'd climbed the rungs, he'd hug him and punch him and tell him he was a troublesome git. Would Joor-Jen be triumphant? She'd deserve to be. He couldn't wait to tell them both about Avena. Perhaps Lento-Fin would allow them some in the refectory to celebrate?

'You go first, Tanun,' said Lento-Fin. 'You should make good time. You've incentive enough. I'll be a rung below you.'

The hatch opened when he was ten rungs below and when he glimpsed Joor-Jen, his heart jumped, but then the thought she and Chyke would have had extra time together made him catch his breath. They'd been matched, after all. Would it all kick off with an argument? Were they in one of Joor-Jen's webs? His legs lost their strength.

'Come on, Tanun.' Lento-Fin had to push Tanun's bottom for the last few rungs. 'Only a few more. Think of a wet room. Proper food. Bed.'

Joor-Jen was waiting for them.

'Joor-Jen.' In their embrace, Tanun asked, 'Where's Chyke? Thought he'd be here to see me.' But they had to separate as Lento-Fin and the SFs reached the hatch.

'I'm sorry, Tanun,' Joor-Jen sniffed. 'Chyke isn't here. The mission failed. He's alive, but still a prisoner. Xen-Lin's dead. So are the two SFs.'

Tanun fell against the wall. Stared at Joor-Jen. Couldn't choose which question to ask. Too many. Too many and more whirled around the hatch room.

While Tanun's limp body pressed against the hatch wall, Joor-Jen turned to Lento-Fin. 'Sorry, Lento-Fin, we were betrayed. Our two infiltrators had been turned and their forces were waiting for us. Bento-Tor, Xen-Lin, and I were captured. Typical Bento-Tor ... he killed an enforcer and released me and Xen-Lin. I got into Chyke's cell. He's Ok, Tanun. But as we left his cell, the door closed, trapping him inside. They'd disabled all access and our stolen rings no longer worked. The three of us had to fight our way to the hatch. Thanks to our SF distracting the enemy, we made it and jumped out. Must have fallen at least twelve rungs. The descent was hell. Pulses from above, pulses from below. Xen-Lin got hit in the shoulder. I reached down for him – for his wrist. I held him, I held him, but he was hit again from the ground and I couldn't hold his unconscious weight. His wrist was sweaty and he slipped from my grasp. He fell.' Joor-Jen wiped her eyes.

'He fell, he fell. Somehow I made it to the bottom. Don't know how. Our SF on the ground was killed. There was an enforcer hiding down there. The one who'd hit Xen-Lin. As Bento-Tor and I were kneeling, saying goodbye to Xen-Lin, the enforcer came for us. Must have wanted us alive. No other reason. He could easily have killed us. Bento-Tor used the enforcer's own knife. You know how good he is with knives. Some sort of justice, I suppose.' Her tears chased each other down her cheeks.

'Joor-Jen,' said Lento-Fin, 'you did well. And so did Bento-Tor. You are the best Special Forces. To have even got into Chyke's cell after being betrayed and to have made it out and got back is incredible. Tell you what, you take

Tanun to his den and tell Bento-Tor I'll see the three of you in the refectory in two hours. Let's go, guys, and get cleaned up.'

Along the corridor, neither Tanun nor Joor-Jen spoke. They didn't speak in the elevator. When Tanun's door whooshed, Joor-Jen followed him in. They didn't speak, then, either. Tanun sat on his lower bunk and put his head in his hands. Joor-Jen sat down beside him and put her arm round his shoulders but he shrugged her off.

'Tanun, I know how you're feeling. I want to help. Let me help.'

He sat up and with blotchy eyes turned to Joor-Jen. 'Was Chyke really Ok? You said you saw him only for a moment.'

'We had no time, but you know Chyke. He's giving them the run-around. Incorrect information, false trails. That sort of thing. There's something else. The KimMorii were there. They're helping the Elders. What the price is, I cannot imagine.'

'Great. They'll torture Chyke, poor git, and find out I have the stone.'

'No. Chyke's too cute for them. He won't reveal anything about the stone. He'll feign ignorance, I'm sure of it. He's good at that.'

'Yeah,' Tanun nodded, 'he is. We've got to rescue him. Could we go? Don't have to involve others.'

'Get real, Tanun. The Governors wouldn't authorise us and to stand any chance of success, we'd need at least four SFs.'

'I don't care about authorisation. I just want to get my brother back.'

'We all do. But the way to do that is working with Lento-Fin and the Council. Not against them.'

Tanun let out a sigh and wiped his sleeve across his eyes. 'You're right. I missed you, Joor-Jen. I was worried you'd have spent a lot of time with Chyke and could have changed your mind.'

Joor-Jen leaned into Tanun. 'I missed you too.'

After a long drawn-out kiss, Joor-Jen said Tanun had better get cleaned up, and reminded him there was a wet room just along from his den. 'I'll wait here, if you'd like.'

'Or come in with me ... if I'd like?'

Joor-Jen smiled. 'I'll wait here.'

\* \* \*

In the refectory, Bento-Tor sat next to Tanun, who was holding Joor-Jen's hand under the table while Lento-Fin sat opposite. He said they both looked better than they had in the hatch room and emphasised to Tanun that if Joor-Jen's mission had not been betrayed, they would have succeeded in rescuing Chyke. Tanun moved his hand from Joor-Jen's and said he understood that, but he couldn't bear to think of Chyke being tortured and they must launch another mission to rescue him.

'We will do that,' said Lento-Fin, 'but we have to find out if there are any other infiltrators who have been turned, otherwise the next mission could end more tragically than the last.'

Tanun asked how you could possibly go about doing that, and Lento-Fin explained it was a complex process of feeding bits of false information to our infiltrators in the enemy dome and seeing how the enemy reacted. Depending on how they did react, we'd know if we were being betrayed.

'We already know who the two traitors were from our own dome who helped with Chyke's kidnap.'

'Yes, good ... but how can you be sure this time who the infiltrators in the other dome were?'

'I had allocated two specific SFs to unlock the hatch and release the cell doors. They did that, but then alerted the enemy which corridors Joor-Jen, Bento-Tor, and Xen-Lin had used. That made it obvious to the enforcers that they were there to rescue Chyke.'

At this, Tanun looked into his lap because he couldn't bear the thought of Chyke stuck in a cell in their old dome.

'Tanun,' said Lento-Fin, 'we can't rescue Chyke until we are confident in our infiltrators, but we might be able to communicate with him via his DD. That would be vastly easier than attempting a rescue.'

'We could?'

'Fraught with peril, but if we could get a signal processor under the dome, tuned to the right frequency, we could.'

'I want to volunteer. I can't live with myself. Joor-Jen could come with me.'

'Joor-Jen is required on another mission, so she cannot. But Bento-Tor could. Would that be Ok, Bento-Tor? Keeping busy is the best thing. You'll need two SFs.'

'Definitely Ok.'

'Good. Sorted, then. I know we've mentioned this before, but why don't you move in with Tanun?'

Bento-Tor looked at Tanun, who nodded.

'Thanks, Tanun. Appreciate it. I promise not to be a pain.'

'Er, Lento-Fin,' said Tanun, 'you said Joor-Jen was required on another mission. What is it?'

'I'm sorry, Tanun, I can't tell you. The Council insisted the purpose be kept top secret.'

'But this is such a liberal dome. I thought the

Governors shared their reasoning behind any decision.'

'We try to. All Governors do, but in matters of intelligence and warfare there are many things we must keep secret. To put your mind at rest, the mission should not be dangerous. It is not a military mission.'

'We'll be away around twenty dark-times,' said Joor-Jen.

'That's enough to get to an enemy dome,' said Tanun, staring at Lento-Fin.

'That's enough chat about the mission,' he replied, 'or any other mission. Tell you what. Let's enjoy some Avena to mark your safe return and honour our dead.'

While Lento-Fin went over to the counter, Tanun turned to Joor-Jen to ask her a question, but she put her finger vertically across her lips.

'Right. Well, if I'm not allowed to talk to you,' Tanun turned away to Bento-Tor, 'do you know how to work this signal processor and when can we set off?'

'No and soon, but I'm good with devices, so I don't think it will take me long. First, though, we've got to get there. Safely. There are missiles all the time now.'

'Yeah, I saw. Will feel really odd going back to my old dome. So much has happened since.'

Lento-Fin returned holding four containers and waving a white bottle. 'This one is nicer than our field version. Tell me what you think, Tanun.'

Tanun sipped from his glass and let the spirit dribble down his throat like before. The others each emptied their container in one action. He looked at them, holding their empty container next to the bottle for a refill, and said they were obviously familiar with Avena.

'Only on special occasions,' said Joor-Jen. 'Lento-Fin?'

He refilled the containers and lifted his towards the

others. 'To you three brilliant young SFs, and never forgetting, respect to our fallen comrades.'

On their way back to their dens, Tanun shook his head as the Avena pulsed in his head. Could he persuade Joor-Jen to stay with him?

'Be great, moving in with you, Tanun,' said Bento-Tor. 'It's when we have time to stop and think that the bad thoughts get in.'

'No worries. After the Avena I won't even notice you're there. Ok if take the top? I'd like to change.'

'I don't care. I'll get my stuff later.'

At Tanun's door, Tanun and Joor-Jen shared a long lingering kiss, oblivious of Bento-Tor.

'Training for your mission at light-time,' said Joor-Jen, wiping her mouth. 'See you at hatch 230-188.' She pecked Bento-Tor on his ear before walking to her den.

'She's an amazing girl, Tanun, and I'm not into girls.'

'She is an amazing girl ... who weaves amazing webs.'

*  *  *

The cell lit up and woke Chyke. Six enforcers dragged him off his bench and onto the chair. One enforcer held him in a strangle-hold. Two others held his legs, and two his right arm. One held out his left arm horizontally and squeezed his bicep. The sixth approached with a syringe and pushed the needle firmly into a vein in Chyke's hand. Chyke watched the clear liquid disappear from the syringe.

'Just a little something to encourage you. You won't even be able to resist telling her how many shits you've had.'

Chyke turned his head to look at the enforcer. 'I couldn't resist before. If you hadn't got the wrong guy, she'd have had all her information by now.'

'Give him some more,' said the enforcer, squeezing his bicep. 'Shut the gobby boy up.'

'We'll do exactly as we were told,' said the enforcer with the syringe as he pulled the needle out. 'She doesn't want him damaged. Too valuable alive, apparently.' The enforcer stared at Chyke. 'Can't think how, except … perhaps … yes, when she's finished with you, you can show us your value in our games room. You'll know you're entering it because of the sign above the door. Dying of Pleasure. All six enforcers sniggered as they turned and left.

Chyke went back to his bench. She wouldn't be long now. Must be letting the drug take effect. At least they hadn't stripped him this time. Not necessary, he guessed, with the drug doing the heavy work.

XorX swept in and stood by the chair.

'Please, Chyke, stay on your bench. The chair won't be necessary. Save that for another session. Remember my friend? She is keen to meet you again. However, let's see if we can resolve my problem this way first. I've gone over it again and again, and I still cannot arrive at a satisfactory explanation.'

Chyke stared upwards and screwed up his face to try to clear his fuzzy head.

'Despite the countless times you have told me, what I cannot reconcile is why you followed your brother after he'd been banished. You believed the outside was poisonous. You had no idea how you would open the hatch. You had no idea you would even find your brother. Yet you left the security of the dome and went after him. I am sorry, but the fact he's your brother really doesn't work for me. Go deep, Chyke. Deep into your mind. You've buried the real reason well, and I admire that, but now I need you to dig it out. Bring it to the surface. Tell me the real reason. The one you've hidden so well. I'll wait. I'll wait for as long as it takes. Why did you follow your brother?'

Chyke's muscles had relaxed. His head was dreamy. This was not so bad. And although the room was distant, the bench had become comfortable. He could sleep forever. XorX's black shape moved in and out of focus. *How long will this last?*

'Why did you follow your brother? Why did you follow your brother? Answer the question. Answer the question.'

Chyke slurred, 'Note. Received note. A note.'

'What sort of note?'

'Roll of cloth. Small.'

'Where?'

'Library. Looking at a knowledge pod. Someone passed my desk and dropped the roll.'

'When?'

'The dark-time before Tanun's trial.'

'Who dropped the note?'

'Don't know. Didn't see.'

'Did you read the note?'

'Course. Unrolled the cloth. Red writing.'

'Tell me what the note said.'

Chyke forced his eyes open but continued to stare upwards, not looking at XorX. '"Tanun to be banished. Follow him. Outside. We'll make it easy for you to escape. Find him and stick close." Not sure it said stick close, but something like that. "You'll be well rewarded." Liked the sound of that. And then it said "Report on what he gets involved in. Who he meets. We'll contact you discreetly. You'll be a major player. Special privileges. One day possibly an Elder. You won't have heard of clones, but you'll get an unlimited supply. Whichever you prefer. Girls or boys." Didn't know what clones were, still don't, actually, but endless supply sounded great. Girls. Oh, yeah – at the bottom it said "The alternative? Stay here, confined to your den for the rest of your life. Do it. Do it. Reply on the back of this cloth. Leave it on this desk after

Tanun's trial has finished." I think that was all of it.'

'Hmm. Why didn't you think it was a fake? A trap?'

'I did at first. Then I thought, the library is so controlled, under constant supervision and observation, how could someone have faked it and delivered it? Why would anyone go to all that trouble? After a food-cube back in my room, I decided it was genuine.'

'Did you consider saying no?'

Chyke closed his eyes. *Please, please could I sleep? Afterwards, I'll answer a million questions. After sleep.*

'Did you consider saying no!'

'Yes, yes. Outside poisonous. Betray Tanun.' He turned his head to look at XorX's shifting shape. 'Then I thought ... he's a git. Always beating down on me. Be great to show him I'm more powerful. Me and loads of girls, and being an Elder ... that would show him. What had I got to lose? I'd been chosen.'

'Who did you think the message was from?'

'The Elders, of course. No one else has that power, or means.'

'What did you do next?'

'At light-time, before Tanun's trial, I scribbled on the back "Count me in. When do I see the girls?" I rolled the cloth up and left it on the desk in the library as instructed.'

'Thank you, Chyke. You have been most informative. Before I go, have a really good think about this next question.'

In the long silence that followed, Chyke began to wonder when the next question would be.

'How would you feel if you were released?'

'Released?'

'So that you could carry on your spying. Pretend you'd escaped. We could easily arrange that. Get to the other dome and report. We'll assign a handler who will look after you. One of our infiltrators. Tell us who Tanun meets. Visitors to the dome. What the dome's strategy is. When will they next attack? Missions and so on. Pretty easy stuff ... and I promise you'll get your girls.'

Chyke pushed himself up to sit on the edge of his bench. Steadied himself by pressing his fists hard against the wooden slats. 'You're serious?'

'I am always serious, you should know that by now. You see, Chyke, I believe you can perform a great service for us. And great service brings great rewards, including great pleasure. Dwell on this, while I verify certain things. Imagine. A secret agent. Important. Powerful. And girls. Sleep well.'

# THIRTEEN: Resolved

In the hatch room, Lento-Fin announced to Bento-Tor, Tanun, and the two SFs, that Bento-Tor would lead their mission. He reminded them they had not tried this type of communication in the field before, but the Signals people had successfully trialled the technique, defeating emulated enemy signal disrupters. Tanun asked if there was any risk to Chyke from sending signals to his DD, and Lento-Fin said the experts had not registered any ill-effects on the test subjects. The worst thing that could happen, he said, apart from being caught, or killed, was that the signals wouldn't synchronize and they wouldn't be able to make any contact with Chyke.

'Keep your missile detectors switched on at all times. The enemy alliances are sending over more and more and you'll be lucky indeed not to encounter a few on the mission.'

'Have there been any from 1279-41130?' asked Bento-Tor.

'No. Being an early smaller dome they have a limited arsenal, although they do have DTGs.'

'DTGs?' said Tanun.

'Dome-to-ground shells. Fifty-metre impact zone. Not nice. All set, Bento-Tor?'

'All set.'

'SFs, down you go. Tanun. Bento-Tor. Good luck.'

Tanun walked through the oat fields, marvelling at how different they looked now the oats had been harvested. He remembered being awestruck at seeing the new dome rising above the stalks and Cassièl telling him and Chyke about porridge and how to press the oat from its casing. Cassièl. Appears and disappears. So powerful, yet not helping them defeat the enemy alliances. There was surely more to the story of Dodecahedron than he had let on. The dull feeling crept up his gut again as he thought about the trial. A lifetime ago. If he'd pleaded for mercy, for clemency, he might still be in his old dome. He wouldn't keep getting that shivery feeling when he felt Joor-Jen was spinning a web. He thought about her all the time, but there was something not right. A distance. A knowing. Was he trapped in a Joor-Jen web? First, you have to know there's a web.

'You Ok, Tanun?' said Bento-Tor from the front of the line. 'You're quiet. Usually you're asking me hundreds of questions.'

'I'm fine. Just thinking.'

'I know it'll be weird for you going back to your old dome. Be great, though, if we get to talk to Chyke.'

'That'll feel weird too. Close but not close. Not sure I'll deal with it very well.'

'We'll look after you.'

Where the oat fields petered out before the wood, the four of them had to stop. A large crater, about ten metres across and ten metres deep, had destroyed the path and surrounding crops. Tanun asked if a missile had caused the crater, but Bento-Tor said it was most likely shrapnel from a nearby DTG. Somewhere close by, he said, would be the impact crater, which would be around fifty metres wide and thirty deep.

'Listen. Incoming. Two, I think. Quick, into the crater.'

The four of them slid down the side of the crater, and when they had come to a stop about halfway down, Tanun asked if the crater was the best place to be. Bento-Tor thought definitely not – but better than in the wood.

'Doesn't matter where you are if you take a direct hit. But if you escape that, it's then about avoiding shrapnel and debris and minimising the effects of the shockwave.'

The thump caused the four of them to slip farther down. Earth and rocks hurtled overhead, although only small stones and branches tumbled down the sides of the crater. The second thump was more distant and only resulted in the sides of the crater crumbling and pouring down to the bottom.

'Think that's it for now,' said Bento-Tor. 'SFs? To the top and throw the rope.'

The two SFs slipped and scrabbled their way up the crater and when they reached the top, threw down a length of carbon rope for Tanun and Bento-Tor to pull themselves up. At the top, Bento-Tor said they should get farther into the wood to make camp.

'But Bento-Tor,' said Tanun, 'what were the targets of those DTGs? Where did they come from? All feels a bit random.'

'They were meant for our dome. Our signal disrupters made them crash short of their target. I don't know for sure, but they probably came from your old dome.'

'Great. And that's where we're heading.'

'Yes. So the closer we get, the safer it should be.' Bento-Tor smiled at Tanun.

'I usually like your sense of humour.'

'The trek back will be much more dangerous.'

* * *

Having asked permission to enter Joor-Jen's den, Lento-Fin stepped through and made for the window. The suns were setting and the harvested oat fields, now a misty-grey hue, had taken on an exhausted demeanour. Joor-Jen stood by the bathroom arch, observing Lento-Fin observing the twilight.

'Always strikes me as an unusual den, Joor-Jen. No bed.'

'Prefer the floor. Like being on a mission. What is it, Lento-Fin?'

He continued to look out the window. 'I feel irresponsible,' he sighed, 'sending them with civil war escalating. Tanun's a quick learner and Bento-Tor's one of the best, but they're effectively heading straight into enemy territory. Active territory. Missiles are increasing and scouts report more DTGs.'

'We discussed this,' said Joor-Jen, 'when the Council was arguing about whether to authorise it. Thank you for letting me attend, by the way.'

Lento-Fin turned from the window to look at Joor-Jen. 'We did. And I know the decision was unanimous. It's just we're risking four for one. With terrible odds.'

'Lento-Fin. The one you speak of is Chyke. Who was in our care. To whom we owed — still owe — a duty of care. He's sixteen. Do you have any idea what he's suffering in that cell? We should be rescuing him, not just trying to make contact.'

'I do know what he's going through. And you know we can't try another rescue until we're confident of our infiltrators. Not after last time.'

'Well, let me go. I'll catch up with them. Gives them a better chance. Improves the odds.'

'Absolutely not. Cannot risk you plus Bento-Tor ... you wouldn't by any chance be letting your feelings for Tanun and Chyke influence you, would you?'

Joor-Jen's face burned. She saw Tanun's face; she saw

Chyke's face. Tasted Tanun's lips; tasted Chyke's lips. Remembered Chyke pressing against her in his cell. Remembered Tanun's long kiss when they sat on his bed. How could this happen? How could she feel this strongly about each of them? She'd grown close to Tanun. He was deep. Layers. More to discover. But she and Chyke were matched. For good reason. She felt the reason every time they got close.

'You haven't resolved anything, have you?'

'I've resolved things a million times. When I'm with one, the situation's resolved. Until I'm with the other.'

'I can't guide you, Joor-Jen, except to say, three youngsters are going to get very hurt.'

'Never considered I could have these feelings for two people. You'd think there'd only be enough for one.'

'Love is virtual. Like time. Anyhow, Joor-Jen, I'm putting you forward for election to the Council. Two Governors are due to step down. We need younger viewpoints and perspectives.'

'Me? I'm an orphan. Speak my mind. Upset too many people.'

'Yes. And now tell me your bad points.'

'Are you sure? I'll refuse if it means I can't fight anymore.'

'You can fight. I do. You'll have to deal with a few macho SFs, but by what I hear you already do.'

'Thank you, Lento-Fin. And I'm sorry about the Tanun and Chyke thing.'

'You don't have to say sorry to me, and it doesn't sound as if you chose the situation ... though I hope all three of you survive it.'

* * *

Chyke opened his eyes to see XorX standing by the chair. Memories like a deck of cards. No chance of knowing which was first, which was second, third, or fourth. Was ace high or low?

'My dear Chyke. We were to work together, and for that ... there had to be honesty and trust. I'm sure you'd agree. Yes? And yet, I am unable to trace the note or the roll of cloth, and believe me I have been thorough. And to compound my difficulty, no Elder will admit to writing such a note. Seems your little story was just a ploy to delay your inevitable suffering.'

'Good.' Chyke stared up into the hood. 'There are bound to be enemy infiltrators here, and to leave that note in existence could have blown my cover. To stand a chance of success, this has to continue to be the most professional operation. I was operating under deep cover in that dome. You should know the risks that entails. Of course, no Elder would admit to writing the note. They can't – they don't – trust each other. Each thinks the other could be an infiltrator. I'd feel my cover was much less secure if someone had admitted to writing the note.' Chyke challenged the inside of the hood.

XorX stared unseen down at Chyke. Neither moved. Silence dominated. Time vanished. Until Chyke thought he could make out a tapping sound. Rhythmic. Growing louder. Out of the corner of his eye he glimpsed it, but he kept on staring into the hood. XorX tapped her "friend" on the back of the chair frame. Harder. Louder. Quicker. The tapping stopped.

'An enforcer will show you who your handler will be in 1279-41618. Right now, your brother and three others are heading for this dome. We believe to attempt to communicate with you. When I deem the moment fitting, you will escape and catch up with them on their way back. Tell them the cell door opened. They will believe their comms device was responsible. Play the suffering but relieved victim and wait for contact from your handler. Did you understand all of that, Chyke?'

'Of course I did. I'm good at this. Don't forget my girls.'
**'You will get your girls. I give you my word.'**

When Chyke looked at his tray after XorX had left, there were six food-cubes plus a flagon of elderflower water. Next to the tray was a torn boilersuit splattered with blood, one flat broken shoe and a bloody bandage, under which was an access ring and a picture of whom he took to be his handler. *That's good, they're doing this properly.* He ran through XorX's reaction to his explanation about the note and her subsequent instructions. What he couldn't clarify and what wouldn't let him settle, was whether XorX and the enforcers knew about his DD. She said Tanun and others were going to try to communicate. How else could they do that except via his DD? *Surely the enforcers would have removed it if they'd known about it? A DD could do so much. Given there are infiltrators in every dome, DDs must be common knowledge. And yet* – they hadn't.

* * *

'There you go, Tanun,' said Bento-Tor. 'Your old dome. Homesick?'

'You've gotta be kidding. I'd like to run in the opposite direction. I'll have nightmares about it. I mean, how can the Elders and enforcers control everyone's life like that? They're evil.'

'They might just be misguided.'

'You didn't live there. You wouldn't say that if you had. And now they're helping the KimMorii.'

'That makes them evil, for sure. Though they probably didn't have a choice. "Thank you but no thank you, KimMorii shapeshifter. We've decided to decline your generous offer of help." Really?'

'Point taken.'

'Wish we could get closer. We'll just have to make a run for it. Swerving of course.'

'I know. Did that with Lento-Fin. Harder than I thought it would be.'

'We'll wait and observe. Confirm timings. Let's make camp.'

Bento-Tor lifted the signaller out of his rucksack and played with the knobs and buttons. In the dark, the little green screen flickered as frequencies and arrows flowed across. 'No chance from here, but everything's working fine. Tanun, listen. Warning. We might not make contact. We'll give it a good few goes, but if we have to call it quits, then we'll need to get away as fast as possible. You'll have to deal with it.'

'I will. I know we haven't got the gear for getting inside.'

The two SFs reported that no one had entered or left the dome for three hours, so now was the optimum time to get under the dome. One SF led, followed by Bento-Tor, Tanun, and the other SF at the rear. The three snaked across the heath, weaving and swerving behind Bento-Tor to keep up with his random change of direction. When they all crowded behind the dish of the leg, each put his hand over his mouth to muffle the sound of his laboured breathing.

'Think we're Ok. Let's wait a bit.'

After half an hour, Bento-Tor pulled out the signaller and knelt behind the dish. Tanun knelt beside him while the SFs scouted the perimeter of the legs and dishes.

'Never done this for real. Worked Ok in testing, but never the same live in the field.'

The screen glowed green. Bento-Tor turned two

knobs simultaneously. Tanun craned closer. Rows of numbers scrolled up.

'There's something. I'm connecting ... although in truth it doesn't look like a DD. Start again.'

Bento-Tor reset the device and twirled the knobs. Arrows turned. A frequency turned red.

'I've got a handshake. Chyke. Don't be alarmed. Bento-Tor here with Tanun. Can you hear me?' Bento-Tor turned the knobs. 'No response. And yet something's registering.'

Although kneeling, Tanun bent double so his head rested in his hands on his knees. Through the gaps between his fingers he caught the flickering green light of the screen as Bento-Tor adjusted and re-adjusted the frequencies.

'What I don't understand,' said Bento-Tor, 'is that although I'm connecting with something, it's not Chyke's DD.'

'Perhaps they're removed it,' said Tanun, straightening up. 'Can't imagine they'd leave it in. Too risky.'

'Possible, but Chyke's and yours were the latest versions and have shields to prevent detection. I'm sorry, Tanun. I'll give it one more go, but then we'll have to leave.'

'How long have we got?'

'Be light-time in two hours. Got to be far into the wood by then.'

Bento-Tor was just about to try a fourth time when the SFs said the suns were coming up and they must leave immediately. Each SF clapped Tanun on his shoulder as they formed the line to snake back to the woods.

# FOURTEEN: Clones

Chyke's door whooshed sideways. He peered left and right along the corridor. Nothing. Turned right and ran along to a hatch. He peeped around the curve to see an enforcer standing guard by the hatch room door. Chyke calculated, but quickly discarded the idea of running around the perimeter of the dome to approach from the other direction. What he wasn't sure of was whether the enforcer was in the know and would let him escape or would shoot on sight and ask questions later. What could he do? The longer he stayed where he was, the higher the chance of detection.

He ran back to his cell and grabbed the flagon of elderflower water. With his hand over the opening, he ran back to where the curve just concealed him and launched the liquid along the shiny floor. 'Look at that,' he said. 'A little goes a long way.' He heard the enforcer run towards the water, which had now covered the width of the corridor. With his hand around the handle, Chyke moved his arm back as far as he could and swung the flagon. The enforcer splashed down. Chyke grabbed the 10/10 from its holster and ran into the hatch room. As soon as he inserted the access ring, the hatch opened. He used his index finger to pull out the ring and slid through the gap to the rungs a moment before the descending hatch hissed shut.

* * *

When the four of them had reached the cover of the woods, an SF said there was movement at the dome. After studying the three legs this side, Bento-Tor passed his binoculars to Tanun.

'There's someone climbing down,' said Bento-Tor. 'Not an enforcer. Could be an SF.'

'No. I think that's Chyke,' said Tanun.

'No way! How could he have got out? You can't see properly in this light. In an hour, yes, but we can't wait that long.'

'It's Chyke, I tell you. Don't know how. Try the signaller.'

'Too far.'

'Try it. Please.'

Bento-Tor took off his rucksack and threw it down. After he'd pulled the signaller out, he pointed it towards the dome. The green screen glowed.

'Gotta fix. Different red frequency.'

'Hello, Chyke.'

Chyke stopped. *Where did that come from?*

'Hello, Chyke. Bento-Tor here. With Tanun.'

'They must've drugged me again.'

'No, they haven't. Keep going down. Don't stop. We're using a signaller to your DD. We're in the woods. How did you escape?'

'Can't believe this. Tanun?'

Tanun knelt next to Bento-Tor and spoke to the device. 'Hi, Chyke. Definitely me. We can see you on the leg. Over halfway. How the hell did you get out?'

'Lying on my bench, the cell door just opened.'

'When was this?'

'Not sure. About an hour ago?'

Bento-Tor and Tanun nodded at each other.

'That was when we were under the dome trying to contact you.'

'We got a handshake,' said Bento-Tor. 'Connected with something, but not your DD.'

'Had to bash an enforcer, but at least I took his access ring.'

'Good,' said Tanun. 'We'll come and meet you.'

'Correction,' said Bento-Tor. 'We can't do that. Too much movement. Too risky. Chyke, listen. When you hit the ground, run like hell, but swerve, keep swerving, keep swerving until you hit the woods. We'll cover you if we have to. Won't be long before they discover what's happened. Good luck.'

'Yeah, good luck,' said Tanun. 'You'd better make it, you git.'

'I'll make it. Just so I can punch you in the face.'

'Signing off now, Chyke. Signal silence. He sounds in good spirits, Tanun.'

'Can't wait to see him. And thump him.'

Bento-Tor posted the two SFs a kilometre apart along the tree line and chose a tree he and Tanun could use as their cover.

'Tanun, this is hard, but it has to be said. Chyke put on a brave face just now. We don't know how brave. Sure, he's been physically abused, but deeper than that, is the psychological damage. He probably doesn't even know it. Be prepared for some irrational behaviour. When we're back, he'll have to do a full debrief. That's for our benefit, but also Chyke's. He'll get a proper psych-eval. A lot of physical wounds can be healed. Much harder for the psychological ones.'

'Thanks for that, Bento-Tor. I know you had to say it. How did you come to have such an old head on young shoulders? Apostle. SF.'

'We need to keep watch on Chyke, but we can talk. Generally, clones have to strive harder than the rest. I guess that's it.'

'What? Did you say clones?'

'Clones, yeah. You obviously haven't covered this yet in the knowledge pods.'

'No, I haven't. And no one's ever mentioned it.'

'They wouldn't. Just part of the normal run of things.'

'I ... I ... don't know what to say. Was Peeso-Lun a clone?'

'We were twins, of course she was. Xen-Lin was a clone. Different issue. Miss him so much. Half the people are clones, Tanun. Got to concentrate on Chyke. About seven minutes to ground. Oh. The hatch door's opening. Do they have spotlights?'

Tanun let out a long huff.

Bento-Tor hissed at him, 'Do they have spotlights?'

'No. No. Never needed any. Outside poisonous, remember?

'Good. He's in with a chance, then.'

'Clones? Why didn't I know?'

'There's lots you don't know.'

In the growing light, Bento-Tor watched the descending figure and passed the binoculars to Tanun. Tanun moved to the edge of the wood and holding the binoculars, leant against a tree for stability. Bento-Tor took out the signaller and pointed it at the leg of the dome.

'Chyke. If you can hear me, they've opened the hatch. They'll be firing soon. When you hit the ground, don't hesitate. Run to your left, but swerve. You must swerve. I'll guide you to us. Chyke? Chyke?'

'He's on the ground,' said Tanun. 'Running. Swerving.'

'I don't know if he can hear me, but I'll guide him in case he can,' said Bento-Tor. 'They're firing. I can see pulses. Come on, Chyke. Run.'

Tanun followed the pulses from their own SFs as they

converged at the hatch. Two enforcers fell, and a third hung by an ankle, flailing around until a pulse hit him.

'Right a bit, Chyke. Swerve. Don't forget the railway track. Jump it. Faster. Six hundred metres. Left a bit. Five hundred. Four hundred. Come on, Chyke.'

Pulses from the dome whizzed past him and trees in the wood exploded as they hit.

'Head down. Swerve, swerve! Head for the black tree to your left.'

Chyke hurtled past Tanun and Bento-Tor into the woods and fell to his knees, wheezing and retching.

Tanun reached him first and knelt on Chyke's left to comfort him. 'You total git. Well done. That was the most amazing run I've ever seen.'

Bento-Tor knelt on Chyke's right and kissed Chyke's cheek. 'Well done. Could you hear me?'

Between gasps and retches, Chyke said, 'Now and again. Swerve. Tree. Faster.'

'Yeah, that was about it. Listen. We can't stay here. As soon as you can, we gotta move. Tanun, give him some water.'

After Tanun had held the flask to Chyke's lips and Chyke had nodded 'enough', Bento-Tor unscrewed a small flat flask.

'Here you go, Chyke. Just a small mouthful.'

'Wow. Thanks, I like, needed that. You'll have to tell me what it is.'

Tanun shook his head as he stared at his brother, remembering the effect Avena had had on him the first time. He pulled Chyke's arm to help him stand and they merged into an embrace. 'Welcome back, you troublesome little bastard.'

'Great to see you too.'

'Tanun, we gotta move again,' said Bento-Tor.

'Ok, I'll run with Chyke. Keep an eye on him.'

'I'm used to it,' said Chyke.

The SFs waved them forward, and as best they could, Tanun, Chyke, and Bento-Tor ran alongside each other without speaking until they were almost at the line of trees before the tunnel. Bento-Tor said they should get to the tunnel where they would camp.

* * *

Joor-Jen checked her camouflaged boiler suit, boots, belt, two 10/10s, knife, binoculars, and all the other essential equipment necessary for a field trip within a war zone. When she was satisfied with the kit inspection, she made for the hatch room nearest Tanun's den.

Lento-Fin was waiting for her and said the four SFs were already descending the rungs. 'Great idea to go and meet them, Joor-Jen. Tanun might be in a state if they failed to make contact with Chyke. He'll need you.'

'He will. I hope I can help. The missiles seemed to have eased. Don't know if that's a good sign or not.'

'Probably can't read too much into that. When you're down there, they'll no doubt start up again.'

Jumping to the ground, Joor-Jen told the four SFs they would make for the woods on the other side of the oat fields and attempt to meet up with the returning party about halfway in. 'I expect they'll be jittery, so let's be careful. Don't scare them.'

* * *

'Move, and you're dead,' said Joor-Jen.

Tanun turned in his insucover to smile up at Joor-Jen.

'And you'd be dead before your first pulse.' Bento-Tor

pressed the barrel of a 10/10 into the back of Joor-Jen's neck.

'And I wouldn't like that!' said Chyke, appearing from behind a tree where Tanun was lying.

'Chyke! How?'

'Lots to tell. Can't remember it all. Desperate to get home.' He flung his arms around her while Tanun looked on until he looked down at the ground.

Joor-Jen pushed Chyke away and turned. 'You got me there, Bento-Tor. Well done.'

'Wasn't you. Those SFs need more training in silent surveillance. They were the ones who gave you away. Anyway, we can talk about that when we're back. Great you came to meet us. Any special reason?' he smiled.

'There's a lull in the missiles. Either that's good and we can get home quicker, or there'll be a bigger offensive quite soon. Seemed the right thing to do to come and help if I could.'

Bento-Tor turned to address all the SFs. 'Ok, listen, everyone. I hope this isn't the calm before the storm, or a trap of some sort. We don't know why the missiles have eased, but it won't be for long. Let's get to the dome. We'll pause at the oat fields and assess, although I'm guessing a straight line would be favourite. So, Tanun and Chyke, no swerving this time.'

When they reached the edge of the wood, Bento-Tor and Joor-Jen walked to the start of the oat field and conferred. Joor-Jen said it was too quiet and something must be brewing. Bent-Tor agreed, but said he couldn't see any evidence. They settled on running as fast as they could in a straight line through the oat fields to the dome. Joor-Jen asked if she could address everyone because she was fresher, and Bento-Tor happily deferred.

'Bento-Tor and I feel uneasy. Expect you all do as well, but we can't stay here. Two SFs at the front. I'll be behind them. Chyke, then Tanun, with Bento-Tor behind him. Four SFs behind him. Stay close, stay fast, stay alive.'

The leading SFs, with Joor-Jen behind, set off at maximum pace. The line behind stretched out for a few seconds but as they all synchronised their pace, Joor-Jen waved everyone to a stop. They watched a surface-to-air missile curl through the air and explode about 750 metres from the dome. Enemy ground forces ran from the left. Enemy ground forces ran from the right. Joor-Jen reckoned at least a couple of hundred on each side. Pulses from the dome drew long coloured lines, embroidering the air and sky.

'We can't make it to the dome!' Joor-Jen called. 'Back to the woods.'

Four SFs led the line, firing continuously at the forces to their left and right, but as they approached the tree line, more than a hundred enforcers ran at them from inside the wood. Three of the party's SFs fell. Two enforcers ran at Tanun. He slashed one, and without thinking pulled the other into a sasae tsurikomi ashi. Chyke fired his 10/10 into the enforcer's head.

'Great work, Bro,' they each shouted.

Bento-Tor had fallen to his knees and was firing both 10/10s into the marauding forces. Tanun stood up. An enforcer ran straight at him. Didn't stop. Tanun fired. The enforcer didn't slow. Tanun side-stepped him as he ran past, but the enforcer turned and lunged. Slashed and lunged. Lunged and screamed. Changed knife hand. Changed knife hand. The air whistled as the blade cut through it. Tanun swerved, bent this way, leant that way, ducked, a feint, bent his knees. As he straightened, the enforcer's knife drew a crimson line from his left shoulder to his right hip. He staggered backwards and fell onto his back, legs flying up from the momentum. Chyke launched and stabbed the enforcer behind the knees, and as he crumpled, slit his throat.

Joor-Jen ripped apart what was left of Tanun's jacket and pressed pads against the yawning wound. 'How did he survive that? His agility somehow saved him. Incredible. Got to get him to medical.'

'I'll stay with him,' said Chyke. 'You fight.'

Joor-Jen hesitated before joining Bento-Tor and their SFs, fighting off enemy forces still emerging from the woods. Eventually, the onslaught eased and they began picking off the remaining fighters.

'Look,' said Bento-Tor, 'DTGs from our dome. Yay. We'll soon be able to cut a path through.'

An enforcer leapt from the oat stalks and flattened Joor-Jen. Straddling her, he pointed his 10/10 at her head. Bento-Tor sliced the enforcer's throat from behind, but as he fell off Joor-Jen he fired; she rolled onto her front and pushed herself up with blood pouring from her left ear.

'Sorry about that, Joor-Jen,' said Bento-Tor.

'No worries. Only an ear. Bastard.'

'Here. Press this on hard. We have to get Tanun to the dome.'

Joor-Jen and Bento-Tor turned to see Chyke kneeling by his brother, pressing red pads onto his chest with his left hand and simultaneously firing 10/10s into the enemy with his right.

'One of our SFs can carry Tanun. What they're trained for.'

Three SFs had survived uninjured, and Joor-Jen ordered one of them to carry Tanun.

'Another at the front and at the back. Not over yet. Let's see how far we get.'

Because of the DTGs, the marauding forces had thinned to around a hundred in total, with half of those attempting to climb the rungs. The rest were making for the dome and paid no attention to the straggly line of six threading through the dead bodies and smashed oat stalks.

At the edge of the oat field, Joor-Jen ordered them to stop. 'Bento-Tor, can you advance and pick off those on the rungs? Take Tanun's 10/10. You'll then have three 10/10s. Keep moving and keep swerving. We'll cover you as best we can from here.'

'I can do that. See you at the dome.'

The three SFs, Joor-Jen, and Chyke, watched Bento-Tor weave across the battle plain, firing continuously at enforcers on the rungs. Most tumbled to the ground, but some fell awkwardly and hung by their leg or arm or strap, screaming for help. Bento-Tor drew closer to the leg of the dome, sometimes having to turn and fire at an injured enforcer who was compos mentis enough to shoot at him. As he reached the dish of the leg, an enforcer, hanging upside down two hundred rungs above, took careful aim. Bento-Tor's left leg flew across the dish and landed on the other side. He hung motionless over the lip. The enforcer tumbled to the ground.

Joor-Jen looked behind to see Chyke lowering his 10/10. 'Look at you. There's not a mark on you. That was an amazing shot, all the same.'

He winked at her. 'When I want something ... I make sure I get it.'

# FIFTEEN: Scar

Lento-Fin stood by Tanun's bed and said that although his scar would be the envy of every SF, there should be no showing off. Tanun assured him he wouldn't and just wanted to get back to normal and when could he leave medical? Lento-Fin replied that unfortunately there was no normal anymore, however, he should be able to leave after four more dark-times.

'You're a very lucky man, Tanun. A centimetre further and you wouldn't be here. Your training and your clear head saved you.'

'Yeah. In the madness of the moment I could just sense how to move the right way.'

After his regular visits to Tanun, Lento-Fin always then visited Joor-Jen. The left side of her head had been shaved so the medics could operate on her left ear.

'I quite like it, Lento-Fin. Might keep it like this.'

'You look even more intimidating than you did before. Ear Ok?'

'It's fine. They've done a great job. I can leave later.'

'Good. We have much to discuss and much to do. Your election to the Council was successful and as soon as you are able, the Council must meet.'

'Thanks, Lento-Fin. I didn't think I would be successful.'

'No one else was even close. The other choices were fine, but no comparison against you.'

'Um, Lento-Fin. Not sure how to put this.'

'Goodness. Must be difficult.'

'That was some battle. We lost a lot. Funny, though,

how Chyke didn't have a bruise, or a cut.'

'That's good, surely?'

'Too good. Almost impossible.'

'What are you saying?'

'Just wondering if the enemy deliberately protected him.'

'He escaped!' Lento-Fin stared into the middle-distance. Turning back to Joor-Jen he reflected, 'Thinking about it, there's another possibility. They could want him back alive. As a hostage – or they believe he can still tell them more.'

'What? A sixteen-year-old?'

'More open. Less to hide. Probably doesn't understand all the implications.'

'Whatever, we should be wary.'

'Right. Well, you're close to him. See if you find out anything. But don't jump to conclusions. Catch you later. I'll see Bento-Tor now.'

'How's he doing?'

'Physically, great. Not so good psychologically. He's such a bundle of energy he's frustrated with his lack of mobility. And the grief has really hit him.'

'After Peeso-Lun, he got very close to Xen-Lin. A cruel twist losing him so soon after. Bonding is strong in the clones.'

'There's a lot of demand after the battles, but at the Council meeting, I'll propose we grow a new leg for him.'

'I'll second that.'

* * *

Chyke sat on the opposite side of the desk from Lento-Fin and investigator Sin-Tun. Lento-Fin commented that Chyke looked much better than when he'd just returned, and Chyke said he was having a good day, but at other times he had panic attacks when reliving XorX's interrogations in the cell.

'That is quite normal, Chyke,' said Lento-Fin, 'and they will never completely go. Your medical report says you have suffered some muscle and skin damage from the torture, although the vein on your hand will heal completely if you follow the treatment regime. Psychological damage will take a lot longer.'

'It wasn't the pain. It was being trapped and having no sense of time.'

'Solitary is the worst. That's why it's used.'

'Chyke,' said Sin-Tun, 'Lento-Fin has told you we have to do a full debrief and this will take many light-times, though we'll stop when you've had enough each time. Let's start at the beginning with your kidnap. Tell us what you recall about it.'

'I know this is funny, but I remember hearing the shower ... a moment before being knelt on. Tape across my mouth. Sharp pain in my neck ... from a cut, I think. Straps round my ankles and hands behind my back. Cloth over my nose and then a hood over my head. Nothing after that. I couldn't remember anything about it in my cell. Only the last few light-times has it come back.'

'Thank you. Now I'd like to leap to the final interrogation in your cell.'

'Oh.' Chyke shuffled on his chair. 'Missing out everything in between?'

'We'll get to in between.'

'The final interrogation was more of a conversation. With XorX. In a previous interrogation, she'd offered me the opportunity to escape. Be a spy for her.'

'A spy?'

'Yeah. I'd made up a story of finding a note before Tanun's trial, inviting me to follow Tanun and report on him.'

'She was convinced by that?'

'Seemed so. Later, she said she couldn't find any evidence of such a note, and no Elder would admit to writing a note. I had to think quickly. I turned it around and said that was good, because leaving evidence around could have blown my cover. Also, I said the Elders didn't trust each other and each suspected the other of being an infiltrator, which is why none would admit to writing the note.'

'Very shrewd of you, Chyke, especially given your circumstances. Thank you, we have enough information, so that will be all this session. Present yourself here next light-time.'

After Chyke had left, Sin-Tun finished with the text on the screen and turned to Lento-Fin. 'He's not telling us everything.'

'Of course he isn't. He's testing us. See how the oats lie. Whether he can trust us.'

'Trust us?'

'Works both ways.'

'Lento-Fin, he could be playing us.'

'He could. But I don't think he is. You know, he's so good at this, we must get him formally trained in espionage.'

'I admire your confidence.' Sin-Tun touched the screen. 'His medical report shows he really did suffer. He's not making that part up.'

'Irrelevant. Many who've suffered have subsequently been turned. Some form of inverted revenge.'

'Next session should be interesting.'

\*\*\*

In the medical centre, Tanun knelt by Bento-Tor's bed, holding his hand. Neither spoke for a long while.

Bento-Tor turned his head to Tanun and smiled. 'Does it hurt?'

'Not so much now. Pulls when I move. What about you?'

'No. But trying to turn in bed is completely bizarre. I can't believe you survived that knife attack. You haven't had nearly as much training.'

'I know, I was lucky. I somehow knew how to move. Have they told you how long you're going to be in here?'

'They won't say. Gonna try crutches next light-time. Well, that's my SF career done.'

'You don't know that. I reckon Bento-Tor with one leg is loads better than most SFs.'

'It's Ok, Tanun. I'm only a clone.'

'Don't say that. Look, I know I reacted badly in the woods when you told me. It wasn't you. It was the whole ... well ... concept. Completely new to me. And I've so many questions.'

'Well, if you get fed up with the knowledge pods, I'm not going anywhere. I'll answer as many questions as you can think up. Thanks for visiting. I really value it.'

'No problem. I wanted to. Um, Bento-Tor, because ... you've not been matched ... because ....'

'Because I prefer boys?'

'Yeah, that. In time, do you think you'll find someone?'

'Too soon after Xen-Lin, and anyway, who would fancy me now?'

'Plenty. I'm sure. You're young – and good-looking. For a boy. Sorry. Didn't mean to qualify.'

'No worries, Tanun. I've had a lot worse.'

Two medics arrived and told Tanun they needed to examine Bento-Tor and he should go back to his bed and wait to be discharged.

'Catch you later, Bento-Tor.'

'Sure. Appreciate the chat.'

* * *

Chyke bounced into the interview room and sat down. Lento-Fin smiled at him, but Sin-Tun was listening to the transcript from the previous session. When he'd finished, he looked at Chyke and thanked him for being on time. This session, he said, he'd like to concentrate on Chyke's first thoughts on coming to in his cell. Take your time, he emphasised. Accuracy was more important than speed.

Chyke looked down. 'Apart from the torture, that was the worst time. As the drug wore off, I could feel I was being carried. But in a sitting position. The enforcers weren't exactly gentle. They pulled off my hood and ripped off the tape. That hurt. I was strapped to a chair. A chair frame, actually, and strapped real tight. One of them fitted an ankle tag. A female enforcer slapped me across the face.'

'How many were there?'

'Five, I think.'

'Think.'

'Four or five. Seemed like five, but probably four.'

'What happened next?'

'They undid my straps and threatened me that if I caused trouble, they'd strap me even tighter.'

'Can you remember exactly what they said?'

'Sorry, no. It was all a bit of a daze. Two enforcers looked at me quite ... er ... well, as if they were undressing me. I didn't know that would come later. After they'd gone, took me a while to move off the chair. I felt desolate. Scared. And sick. When I did move, that's when I saw it was just a chair frame. Then, I didn't know why it would be a frame and not a proper chair. I do now. As soon as I'd got onto my bench, the light went out. Absolute blackness.'

'Thank you, Chyke. That was tough for you. Next session, I want you to describe your cell. Dimensions, shape, colour, light, door, floor, ceiling, bench, furniture, food, water, waste, and where the cell was in the dome. Every single detail.'

\* \* \*

Tanun lay on his top bunk and ran his fingers up and down the angry scar. About half a centimetre wide and proud by about the same. While he pondered if it would ever fade enough to be ignored, he recalled the enforcer running toward him. Determined to get him. Nothing stopped him. Slowed him. Almost as if he'd been programmed. One task. Nothing else mattered. As the enforcer had slashed, changing hands mid-sweep, Tanun had known – he'd just known – which way to swerve, which way to feint. He sat up on his bunk in a sweat. Where was Joor-Jen? Chyke was in the debriefing room, so she wasn't with him. She would probably be there straight after, though. She seemed oblivious to any hurt she caused. He decided he really would have to confront her and sort out the whole mess with Chyke.

'Tanun? It's Cassièl. Please may I enter?'

'Suppose. Hi. Where have you been? So much has happened. Is happening. War, deaths. You just disappear. Lento-Fin must think it's Ok. Is Ennti all right? Actually, I need your advice on something.'

'One thing at a time, Tanun. Appreciate you are

stressed and I am so sorry but I cannot stay here, on Lemtor. There is turmoil across the universes, yet there is so much I need to tell you. First, I have to say, you have done exceptionally well. Without me. You have fought skilfully, plus you helped rescue Chyke. And all the while kept Dodecahedron safe.'

'I nearly died. Look.' Tanun opened the top of his boilersuit.

'Your skill ... and Dodecahedron.'

'What's the stone got to do with anything?'

'You are a good fighter, Tanun, but that enforcer was an experienced knife man. The major in charge. Dodecahedron helped you anticipate.'

Tanun stared at Cassièl as Joor-Jen and Lento-Fin's voice echoed about his agility and quick-wittedness. 'I see it now, Cassièl. Sorry. My world has changed. Not changed. One world has been destroyed and another has taken its place.'

'A fair summary. Tanun, you must realise, this would have happened even if you had not found the stone. You had been banished. You did not know there were other domes, and if you had, you did not know how to find them. Same for Chyke.'

'Chyke. Do you know what happened? He was kidna—'

'I know. And he has been as amazing as you are. Dodecahedron could not have found better boys. Are you hungry? We could go to the refectory and you could get something. Fancy some Avena?'

'Are you allowed? I thought only Lento-Fin was allowed.'

'Well, being an Amnian does have certain advantages.'

'Brilliant, I'm starving. And some Avena would go down a treat.

'Right. Down you get and lead the way.'

\* \* \*

'Thanks for suggesting that, Cassièl, I was starving.' Tanun leant across the table. 'Do you know what's going to happen to us?'

'We Amnians can see all possible futures. What we cannot tell is which one will come to pass. Since the beginning, we have had a policy of not interfering in other worlds, so we cannot say which future will transpire.'

'Ok, but the KimMorii shapeshifters interfere.'

'Unfortunately, they do. And if we also interfered, we would end up confronting them in both the spiritual and the physical universes. That would, without exception, result in catastrophe.'

'So difficult, Cassièl. My world – what I understood of it, anyway – was so small, and thinking about it, Lemtor is small on the scale of things, isn't it? Alters my entire view of everything. I mean, how many other planets are there?'

'That would be a number you couldn't grasp, Tanun. Think of out there as teeming with lives. And those are just the physical universes. There are even more spiritual universes, and I would have loved you and Chyke to have experienced Amnia, but the problem with Dodecahedron has prevented me.'

'Have the other stones been a problem?'

'Dodecahedron is the first we have found. I hope the others will not prove so difficult.'

'Why didn't the KimMorii take them all back to their universe?'

'We are not sure, but we think the Nuclei would not let them. We have learnt that the KimMorii found they could not transpose to their universe – KimMoriN – when in possession of a Nucleus. And with us InQuisitorii – searchers of stones – pursuing them, we believe they were forced to hide each stone on a different planet – within the physical universes. I do not expect you to remember this, but after we had first met, I mentioned the thirteen Nuclei form the Master Circle.'

'I do remember.'

'Well, I did not trouble you with this then, but the Master Circle is just part of a mysterious entity called Principium. Principium is the source and driving force and creator of all universes, energy, and life. We have studied this since the beginning and we still do not comprehend how it came to be, or how it creates all existence.'

'Right. Any chance of that Avena?'

Cassièl went over to a serving bar and collected a bottle and a container.

'So, you were allowed.'

'Try this. One of the better ones. You said there was something you wanted advice about.'

Tanun drank back the Avena and shook his head. 'Brrr. This is difficult. Embarrassing, really. Don't know where to start. How to start.'

'Try saying, I'm very fond of Joor-Jen.'

'Yes, thank you. Cassièl. Sorry.' Tanun huffed out a breath. 'I'm very fond of Joor-Jen ... I think she's fond of me, too. Great, you might say, but she seems equally fond of Chyke. He doesn't see a problem with it. Joor-Jen doesn't either, apparently, so I'm the one who's all screwed up. Sometimes I feel ... I dunno ... used.'

'I appreciate your confiding in me, Tanun. Unfortunately, I do not have a solution to this. There probably is no satisfactory solution. However, a story might help. Before that, try to understand that the feelings

Joor-Jen has for you ... and for Chyke, are genuine. She is probably just as conflicted and cannot see a way of avoiding hurting one or both of you.'

'She doesn't show it.'

'Joor-Jen might say the same about you.'

'How do you—?'

'The story. There was once a great ruler. Stern, but fair. One light-time in winter, his servants brought two mothers to him. Each claimed the same new-born baby, and each seemed as sincere as the other. So, the ruler asked the servants to pass him the baby, and he held the baby in his arms. He said to the two mothers, they must each stand in front of him and look him in the eye. The first to look away, he said, would prove she was false and would forfeit the child and her own life. So, on a drumbeat, each mother looked the ruler in the eye. Time passed. Drums rolled. The fire roared. The ruler looked from one mother to the other. The drums grew louder, faster. The flames higher. Still the mothers stared. After an age, the ruler raised the child above his head and made to throw her into the roaring fire. One mother continued to stare the ruler in the eye as commanded. The other, though, broke her stare and looked in terror at the child. She fell to her knees, begging the ruler not to harm the baby. By this, the ruler knew she was the genuine mother, for no mother could abide this for her child. You see, Tanun, sometimes your feelings for someone mean you have to bear your hurt ... for the sake of their happiness.'

Tanun wiped away a tear with the back of his hand and held out his container to Cassièl.

'My price, Tanun, is to see Dodecahedron.'

Tanun reached into his pocket and showed Cassièl the stone. 'If I put it on the table, perhaps you could pick it up?'

'I fear not, although there would be no harm in trying.'

Using his thumb and middle finger, Tanun gently placed Dodecahedron on the table midway between himself and Cassièl. Cassièl stared down at the stone before reaching for it.

'Dodecahedron might as well weigh a trillion stars. It does not wish me to retrieve it. Thank you, though, Tanun, for suggesting that. Best hide it away again.'

While Cassièl poured some more Avena into Tanun's container, Tanun said, 'Can I ask you something else?'

'Of course, you can. Ask away.'

'Bento-Tor's a clone. So was his sister, and Xen-Lin.'

'You have recently discovered this.'

'Why, though? Why create clones? How did cloning start? Who controls it? Who decides?'

'Use the knowledge pods for the background, Tanun. This dome wasn't the first, by any means, to create clones. After the poisoning of the environment, reproduction rates plummeted. Something had affected the DNA. Other domes wanted to build up their military but were desperately short of people, so they recommenced cloning to create compliant combatants. Cloning had been going on long before the religion wars. As a means, as they saw it, of removing imperfections. As the domes formed into alliances, this liberal alliance also decided to create clones in an attempt to match their numbers. They discussed the issue for many years and the vote was close.'

'But are they like normal people?'

'What are normal people like?'

'Point taken. Are they treated the same?'

'In this dome they are, I believe. Not so much in the other alliances.'

'Who controls the program? Who decides how many?

Can they determine the sex of the clone?'

'In this dome and the other domes in the alliance, the Council for each dome approves each phase of the program. The rule here is for fifty percent male and fifty percent female.'

'Do the clones mind? You know, being created?'

'We are all created.'

'I think I need to work out my questions a bit more.'

'You are doing great, Tanun. This is a big subject and the important questions are hiding below the superficial. Learn a bit more about the subject and we can talk again.'

'I will. Can't wait to ask you more. I'm to have more training next light-time so I'd better get back.'

'And I need to speak with Lento-Fin. I will disappear again, Tanun, though I shall return.'

# SIXTEEN: A Little Roll of Cloth

Chyke was again on time, prompting Lento-Fin to thank him for cooperating so enthusiastically. Chyke replied that at least while the debriefing was going on, he didn't have to work in the fields or have more training. Lento-Fin told him to enjoy it while it lasted because they would soon be on a proper war footing.

'Chyke,' said Sin-Tun, 'this time I want you to tell us about your interrogations after the failed attempt to rescue you.'

Chyke shuffled around and wiped his face with his left hand. He looked straight into Sin-Tun's eyes. 'I really thought I was in for it. As it happened, I was given a truth drug.'

'From XorX?'

'Come on. She doesn't bother with stuff like that. From enforcers. Hurt.'

'After the needle, what then?'

'Some of them wanted to give me more, but the top guy was adamant they obey instructions. I was getting dreamy. Sleepy. When they'd gone, I went back to my bench – they hadn't strapped me to the chair, or stripped me. Guess they didn't need to. Sleepiness got worse and worse. When I opened my eyes, there she was, by the chair. Blurred.'

'And?'

'Whether she was toying with me, I don't know, but she was fixated on why I left the dome to follow Tanun. She said she couldn't understand why I would do that. She insisted there must have been a reason other than I was his brother. Kept insisting. Told me to go deep. Deep down, below the layers. Dig it out.'

'How did you handle this?'

'I was really dreamy. All I wanted to do was go to sleep. She kept on and on at me. Couldn't think what I could do to convince her, and for no reason I said, "Note. Received a note." This really piqued her interest.'

'Did you make this up, Chyke? Or did you perhaps … please think very carefully before answering … really receive a note?'

'Sin-Tun.' Chyke closed his eyes. 'I made this up, I swear to you. Of course, then I had to play along and build my story.' Chyke opened his eyes.

'What I don't understand, Chyke, is after you'd had a truth drug, how could you possibly think so coherently as to construct such a story?'

Chyke stood up and moved behind the chair and held the top of the back. 'I'm not as big as my brother. Or others my age in my old dome. I've had to think quickly and use my wits. I viewed this situation like all those fights with my brother, which I won nearly equally. Gits like XorX can't think openly. They're obsessed with proving *their* interpretation of the situation. Unlike you, Sin-Tun, if you don't mind my saying so. You are neutral and as a consequence gather much more information than bastards like XorX.'

'Astute as ever, Chyke. And what form did this note take?

'A small square of cloth.' Crimson crept up Chyke's face and he spoke curtly. 'Rolled up. Red writing on the inner face – just like the decrees from the Elders.' He ran his hands over his face.

'Chyke, would you like a break?'

'A drink of water would be great, then I'll be good to carry on.'

'I'll get the drinks,' said Lento-Fin and he clapped Chyke on his shoulder as he went past.

* * *

Joor-Jen apologised to Bento-Tor for all the to-ing and fro-ing from one room to another as she followed him along the corridor. He moved almost as fast on crutches as a two-legged person and Joor-Jen had to march along to keep up.

'This is the one,' she said. ' We thought it best not to use your previous den.'

'Good thinking. His absence would still be loud. Coming in for a while?'

'Sure.'

Bento-Tor threw his crutches down and crashed onto his bed. 'That was more tiring than I'd realised.'

'You were going fast, for a beginner.'

'Didn't want to be defeated. Show weakness.'

'Nothing wrong with that.'

'That's funny coming from you, Joor-Jen.'

'I know. Anyway, now you're settled, I've some good news.'

'Oh yeah. Like I can have a new leg?'

'Like, yes. You can.'

'Don't piss me around.'

'I'm not. The Council agreed. Helped that Lento-Fin and I voted for you as well. Don't cry, Bento-Tor. I'm not good with that.'

'Give me a bloody big kiss, then.'

Bento-Tor hugged Joor-Jen until she complained about her neck.

'Do you know when?'

'A few light-times. There's quite a queue after the battle. Your leg is doing well. This wasn't just generosity. You're the best SF. Not only fighting, but signals. We need you.'

'Thanks, Joor-Jen. And thank Lento-Fin.'

'I will. Now get a good sleep. Need to build up your strength for the op.'

* * *

Chyke drank two containers of water and slumped back down on his chair. While Sin-Tun was checking some text on the transparent screen, he turned to Lento-Fin, 'Over to you.'

'Ready to go, Chyke?'

He nodded.

'Tell us what you told XorX was written on the cloth.'

'I told her it said, "Tanun to be banished. Follow him. Outside. We'll make it easy for you to escape. Find him and stick close.". I said, it didn't say stick close, but something like that. Couldn't be too perfect. Wouldn't sound genuine, would it? And I added, "You will be well rewarded. Report on what he gets involved in. Who he meets. We'll contact you discreetly. You'll be a major player. Special privileges. One day, possibly, an Elder. You won't have heard of clones, but you'll get an unlimited supply. Whichever type you prefer.".'

'You are a very cool customer, Chyke,' said Lento-Fin.

'Thanks. There's a little more. I added that it said at the bottom, "The alternative? Stay here – confined to your den for the rest of your life. Do it. Do it. Reply on the back of this cloth. Leave it on this desk after Tanun's trial.".'

'Incredible,' said Lento-Fin.

'XorX will have checked out your story,' said Sin-Tun. 'If you made up the note, wouldn't your story have collapsed? What convinced her?'

Chyke exaggerated taking a deep breath and letting it go. 'When she told me she couldn't trace the note and that no Elder had admitted to writing said note, I said to XorX, "Good. I didn't want my cover blown by a note left lying around. This had to be a professional operation. I was taking a monumental risk going back to the other dome, under deep cover." And I added, "The Elders don't trust each other, so I'm not surprised no one would admit to writing the note.".'

Chyke looked from Lento-Fin to Sin-Tun as they stared at each other with wry smiles.

'That took some balls,' said Sin-Tun.

'Yeah, well. I gambled everything. And I definitely would have lost them if it hadn't have worked.'

'And it did work?' said Lento-Fin.

'She tapped her "friend" on the back of the chair. I thought I was done for. I didn't look away, though. I carried on staring into the hood. I was challenging her. After an eternity, she asked why I didn't think the note was fake. I said I did at first, but then I thought only someone important with access could have dropped the cloth on the desk in the library. And the red writing reminded me of all the decrees the Elders issue. I said I scribbled on the back, "Count me in. When do I see the girls?". For some reason, this seemed to change XorX's mood. Perhaps she felt the same way about the Elders. Couldn't trust them.'

'Anything else?' said Lento-Fin.

'She told me I'd be shown who my handler would be in this dome. I was to report on the same sorts of things.'

'Same sorts of things?'

'Oh, you know, who Tanun met, plans I might hear about attacks, who's who on the Council. Oh, yes, and the cloning schedule. The most important thing seemed to be reporting any unusual visitors to this dome.'

'She'll have meant Amnians, Chyke. She'll have meant, Cassièl.'

'I said I'd never heard of her. Thought that was quite clever. When XorX had gone, apart from lots of food-cubes, I was left a blood-spattered boilersuit, a broken shoe and a bloody bandage. Oh, yeah, there was a portrait drawing of my handler and an access ring. By the way, I told the others I took the ring from an enforcer I'd clouted. All good stuff, and I took that as a sign they believed me and were going to support me. After escaping, I was to wait for contact back here. The thing I couldn't understand and still don't, is why didn't they remove my DD? They must have known about it.'

'We hoped they didn't,' said Lento-Fin. 'You and Tanun have newer versions. Deeper, and with shielding. They obviously haven't caught up with our technology. Chyke, this has been a very long, very tough session. Thank you. We'll assign three SFs to you for safety. Don't worry — they'll be discreet. Only myself and Sin-Tun know about this ... this charade, if you will, and we must keep it that way. You must not divulge anything about it to anyone. That means anyone, Chyke. Keep your wits about you, because people with suspicions will try many subtle ways to get you to lower your guard. Report only to Sin-Tun or me. And let us know when they've made contact.'

'Chyke,' added Sin-Tun, 'you have shown a remarkable presence of mind in the most terrifying of circumstances. We would like to train you in espionage. We believe you could become a formidable intelligence officer. 'Your basics are strong, but there are many techniques to learn.'

'Wow. Thanks. That bit won't be secret, presumably?'

'No, it won't,' laughed Lento-Fin. 'Have a shower and relax in the refectory. But remember ... nothing. To anyone. I mean – anyone.'

Chyke left the debriefing room and took a long route back to his and Tanun's den. After each session, he needed longer and longer to recover, but the last one had been the worst. Had he convinced them? Had he played it just right? Walking the corridors and travelling up and down in elevators created a mind space where he could pack the memories away. Not that Sin-Tun was unpleasant, or Lento-Fin for that matter. No, it was reliving the interrogations and convincing them of his story that really screwed him up.

After his door had whooshed open, he flopped face down on his bunk. When he turned onto his side to face the wall, he saw something. A little roll of cloth nestling between the bed and the wall. Using his thumb and forefinger, he lifted the little cloth tube up. No label. No writing. After unrolling the cloth, the red writing leapt out.

Waste hatch
Early next light-time
Bring this

So, it had begun. *How am I going to get all the way down there unnoticed? And where can I hide the cloth in case I'm caught?* Chyke pushed his hand against his chest to smother the thumping, but the questions kept piling in. *Should I tell Lento-Fin? What if I'm already being watched? That could give the game away. No. For the first meet I have to do it on my own. Then I can tell Lento-Fin. That way, I'll most likely have the name of my handler to tell them.*

The door whooshed open. *Shit, shit, shit.* Chyke

pushed the cloth under his shoulder.

'You Ok?' said Joor-Jen? You look pale.'

'Yeah, I'm Ok. Just got back from a debrief. Reliving the experiences stuffs me up.'

'Let's go to the refectory. Have a chat.'

'Ok. Hold on – need the bathroom.'

What could he do? As he turned to sit up, he pushed the cloth under his pillow. *Should be all right there.*

In the elevator, Joor-Jen pulled Chyke to her and they kissed for several minutes.

'I missed you in that dome,' said Joor-Jen, 'but I miss you more now you're here and in that debriefing room all the time. You're closer, but unavailable.'

'I missed you, too. I think the last session might have been it. I hope so. Two of them taking me to pieces. They're nice enough, but each session is knackering.'

When they had both collected plates of food, Joor-Jen sat opposite Chyke, studying his olive skin and blonde hair, short now it had been cut, before asking, 'What's the format in the debriefing? Is it the same each time? And do they go through the timeline, or jump about?'

'Follows the same process, but for some reason, Sin-Tun jumps around the timeline. I think he does it to try to catch me out.'

'Catch you out at what, though? You don't have anything to be caught out about, do you?'

'I don't think so. Perhaps he has another reason. Joor-Jen … have you put Tanun right? I don't want him to think he still has some option on you.'

'Not exactly. We've both been on missions and training and there hasn't been a suitable opportunity. I- '

'Did you … while I was away?'

'No.'

'Ok, then. Well, don't leave it too long.'
'I won't, Chyke. Soon be sorted.'

\* \* \*

At first-light, Chyke slipped from his lower bunk as silently as he could and pushed the little roll of cloth down the front of his pants. When he turned, all he could see of Tanun was a shape under the blanket and a wisp of fair hair. After debating every permutation with himself, he decided he would walk purposefully along the corridors and stand confidently in the middle of the elevator. He reckoned if he should encounter anyone this early, it would likely prompt questions as to what he was up to if he appeared timid.

His nerves grew, however, as the elevator descended beyond the medical level and he heard the numbers count down to zero. When the door slid aside, the noise, heat, and smell of oil hit him. There seemed to be little space between the thousands of pipes bending this way and that, and steam or spray spurted from various bends and joints. He couldn't place the smell, which seemed to be a conglomeration of food, sweat, socks, oil, and shit.

He stepped into the narrow gap between the elevator door and columns of grey pipes zooming up to unknown levels, recoiling from their radiated heat. He had to shuffle sideways to his right until a left turn enabled him to walk along a narrow parting between engines, motors, pumps, and filters. The floor was a lattice of metal through which he could just make out more pipes and pumps. Was this the right way? Perhaps he should have gone left. What he really had to make sure of, though, was to remember how to get back to the elevator in this bewildering maze.

A hand on his shoulder made him jump. He turned to

see an arm, apparently emerging from another column of pipes. When he took a step back he could see there was another walkway in the confusion of engineering, and standing there was someone he recognised as his handler.

'Cloth?'

Chyke reached into his boilersuit and produced the little roll of cloth.

The man took it and put it in his pocket.

'How do you get from that dome to this dome?' said Chyke 'And how do you get in? Do I get a name?'

'All stuff you'll learn if you give us what we want. Next time might be dark-time. Could be anytime. Cloth could be anywhere. Make sure you find it before anyone else does. Call me Pen-Nan.'

'Great. Can't you give me any clues?'

'Try the clothes chutes, or the piles of towels. Could be in a container in the refectory. Bring the cloth with you. Don't want an identical clone in your place, do we? Now, this is what you need to tell us. I wouldn't get this wrong, sunshine, because she'll get very annoyed. If that happens, you'll find yourself back in your cell quicker than you can say truth drug.'

'You don't have to worry about that. I'm good at doing this. Doesn't mean I can get you everything every time.'

'We know that.'

A loud clanging made them both retreat farther along the narrow walkway. After about twenty clangs, they stopped while a jet of steam hissed across between them.

'Great place. My worst nightmare,' said Chyke.

'Your worst nightmare for you would be back in your cell with XorX on the rampage.'

'That won't happen. I'm all set.'

'Right. Remember these points. Weapon status.

Planned attacks. Council meetings. Who are the hawks? Who are the doves? Cloning schedule. Most important of all, we want to know of any strange visitors.'

'Strange visitors? What, like green people or any with two heads?'

'Anyone.'

'Is that the list? Not asking much, are you?'

'That's the list for now. Do I need to stress how careful you need to be? How discreet? And we'll be watching, so no funny business. You won't be able to hoodwink us.'

A motor next to Pen-Nan's right knee started up, which made listening impossible, so he pushed Chyke back the way he'd come. When Chyke reached the elevator door he turned, but there was no sign of Pen-Nan.

Why was it, when you really needed an elevator, they never seemed to turn up? He kicked the door, which didn't help but calmed the nerves in his stomach. While he was considering all the machinery and the expertise to design and maintain the complex collection of processes, the door slid open. He decided to make for the refectory, rather than heading straight back to his den. Too obvious. After some food, he'd track down Joor-Jen.

*  *  *

Tanun stared at the transparent screen. The image of Level 299 with its thousands of pipes, pumps, probes, and purifiers feeding into and from the rows and rows of incubating clones had gone, but the impact had remained, burnt into his vision. A whole level, he thought, even a lower level, was still an incredible enterprise. He'd ask Joor-Jen if he could actually visit, although even if he were allowed, he'd have to be scrubbed clean and wear all that protective equipment he saw the medics wearing. He tried to imagine Bento-Tor in one of those jars with all the coloured tubes wiggling every which way. How did they start one off? Did it spend all its growing time in the container? Did things go wrong? And what if they did – what could be done?

Tanun left the knowledge centre and went to the refectory. Perhaps Joor-Jen would be there and he could ask her some more questions. He searched the usual places and tables, but with no sign of her, after eating he went back to his den.

* * *

When they slid apart, Chyke flopped onto his back and Joor-Jen kissed his sternum before laying her head on his damp chest. She stroked his smooth face and neck, breathing his spicy scent.

'Don't take this wrong, Chyke, but … you're not the same. I can tell. Realise that's hardly surprising. Your experience in that cell must have been truly, truly awful. You're so lucky to have escaped. Thank goodness Bento-Tor's signaller opened your cell door. I'm so lucky too, so please don't ever get kidnapped again. Are you Ok to tell me about some of your interrogations? Only if it's not too distressing.'

'Do you really want to know? Sometimes I feel I can, other times it's as if I'm reliving it all for real … and I can't. You know, the pain was indescribable, but worse than that was losing track of time and light-time and dark-time. Doesn't take long before you're completely disorientated. I used to count – trays, light-times, dark-times, chair frames, shits.'

'How would XorX's interrogations go? Were they always the same?'

'Nearly always the same. She'd feign a lack of understanding, or confusion over a piece of information, or a missing piece of information. "Could you help me?", she'd say. If I just looked at her, or shook my head, she'd produce her "friend", as she called it.'

'I saw it. Threatened with it. Thankfully, didn't experience it. Can you describe its effect?'

'All I can tell you is, you don't know pain until that thing is pressed into you. XorX knew all the places. You'd swear to do anything, anything, kill anyone, betray your best friend, to make it stop. I threw up, loads. Passed out sometimes.'

'You'd probably agree to anything.'

'Other times, I was injected with a truth drug. Made you dreamy at first. Later, really sleepy. Lost track of my counting then. When she's asked you the same question a hundred times, you can't resist. The truth comes babbling out faster than you can control it. The truth drug also made you more amenable to suggestion. She'd suggest things and you'd agree to them. What she said would seem so rational. Logical. Obvious.'

'Didn't realise a truth drug might do that. Did XorX suggest anything to you?'

'Loads of things. Can't remember most of them, though. That drug really does your head in.'

'Can't remember even one?'

'Oh yeah, there is one I remember. She suggested – I know this is hard to believe – she suggested I could escape.'

'Escape? How? Why?'

'With her help, of course, to act as a spy for her. Under cover. You know, pretend to be normal, but actually be spying. Can you believe that? After what I'd suffered?'

'What did you say to her?'

'Can't remember exactly. Sort of, I'd rather die in here than betray my friends.'

'I guess she wasn't too happy about that?'

'You guessed right. She wasn't angry. Well, not loudly. But her voice took on an even colder tone. She said when she'd finished with me, she'd leave just enough for the enforcers to have their fun with me in their games room. No idea what that's about, but I don't suppose there are many laughs in there. When there's nothing left, when she's drained you of all energy, all will, all control, she leaves you alone to recover, to reconsider. To regret. You know, Joor-Jen, being in that cell, you have no idea how much you've deteriorated until you're out. Everything goes too, too fast.'

'My poor Chyke.' Joor-Jen ran her hand across his lower stomach. 'I hope I can make up for some of the pain. Perhaps lots of pleasure will cancel it out. Willing to try?'

# SEVENTEEN: Maze within a Maze

In a clipped tone, Joor-Jen ordered the elevator to Level 1240. She hoped to get a few minutes with Lento-Fin before the Council meeting. Vital she passed on to him what she'd learnt. Time was critical. Goodness knows what damage had already been done.

'Hello, Joor-Jen. You look determined.'

'We must speak.'

'Seems we must.'

'You know I mentioned when we were in the woods, fighting to get back to the dome, lots of our forces were killed. In our group most of the SFs were killed and all of us got injured.'

'Except for Chyke.'

'Yes. Except for Chyke. No enforcer went near him. Didn't see any pulses close by, either.'

'The chaos and randomness of battle.'

'No. Something more than that.'

'What are you saying, Joor-Jen?'

'It upsets me to admit this, Lento-Fin, but I think Chyke has been turned. Poor thing. I don't blame him. They broke him – they broke him. Anyone would break in that cell.'

'Not necessarily. We all have a different threshold.'

'Chyke was telling me about the truth drug they used. He admitted it made him more amenable to suggestion.'

'Where and when was he telling you this?'

'Oh, in my den. Not long since.'

'Right.'

'Hear me out. I can tell he's different, Lento-Fin. What

really convinced me was that he admitted XorX had tried to turn him.'

'So? And?'

'Think about it. He admitted it to me ... so I would think, no way would someone who'd really be turned volunteer that information. You know ... and risk putting the idea in my head? When all along, of course, he had actually been turned. He's been coached. Double-bluff. Clever.'

'That is clever. Not proof, though.'

'But he's young. The disorientation. The drugs. The suffering. I just know XorX has turned him.'

'A woman's intuition? We need more than that, Joor-Jen. And I'm not sure age is relevant in these matters. Are you going to pursue this?'

'Shouldn't I?'

'Let's just say for a moment he has been turned – he'll have been well-conditioned. Not sure you'll get him to slip up. Make a mistake.'

'Oh, I dunno. I'm a girl – I have ways. He might lower his guard ... just for a moment. All I need.'

'Pillow talk is not always reliable. You should know that.'

*  *  *

After a selection of root vegetables with plenty of delicious blue sauce, Chyke went back to his den. 'Hey, Tanun. Where have you been? How's your scar?'

'The knowledge pods, mostly. Scar's Ok. Look.' Tanun climbed down from the top bunk and pulled open his boilersuit.

'Wow. Impressive. That should get the girls.'

'Doubt it. More to the point, where have you been?'

'Debriefs, debriefs, debriefs. I think I've done the last one. They want to train me up in espionage. Not sure I fancy it if you have to do a debrief after every mission.'

'But you'd be good at espionage. You're good at sneaking.'

'Thanks. Training starts next light-time. Look, I need a shower. After, tell me about what you've been learning from the pods.'

* * *

Lento-Fin announced the start of the Council meeting and the agenda. He welcomed two new Councillors: Joor-Jen and Cen-Por.

When they reached the last item on the agenda, Lento-Fin said from that point the meeting was a closed session. A record would be kept at the highest security level, he said, but nothing must be divulged.

He stood up. 'We have received a message from the Dicio Alliance. They have made a tentative offer of peace talks with the Liberal Alliance and request we send a delegation – under full diplomatic immunity – to explore how a peace deal might be developed.'

After much discussion, disagreement, argument, and impassioned speeches, the Council voted by a two-vote majority to send a delegation. They agreed Lento-Fin and Joor-Jen would lead, accompanied by four SFs as witnesses and for protection. The mission would be secret and therefore no one outside the Council would be informed of the decision. The Council set a time-limit for the mission of 90 light-times and agreed to record the Council's best wishes for the success of the talks.

Once the meeting was over, the councillors left quickly, only the Clerk to the Council remained, sitting at the top table facing four screens, two displaying moving pictures and two displaying scrolling text. Chyke strode into the empty meeting room.

'How may I help you?'

'Are you official? I wanted to see Lento-Fin.'

'And you are?'

'Chyke. A newcomer.'

'Ah yes, Chyke. I'm the Clerk to the Council, so yes, you could say I'm official. Lento-Fin is not available at the moment. What was it about?'

Shit. Chyke cursed himself for not thinking of this situation. 'I've just remembered something to add to my last debrief.'

'Would Sin-Tun be able to help?'

'Good idea. Thanks. Where would I find him?'

'Usual place. Medical level 297, room 103.'

'Know it well. Thanks.'

After Chyke had told the elevator Level 297, he leant against the back wall. Would Sin-Tun just accept his version of events, or would he interrogate him like he did in the debriefs? What if Sin-Tun suspected him of being a double agent and therefore fed him info his handler and XorX would discover was false? The potential dangers of being mistrusted by both sides rose from his gut to his face, which burned in response. Nothing for it. He had to play it straight – that was all he could do. Think of the girls.

'Hello Sin-Tun. I need to speak to you. I went to the meeting room to tell Lento-Fin, but he's not around.'

'Did you speak to the Clerk?'

'Yes. He seemed to know of me. I said I'd remembered something that should be added to my last debriefing session.'

'Excellent. Well, sit down.' Sin-Tun waved his hand at

the screen, which cleared. 'I'll record this, but it will be filed at the highest possible level of security.'

'Good. I'm getting a bit spooked about everything.'

'Spook is a good word. If you weren't nervous, I'd be worried. Those who are blasé make the mistakes. We'll protect you.'

'Right. I hope so. Well, I've met my handler.'

'Why didn't you tell us they'd made contact?'

'Because there wasn't time and I thought I'd be able to tell you more useful stuff once we'd met.'

'Method? Name?'

'A little roll of cloth. Down the side of my bed. Bottom bunk. Tanun and I have swapped. He said to call him Pen-Nan.'

'I'll check it out. Might be genuine. Do you have this cloth?'

'No. I had to take it to the rendezvous and hand it over.'

'Where?'

'Level 0.'

'A little predictable.'

'Could hardly be the refectory.'

'Has been.'

'You'd have to be really clever to pull that off.'

'They were. Not quite clever enough, though. Caught them all. Ok, Chyke. Now the basics are out of the way, let's go through the whole thing detail by detail.'

* * *

'Very good. You handled it well. However, there was enough time to tell Lento-Fin or me, wasn't there?'

'I suppose so.' Chyke looked down into his lap. He looked up at Sin-Tun. 'But if I'd left my den, Tanun would have asked me what I was doing. That would be another story I'd have had to concoct. I had to sneak out as it was.'

'You've just about managed to make a fair point.'

'So, how am I supposed to tell them our weapon status and about any planned attacks?'

'You're not.'

'But, Sin-Tun, Pen-Nan will expect- '

'It's a test. Of course they know you couldn't get that quality of info. Not after your first visit. If you brought that information to the next rendezvous they'd know either you were inventing stuff and playing them along, or you were being fed false facts by us – in which case they'd conclude we'd know you were spying. Either way, you would have failed the test. And your corpse would probably be decaying amongst the pipes in the heat of Level 0.'

'Crap. I'm in a maze within a maze. What can I do?'

'Make sure you keep our confidence in you. I will give you the information to provide … and the reasons. Don't do things unilaterally, Chyke. The cost of failure would be very unpleasant.'

'Right, right, right. Got it.'

'Get your mind into gear. Remember the following. You tried to find out when the Council meetings were, but everyone stalled you, saying that was confidential and why did you want to know? You asked around in the refectory about the planned attacks because you wanted to be involved, but the SFs laughed and said you had to finish your training, and anyway, only the military committee knew when any attacks were planned. You can tell Pen-Nan the next Council meeting is in 30 light-times. And you can tell him Lento-Fin and Joor-Jen are missing.'

'Are they?'

'Not yet.'

'I need to know. I … Joor-Jen …'

'Yes. Well, you'll learn soon enough. And tell him that Joor-Jen and Tanun have grown quite close.'

'No. I'm not telling him that. They haven't.'

'Chyke. This is a façade. To confuse the enemy. You'd better learn quickly to keep your feelings separate from your duties.'

'Ok. I get that. They're still not, though.'

'And that you reckon by next time you'll have the cloning schedule.'

'How would I have got that?'

'Because your brother is obsessed with the whole concept and you'll be able to get him to reveal what he's found out, including the schedule.'

'Oh, crap, crap. Another maze. Why don't you arrest Pen-Nan, now you know who he is?'

'Chyke. Think. We can learn a lot more about them, what they're interested in, the enemy alliances, XorX, while they think they're learning a lot more about us. All depends, though, on how good you are at this. One last thing. This should keep them on the hook. Right at the end, tell Pen-Nan you've been selected for espionage training. He and XorX will see this as you getting closer to much richer information. The mole climbs higher. Their mole.'

*\*\*\**

It wasn't her breath on his face. Or her lips gliding across his. It was her hand rubbing his lower stomach that woke Tanun. 'Joor-J ...?'

His question was lost in the kiss and 'Uh,' the only sound as her fingers closed around him. He clasped her face and eased her away. 'What are the rules?'

'You're such a control freak, Tanun. The rules are 'I want to'. You do too, it seems. Shall I climb up?'

Joor-Jen didn't wait for an answer. Tanun turned onto his back as Joor-Jen reached the top bunk and straddled him, her boiler suit open. She pushed the waist of his boilersuit past his hips. Traced the scar with her finger from his left shoulder across and down, up and across and down to his right hip. Brushed his hardness. Leant forward to explore his tongue with hers. Impatience ruled. Her tongue traced a line to his left nipple. Kissing. Flicking. The eager right. Down, over his scar, down across his stomach. Big kisses. Little kisses. Drawing little circles. She shuffled backwards so her mouth could consume him in soft wetness. Bobbing, hesitating, engulfing, suckling.

Tanun's legs twitched. 'Stop, stop!'

Joor-Jen wiped her mouth and chin. 'Ok, but only because it's my turn.'

She slid to the side and eased her boiler suit down her arms and legs. Tanun climbed across. Pulled the boiler suit from her ankles. Kissed her neck. Sucking a little, tonguing circles. As light as a butterfly's wings his nails grazed across her breasts. His tongue sought the inevitable path to her right nipple. Toyed. Gripped. Circled. Sucked, complying, as the hardness demanded. Then the other. Harder, softer. Toying, teasing. Her right, again. Both begged for more, but a stronger hunger summoned. Slid his hands under her bottom and raised her to his face. Traced her contours. Licked the folds. Probed the willing places. Settled on her stiffness. Fast, slow, slow, faster, slower.

'Stop. Stop. Now, Tanun, now.'

He eased her down and lifted her ankles onto his shoulders. The willing and the wet, the wet and the willing. Impatience agreeing with impatience. Flesh seeking, flesh consenting, racing as one to the inevitable consummation.

\* \* \*

After the last session with Sin-Tun, Chyke again needed to go via a long route to the refectory to recover. The risks and thoughts of capture and torture seemed to smother the excitement of playing one side off against the other, and all the time, while prodding the spheres, cubes, and pyramids, he wondered where Pen-Nan would leave the next roll of cloth.

'Shit.' Chyke's knife squealed as it slipped and swept a sphere with blue gravy onto the table. He reached into his pocket and pulled out his handkerchief. Except it wasn't. It was a square piece of cloth. Folded in half. He stuffed it back into his pocket and reached into his other pocket. Nothing. All he could do was slide his knife under the broken vegetable sphere and lift it onto his plate. He wiped the mess of gravy with the arm of his boilersuit.

*Yuck. Why did the knife have to do that? And how did the cloth get into my pocket? I haven't seen anybody since Sin-Tun.* His left hand played with the cloth. *Could I read it here? Who would know? Just a piece of cloth. Easier than in the den with Tanun around.* Chyke eased the cloth from his pocket and unfolded it. Red writing again. Not very discreet.

> Before dark-time
> Same place
> Important you bring all you know
> And the cloth

*Is that it? Hasn't left much time to find out anything. Just have to remember Sin-Tun's instructions. Should I wait here and then make my way down, or would it look less suspicious to go back to my den?* Chyke squirmed in his dilemma. *The only thing is, if Tanun's there, I'd have to think of a reason to leave at dark-time.*

Meanwhile, Lento-Fin, Joor-Jen and the four SFs

waited in the hatch room. Sin-Tun and seven other Governors had come to see them off and waited in a semicircle outside the room.

'Our best wishes go with you both,' said Sin-Tun. 'We hope the Dicio Alliance and the Elders are sincere in their approach and desire for peace. You will of course have little protection should things go awry. However, in the past thousand years, Dicio has proved the more genuine in its dealings and has developed a sophisticated diplomatic service.'

'Together with sophisticated espionage,' said Joor-Jen.

'As have we, as have we,' said Lento-Fin. 'We'll approach these talks in a positive way, and if that is reciprocated, all Lemtorn will benefit. I wish you good fortune, Sin-Tun, in our absence.'

'Thank you. I shall miss your wisdom and guidance. Let us hope there are fewer missiles and no more kidnappings.'

'Especially the latter,' said Joor-Jen.

With a nod from Lento-Fin, two SFs began their descent. Joor-Jen followed and then Lento-Fin. Above him, the other two SFs. Sin-Tun watched them until darkness consumed them.

Lento-Fin checked his compass. 'So, south-east until light-time. If we suffer no disturbances, let's try to get there before the tenth dark-time. Ready for a hike, Joor-Jen?'

*  *  *

Tanun was listening on his DD to a pod about the ancient railway network when Chyke bounded through the doorway.

'Hey, Chyke. More debriefs?'

Chyke crashed onto his bottom bunk. 'Thought they

were done, but they always think of something else to ask. What are you listening to?'

'They had an amazing railway network. I'd learnt a lot from the old books in the library, but these pods have so much more. People used to travel all over the planet. Fast. Used fusion power. Then of course the trains got used for moving soldiers and munitions. No wonder there's hardly anything left.'

'But that's just around here. Other parts of Lemtor might have loads. You could ask Cassièl.'

'Yeah, he'd know. Just never know when he'll appear.'

'When did you last see him?'

'I lose track. A good few dark-times ago. We went to the refectory and he let me have some Avena.'

'D'you know, Tanun? I could do with some of that right now. Shall we try? I'm starving.'

'Not sure we'd be allowed. Could give it a go.'

'But you must be nearly eighteen.'

'Is that the rule? I don't know. Tell you what, Bento-Tor's just along the corridor. Let's knock him up. If anyone could get us some Avena, he could.

Tanun knocked on Bento-Tor's door and called, 'Hey, Bento-Tor, Chyke and I want to go to the refectory. Get some Avena. Probably need your help with that.'

Tanun listened. Thought he heard something. 'He's not answering.' Tanun put his ear to the door. His face reddened as he recognised the little grunts and giggles and ragged breaths. Thought he heard Bento-Tor say, "more". 'I reckon Bento-Tor's busy.'

'With what?' said Chyke.

'He's just busy.' Tanun called through the door again. 'Sorry, Bento-Tor. Didn't mean to interrupt anything. See you later in the refectory. Don't forget! Come on, Chyke.

We can get something to eat and you can tell me about your debriefings.'

* * *

With Septies to his left, and Ellye to his right, Cassièl faced Anselm in the Forum. After explaining he still could not retrieve Dodecahedron and neither could Ennti, he warned that not only was civil war brewing on Lemtor, the KimMorii would soon invade. 'Civil war is the perfect distraction. I believe they are already helping the two aggressive alliances. Little do the Elders in those alliances know how the KimMorii repay loyalty.'

'I do not want us to lose track of Dodecahedron, Cassièl,' said Anselm. 'It has taken a lot of effort to track it down. Your effort mostly. And this is only the first Nucleus. In the chaos of war, the KimMorii are more likely to trace Dodecahedron and take it.'

'And that would be ... unjust for poor Tanun.'

'The KimMorii do not deal in justice, as you know. Are you no wiser as to why you cannot retrieve?

'I believe there are requisites. Children. Possibly siblings. Twins, possibly. Estrangement, blood ... and death. I do not know the combination.

'That,' said Septies, 'is a difficult conundrum.'

'ForumPrinceps, would you like me to keep a close watch on Tanun?' said Ellye.

'Thank you, Ellye. I will leave this in Cassièl's control for the moment.'

'He is suffering,' said Cassièl. 'Not only because of possessing a Nucleus, but his life had changed completely and he's experiencing the usual adolescent traumas.'

'Please visit him again and help him to feel loved and appreciated.'

'I will, Forum Princeps. Thank you.'
'We shall reconvene when the situation on Lemtor has changed.'

# EIGHTEEN: Elbows, Legs, and Foreheads

Tanun and Chyke had just finished their coloured vegetables and cylinder-shaped fruit when Bento-Tor arrived and sat down next to Tanun, opposite Chyke.

'Thanks for coming over, Bento-Tor,' said Tanun. 'Sorry about earlier. Hope I didn't spoil anything.'

'Far from it.'

'Have you found someone?'

'Not sure. Nice enough, but not sure he's sure.'

'And I thought girls were difficult enough.'

'Relationships,' said Bento-Tor. 'Doesn't matter what sort.'

'Deep as ever. Look, Chyke and me really fancy some Avena. He's had a tough debrief and I've been at the pods all light-time. Trouble is, I don't think we're allowed.'

'Have you tried? You probably can. Anyway, I'll get us some.'

While Bento-Tor went over to a serving bar, Tanun said to Chyke he'd try next time. 'After all, if Bento-Tor can, I should be able to. I'm older.'

'Yeah, but he's a top SF. We're newcomers.'

Bento-Tor didn't bring the bottle of Avena to the table, or any containers. A girl about Bento-Tor's size, with black-ringleted hair down to her waist, carried a bottle and four containers and sat down next to Chyke. She pressed against him.

'Thanks,' said Bento-Tor. 'Long time, no see.' He then explained unnecessarily to Tanun and Chyke, 'I couldn't carry the stuff with my crutches, so Sreen-Gar here helped me. Tanun? Meet Sreen-Gar. Chyke? Meet Sreen-Gar.'

The girl put down the bottle a little too hard and distributed the four containers. When she'd finished, she pressed harder against Chyke and put her hand on his thigh.

'Great to meet you boys. Joor-Jen never stops talking about you both and I can see why. I reckon you're top of the good-looks chart around here. Agreed, Bento-Tor?'

'Definitely.'

Chyke stared at her. He looked over at Tanun. Tanun stared at her. He looked back at Chyke.

'Thanks, Sreen-Gar,' said Tanun, 'If we are, you must be too.'

'We have a charmer, Bento-Tor. You never mentioned that.'

'If he's the charmer,' said Chyke, 'I'm the troublemaker.'

'Troublemakers are my absolute favourite. Are you ever gonna pour that drink, Bento-Tor?'

'Yes, sorry. Got absorbed in the introductions. There we go. Let's drink to my new leg.'

Bento-Tor downed his drink in one swallow. Sreen-Gar copied him. Chyke drank half and Tanun sipped a little.

'Did I hear that right?' said Tanun?

'Dead right. In three light-times.'

'That is just fabulous news.'

'Leg's ready. Just the op to fix it.'

'That's such good news, Bento-Tor,' said Chyke. 'I felt so responsible. You know, you coming to communicate with me.'

'That's really stupid, Chyke, and you know it. Don't ever say that again. We all do missions for goodness knows what reasons. Not the mission's fault, or yours, if something goes wrong. People get killed. Luck of the draw.

Think of Peeso-Lun.'

'He's right, Chyke,' said Sreen-Gar. 'You shouldn't blame yourself.'

Sreen-Gar held out her glass to Bento-Tor, and after he'd topped her up he poured Avena to the brim of the other three containers. 'Just enough, I reckon, for one more round. We should all sleep well this dark-time.'

'Oh, not yet, I hope,' said Sreen-Gar. 'Let's go to my den. I've some fantastic Avena – and some special treats. So much I want to learn about these lovely boys.'

'Her den is something else,' said Bento-Tor, smiling at Tanun and Chyke. 'You can't see the floor, or the ceiling, or the walls for that matter. Masses of floaty curtains and fluffy pillows and soft cushions and shaggy rugs. And then there's the big bath – can you believe that? Only one in the dome, as far as I know. Room for three in it … so I've heard.'

'And I reckon us three would fit in there very well,' said Sreen-Gar, putting her arm across Chyke's shoulders while smiling at Tanun. He, however, was staring at Chyke as determinedly as Chyke was staring at him.

'That's very generous,' said Tanun. 'Unfortunately, I have advanced training first thing and I need a good sleep. Would love to see your den, though – another time.'

'He's got training,' said Chyke, 'and I've got another debrief. I'd love to see your den too – and that bath.'

'Seems I'm out of luck this dark-time,' said Sreen-Gar. 'We must make a date. Shall I see you back to your den, Bento-Tor?'

'Please. Tanun and Chyke? We'll do Sreen-Gar's place another time.'

'Sure,' said Tanun. He stood up and sat straight down. 'Goodness. Too much Avena.'

'Come on, Brother. I'll get you back to our den. Up you

get.' Chyke helped Tanun to stand, and supporting him with his arm, led him towards the door of the refectory.

'Wow, Bento-Tor,' said Sreen-Gar as Tanun and Chyke headed toward the nearest exit. 'How hot are they? Fancy each as much as the other. Impossible to choose.'

'I think I've heard that somewhere before.'

'I'll get them both into my den if it's the last thing I do. Just imagine ... together.'

'Honestly, Sreen-Gar, that's enough. If you would see me back to my den, I can leave you to your imagination.'

'Er, sorry, just seen someone I need to speak to. Catch you later.'

'Hey, Tanun! Chyke!' Bento-Tor shouted.

Both turned from the door to look back.

'Give us a hand. Apparently, Sreen-Gar has other priorities.'

After Chyke had led Tanun back to the table, he helped Bento-Tor up and gave him his crutches. 'Tanun on my left and you on my right. Let's go.'

'Phew. That was a lucky escape,' said Tanun. 'Why have we never seen her before?'

'Because she's always training SFs. This is her short shift-break. Only takes one every 90 light-times. Lives out in the fields with trainees most of the time. Neither Joor-Jen nor I would be alive except for her. She's the best.'

'She's a military trainer?' said Chyke incredulously, letting out a long sigh. 'What does she do with them afterwards? Leave a little pile of bones in the corner?'

'You're not far away from the reality. Not for me to say, but be careful. Don't play with fire unless you want to get your fingers burnt. Trouble is, like in the field, when she's got someone in her sights, they don't escape.'

'Can't believe she's friends with Joor-Jen,' said Tanun.

'They're complete opposites.'

'Like north and south magnets?' said Bento-Tor.

'Too much Avena. But good point.'

After helping Bento-Tor into his den and thanking him for the evening and everything, and congratulating him on getting authorised for a new leg, Chyke helped Tanun backtrack to their den. Tanun said he was going to crash out and shower in the morning.

'Good move. The stuff doesn't seem to affect me the same way.'

When Tanun had climbed up to his top bunk, Chyke listened until his breathing had changed. *Crap, crap, crap. This is all I need right now. Thank goodness I can handle Avena better than my brother.* He checked for the cloth in his pocket, and while he strode along the corridors he began rehearsing what he had been told by Sin-Tun.

He decided he ought to take a different elevator from last time, so walked to an interchange with another corridor. When the elevator door whooshed sideways, though, Chyke had to step aside smartly as five SFs with Sreen-Gar somewhere in the middle of the melee, staggered out singing and meandering along the corridor. Before the door closed, Chyke caught something about Mary and a little lamb. He blew out his cheeks. *Stroke of luck Sreen-Gar didn't seen me because after all that Avena I don't think I could quickly have thought up a reason why at this time I'm getting an elevator so far from my den. Seems my brain isn't functioning that well after all.*

The heat hit him. The place felt hotter and noisier than last time. Was it because of the different time? He had no idea, but after a while he realised he'd stepped out into a different part of the basement level. Pipes. Pipes everywhere. The narrow gaps leading away left and right made no sense. *Which way? Which way? I went right last time. I'll go left this time.* As he edged along the gap, he scorched his right elbow on a pipe. When he rubbed the burn with his left hand, his left elbow caught the sharp edge of a cooling fin. 'Shit. *Can't leave blood on the floor.*' He pulled the message cloth from his pocket and although it hurt his burnt elbow, wiped off the blood. He wriggled down with just a centimetre of space on either side, and while keeping his elbows against his body wiped the red blobs from the floor.

The cold barrel of a 10/10 pressed against the vertebrae in his neck. He shivered, even in the oppressive heat.

'Luckily for you I'm on your side. Get up.'

Chyke straightened as best he could within the restricted walkway and started to turn.

'Don't turn. Walk.'

'It's difficult enough without a 10/10 in my neck.'

The barrel was gone.

'Thanks.'

'Right. Five metres. There'll be a bit more room.'

When Chyke reached an intersection of mini-corridors, he stopped. Pen-Nan pushed on his shoulders to turn him around.

'Have you been drinking?'

'No. Yes. A little. Just met up with some friends.'

'What? When you knew you had a rendezvous?'

'It wasn't arranged. Just happened. I didn't plan it.'

'You told us you were good at this. Don't ever drink when on duty. I'll whip your face with this 10/10 until you wouldn't recognise yourself a nose from the mirror. I should whip you for leaving yourself defenceless on the floor.'

'You're right. Got it.'

'Cloth?'

Chyke held out the bloody cloth between his thumb and forefinger. 'Had to wipe up the blood. Only thing I had.'

Pen-Nan snatched the cloth away, shaking his head as he stuffed the cloth into his pocket. 'Before we start, anything suspicious I should know about? Met any new people? Anyone in places you didn't expect them?'

'I don't think so.'

'You don't think so?'

'No. No, there hasn't.'

'Are you still being debriefed?'

'Yes. I sodding well am. We've been over everything a million times. I wish they'd stop.'

'Lento-Fin and Sin-Tun?'

'Yeah.'

'They're good. Means they're not happy with some aspect of your recollection. Or your story. Be careful.'

'I intend to be.'

'So, have you got everything I asked for?'

'Sorry, no. Just can't get access to that level. But I will.'

'So what *have* you got?'

'Lento-Fin and Joor-Jen are missing. Don't know why. Don't know where they've gone.'

'Thank you, Chyke,' said Pen-Nan in a gentler tone. 'That's very helpful.'

'Also, there's a Council meeting in 29 light-times. Whether Lento-Fin and Joor-Jen will be there, who knows? And I reckon I can find out the cloning schedule.'

'How would you find that out? That would have a high security level.'

'Tanun, my brother. He's obsessed with the whole cloning concept. Spends hours at the knowledge pods.

He's questioning everyone involved and wants to visit the facility. I reckon he'll find out the schedule in all his investigations, and I'm good at getting information out of people without them realising it.'

'Not bad.'

'Also – this might be just tittle-tattle – don't know if you need this stuff – but Tanun and Joor-Jen have got quite close.'

'That is precisely the sort of thing we need. Knowing who's with who and who has influence over another is vital. Helps us paint a picture. Does it bother you?'

'What?'

'Tanun and Joor-Jen?'

'No. Should it?'

'Time to go. Work on the cloning schedule. Find out where Lento-Fin and Joor-Jen have gone. And always let me know about any visitors. How are you going to explain your elbows?'

'Too much Avena. Thought I was Ok but took a fall. Oh, yeah, I nearly forgot. They want to train me in espionage.'

'Do they? That *is* good news. Play along. That will get you to classified information. XorX will be pleased when I tell her. Just make sure you keep passing the grades. If you don't, your value will decline. Who knows what could happen to you then?'

'I told you, I'm good at this. Any sign of those girls?'

'You'll get your girls. Soon as we can sneak you out and back safely. Off you go.'

'I'll have to go back the way we came. You'll have to move.'

'No, you don't. Down there. Second left.'

* * *

Sin-Tun strode into Tanun and Chyke's den and clapped his hands. Several swear words emerged from under Chyke's cover and 'Shit, my head,' from Tanun's bunk.

'You can have as much Avena as you can stomach ... on the understanding you're ready for action when required. Tanun - get yourself to the interrogation rooms. 298-131 for you. Explosives. Chyke to 103. The one you know so well. Espionage. You both might want another drink by the time you've finished. You'll have to shower later. Everyone's waiting.'

After much mumbling, grumbling, bumping into each other and hopping around while they dressed, Tanun and Chyke clapped each other on the shoulder and headed out of their den. When the elevator had closed, neither spoke, but each was desperate to ask the other if they knew where Joor-Jen was. Tanun was convinced she was staying away from him after their surprise love-making session. Chyke had concluded she was waiting for the right moment to pounce and probe his loyalties again, probably on the floor of her den.

'I can't imagine what the first thing you'd cover on an espionage course would be,' said Tanun.

'Nor me. Same with your explosives course. Bet it's all about safety and boring stuff. No way would you get to blow up something on the first session.' Chyke couldn't contain himself any longer. 'By the way, have you seen Joor-Jen? She seems to have completely disappeared.'

'No. I was going to ask you the same. Perhaps she'll be on your course.'

'Perhaps she'll be on yours.'

'I'll let you know. Here's yours. I'm farther along. Catch you later.'

\* \* \*

Emerging from dense forest, Lento-Fin said the next two light-times and dark-times would mostly be in open terrain, except for clumps of scrubby stunted trees dotted here and there. He admitted they would no doubt be discovered and tracked despite their camouflage and skill at walking undetected. They'd better hope it was the Dicio Alliance who had promised diplomatic immunity and safe passage rather than the Percutio Alliance who probably wouldn't approve of any peace talks, and in any case, always attacked first and asked questions afterwards.

'When we find a suitable clump of trees we'll make camp. Not much protection — more of a psychological thing. Could, though, help a little if there were reconnaissance drones in dark-time.'

In first-watch, Joor-Jen was sure she could hear scouts, not too distant, and kept her 10/10 and knife ready. Her shift, though, was uneventful, but she reported her suspicions to Lento-Fin when he took over from her.

In the twilight at the end of the eighth light-time, as they sheltered from viscous grey rain under a copse of five trees, four male and five female scouts appeared out of the gloom and surrounded the copse. The uneven spacing marked them out as trained fighters.

'Greetings, friends,' said Lento-Fin. 'Not a clement time to be scouting.'

'And who walks unannounced in our territory?' said one of the men.

'I am Lento-Fin.' He slapped Joor-Jen on her shoulder. 'This is Joor-Jen.' He swept his arm to the SFs. 'And four of my best Special Forces. We are returning to our dome in the Dicio Alliance. And who addresses me?'

'I am Kin-Bor of the Percutio Alliance.' His gaze was

forbidding. 'We find it unusual for any from Dicio to venture this far.'

'We find ourselves in unusual times, I fear. And ... if I am not mistaken, we are in Dicio territory and not Percutio territory. So, I might return your question – who walks unannounced in Dicio territory?'

The other eight scouts tensed.

'We cooperate in policing these lands,' said Kin-Bor. 'Strange visitors have been seen, and spies and infiltrators are everywhere. There is rumour of a powerful artefact being found which is now in the possession of the Liberal Alliance. With this new power they are planning to attack our alliances.'

The sticky grey rain fell harder and the nine scouts on the periphery of the thicket merged into the murky mist and twilight.

'You are right about spies and infiltrators, my friend,' said Lento-Fin. 'Eleven light-times ago we unmasked two infiltrators in our dome. Thankfully, the Liberal Alliance is not the only alliance to have spies. I hear there is some debate about how ready the Liberal Alliance is.'

'Only amongst the weak. One of our domes was destroyed recently. The enemy deployed signal disruptors. Not the actions of a peaceful alliance. Our best chance of protecting the two alliances is to attack. In my view, the sooner the better.'

'Wise words,' agreed Lento-Fin, nodding. 'Because of the rain, we shall rest here until the rain eases. Will you share porridge with us?'

The five women and three men looked to Kin-Bor.

'Your generosity is welcome, Lento-Fin. We would appreciate that.'

* * *

Bento-Tor opened his eyes. Darkened room. Soft lights. Tubes, tubes, tubes. How many tubes could there be?

'Everything is fine, Bento-Tor,' said the medic. 'Soon be dark-time. In light-time we'll check all the nerves and muscles are functioning. If you successfully complete the running and climbing tests, you'll be able to leave.'

'Thank you, thank you, thank you.'

'You're the perfect patient. Close your eyes for a moment.'

'Hey, Bento-Tor, you look great,' said Tanun, pushing open the door.

'The tubes definitely help,' said Chyke.

'Guys! Thanks, thanks for coming to see me.'

'You must not sit on his bed,' said the medic. 'And no touching.'

'Who'd want to touch that?' grinned Chyke. 'Even with two legs.'

'You'd be amazed,' said Bento-Tor. 'I have to fight them off.'

'You can have five minutes,' said the medic. 'The patient has to sleep.'

The three of them chatted about when Bento-Tor could leave the medical level and Tanun described his explosives course. Chyke feigned ignorance about his espionage course, but relented when Bento-Tor teased him about it and that even denying he was on an espionage course would have blown his cover.

'I'm surprised Joor-Jen isn't here,' said Tanun. 'I haven't seen her for many light-times.'

'Don't look at me,' said Chyke. 'I haven't, either.'

'Weird that Lento-Fin also hasn't been around,' said Bento-Tor. 'I'll see what I can find out.'

'How are you going to do that in here?' said Chyke.

'I pick up lots of gossip, and anyway, if I pass my tests, I'll be out next light-time. Then watch me go.'

'Ok, boys. Time to leave,' said the medic.

* * *

After dishing out the porridge, the nine scouts crouched in a semicircle holding their bowls. Lento-Fin made to serve Joor-Jen, but instead let the ladle sink into the pot. His two 10/10s, together with Joor-Jen's two 10/10s, and their four SFs each with two 10/10s, aimed simultaneously and fired at nine foreheads.

'Looks like we've double-rations this dark-time,' said Lento-Fin.

'And extra 10/10s,' said Joor-Jen. 'That was a masterclass in deception, Lento-Fin.'

'All I could do in the situation. We would have suffered in a fight.'

'Were they convinced?'

'They were not. They would have waited until one of us was asleep and done the same. Useful intelligence. They were slack there.'

# NINETEEN: Rumours

Bento-Tor and Tanun wandered along the rows in the refectory trying to find an unoccupied table. Many training courses had finished and groups of SFs had returned from scouting missions. Tanun spotted a table, the farthest from a serving bar and up against the wall, which he hoped would offer a degree of privacy for whatever Bento-Tor was about to tell him.

He'd earlier confided in Bento-Tor he was really missing Joor-Jen and had speculated out loud he suspected Joor-Jen and Chyke were meeting secretly and making love behind his back. Bento-Tor had retorted that perhaps Chyke might accuse Tanun of the same.

'What are you talking about?' he'd said, immediately regretting the hint of aggression that had crept in.

'Bad try, Tanun. No wonder Chyke's doing espionage and you're doing explosives.'

'Thanks for that. But why the hell do you know everything?'

'Small dome. People gossip. Keeps them going. My job. Anyhow, I have some information. Let's get some food.' He told Tanun to stay at the table while he went to the serving bar. 'Billions easier without crutches,' he remarked on his return, and slid two plates, two forks, and two containers onto the table.

'Do you notice you've got a new leg, or does it feel just like the old one?'

'Just the same. Took a few light-times to get the nerve signals coordinated. Now it's as if I never lost the old one.'

'You're amazing, Bento-Tor. I mean, sixteen and you're

an SF and a signaller, lost a leg– '

'And a twin sister.'

'Yes. Sorry. And your best friend.'

'Each hurts as much as the other, but differently.'

'Doesn't compare to you, but I get so hurt when I think of Joor-Jen with Chyke.'

'I know. And guess what? I think Chyke feels the same when he thinks about her and you. He just has a different way of dealing with it.'

'I'm scared for him with this espionage stuff. Not exactly straightforward – I mean, in a battle you know your enemy. In spying, your enemy could be anyone, anywhere.'

'You don't know how accurate that is. Tanun … don't react – whatever you do, don't react – but there's a rumour Chyke has been turned and is working for your old dome. XorX … through torture and psychological blackmail, has broken him and persuaded him to work for her.'

Tanun stopped eating, even though his mouth was full of vegetables. He stared at Bento-Tor, put down his fork and gripped the sides of the plate.

'Finish off that mouthful, then we can talk.'

Bento-Tor laughed as Tanun half-chewed, half-swallowed, half-choked and half-coughed away the vegetables. He offered Tanun a container of water.

After Tanun had drunk every drop and wiped his eyes, he said, 'There is no way Chyke would do that. I absolutely know. He's my brother.'

'In the history of Lemtor, there probably has been a spy who was also a brother.'

'Not this one.'

'You underestimate him. It is possible he is playing the old dome at their own game.'

Tanun directed a puzzled look at him across the table.

'I'm only surmising, but knowing Chyke, he is probably acting as a double-agent.'

'Come on, Bento-Tor, what the hell is a double agent?'

'The old dome sent him back here— '

'He escaped!'

'Coincidentally? While we were nearby? They let him escape so he could come back here pretending to be the suffering prisoner, while reporting whatever information he could obtain back to XorX. Perfect cover.'

'No, no.'

'But perhaps what he's really doing is feeding them false information – whatever Lento-Fin or Sin-Tun wants them to have.'

'Thinking about it, he has kept disappearing at odd times.'

'Exactly. In addition to his debriefs, he's meeting his handler. Goodness knows what they've promised him. The problem, Tanun, with all spies, is … who are they really working for? Everyone in espionage knows a spy works only for herself, or himself. And the risk is that Chyke might be pretending to work for us by pretending to work for the old dome, when in fact, he is really, really, really, working for the old dome all along. A triple agent. He's clever enough.'

'Double agent was hard enough to grasp. But triple agent? I'd never considered anything like that, Bento-Tor. Thanks. But I so cannot believe Chyke would betray us. He just wouldn't.'

'And I happen to agree with you. But always keep in mind, things are rarely as they appear. Ready for a real rumour?'

'Honestly, Bento-Tor, wasn't that one enough?'

'Lean closer over the table.'

Tanun and Bento-Tor leant across until their noses were almost touching.

'The reason you haven't seen Joor-Jen is not that somewhere in the dome she's making mad passionate love with your brother- '

'Don't.'

'It's that she's not even in the dome. Nor is Lento-Fin.'

'Oh, crap. Go on.'

'They've gone to a dome in the Dicio Alliance many light-times away ... to pursue peace talks.'

'Well, that's a waste of time. How d'you find all this out? If it's true, it must be top secret.'

'It is definitely top secret.'

'Well how, then?'

Bento-Tor leant back in his chair, causing Tanun to do the same. Bento-Tor screwed up his face in embarrassment.

'Um. Pillow talk, you might say.'

'Shit. I ... I, Bento-Tor, please be careful with your feelings. You've been hurt too much already.'

'Look, Tanun. If I derive some comfort from my ... activities and I find out things at the same time, well, that just increases the attraction of them.'

'You could be in danger of being accused of being a spy.'

'Let me just decode that last sentence. Too many verbs.'

'I don't suppose I should ask who?'

'No, I don't suppose you should. Look, I really do value your concern, Tanun, but I know what I'm doing.'

'Hope you do. I could really do with some Avena. Any chance?'

'Sure. I'll get it.'

While Bento-Tor was fetching a bottle of Avena, three SFs appeared and lurked by Tanun's table. One sat down on Bento-Tor's chair and another sat on the spare chair facing the wall. The third stood behind Tanun, pressing up against him.

'Mind if we join you?' said the one behind Tanun.

'Yes, actually. Bento-Tor and I are having a private chat.'

'Private?' said the one sitting on Bento-Tor's chair. 'Whispering sweet nothings?'

'Playing hard to get?' said the one facing the wall, making the other two snigger and send each other looks.

'Don't be boring,' said Tanun, looking straight ahead. 'Go and intimidate someone else because you're not intimidating me.'

'Here he is. The one-legged, boy-loving clone.'

Bento-Tor slipped the bottle of Avena into his pocket and stood behind the SF facing the wall. 'Piss off, guys.'

'Not 'till we know who's taking who back to whose den,' said the SF standing behind Tanun. He stuck his tongue out and wiggled it at the other two SFs.

Bento-Tor reached towards the table and picked up his and Tanun's drinks containers. He cracked the tops against the edge of the table and pressed the broken edges against the throat of the SF facing the wall. 'If you three don't leave now, I'll take his throat back in these.' Bento-Tor gave the containers a twist, which produced a lattice of crimson that meandered into the SF's collar.

The SF's face reddened as Bento-Tor pressed harder.

'Come on. They're not worth the bother,' said the one behind Tanun. 'The clone'll get his due for using violence in the refectory.'

Bento-Tor gave the containers a jerk before pulling

them away. The SF stood up, and holding his throat, rasped at Bento-Tor that he'd remember, and vowed revenge.

'That's two of us.'

When the three SFs had shuffled off, cursing and looking back, Bento-Tor smiled at Tanun's face, frozen, with his mouth open.

'You don't mind sharing, do you? Save getting more containers.' He passed Tanun the bottle. 'You go first.'

* * *

The dome rose from the horizon as Lento-Fin, Joor-Jen, and the four SFs trekked through the approaching oat fields, causing Joor-Jen to say the dome must be at least twice the size of their own. Lento-Fin said intelligence reports had calculated the diameter to be fifty percent wider than theirs. He paused and took a moment to tell the others that they would already been detected, and that any accommodation they might be offered would likely have hidden microphones and every communication recorded.

'We must maintain our integrity, be discreet, sincere, and act professionally at all times. I suggest we talk confidentially only when we are in the meeting room, where the usual protocols should be observed.'

After walking for another two hours, the fields gave way to a neatly swept circle of brushed earth, circumscribing the six legs and their dishes. The soft circle extended about ten metres beyond the leg dishes. Lento-Fin held out his arms to bring the group to a halt just before the demarcation line.

'Your party is welcome here, Lento-Fin,' said a voice emanating from the dome. 'Please proceed to the leg to your left. The earth is soft, so you will need to lift your feet, but the mines have been deactivated.'

When the six of them set off, their feet and legs sank about half a metre into the enveloping soil, which made the going very slow.

'Right, everyone,' puffed Lento-Fin as they reached the leg-dish. 'The climb is higher that we're used to, but let's show them what we can do.'

One SF set off, followed by Lento-Fin. The second SF followed him, Joor-Jen behind. The remaining two SFs followed Joor-Jen. The group's experience of climbing rungs meant they set a slow, steady pace and did not stop until they reached the hatch, which then opened. A man of short stature but exceptional width, with an ammunition belt diagonally across each shoulder and a 10/10 in a holster on each hip, offered his hand to help Lento-Fin into the hatch room.

'I made that 6,999,' said Lento-Fin.

'Your counting is correct, Lento-Fin. I am Ban-Ten, Chief Elder. My Elders and I welcome you and your party to our dome.'

'Thank you. I am Chief Governor for my dome. This is Joor-Jen, Chief Apostle. My four top SFs are for protection on our journey. Thank you for allowing us into your dome. We are very grateful.'

'My Clerk will show you to your accommodation. You will find clean things. As we are approaching dark-time, we shall enjoy food together in the conference centre and commence our talks early next light-time. Is that agreeable?'

'Most agreeable, Ban-Ten. Thank you for your welcome. Your generosity is much appreciated.

'Please, follow my Clerk. She will collect you all in two hours.'

*  *  *

Before the peace talks officially began at light-time in the conference room, Lento-Fin presented Ban-Ten with a selection of vegetables from the fields around the group's dome.

'We trust our offering will illustrate our thanks for inviting us to these peace talks, but also show our sincerity and good intentions, regardless of any outcome.'

'Your gift is much appreciated and I have pleasure in accepting it on behalf of this dome in particular and the Dicio Alliance in general. To business.'

Ban-Ten described the famines caused by missiles from the Liberal Alliance damaging the farmland, and the resultant pressures from other domes demanding severe retaliatory action. Lento-Fin assured the conference the only missiles his dome had launched were DTGs in defence of his dome when under threat of invasion by the Percutio Alliance.

'I cannot vouch for other domes in the Liberal Alliance. We do not have a ruling Council for our alliance.'

Ban-Ten said that made reaching any agreement difficult if enforcement of terms would be hard to police. Lento-Fin responded by saying if the terms were mutual and fair, he believed he could convince the other members to sign an alliance-wide treaty.

After three light-times, both sides had reached outline terms and were ready to move to the final agenda item.

Ban-Ten said before they did so, he would speak frankly and trusted no conversation would be reported outside the dome. Lento-Fin gave his word all communications would remain within the dome.

'I value your word, Lento-Fin. There are, however, many in the Percutio Alliance who do not. They seem to be war-seekers, regardless of the resulting death and destruction. Lemtor has surely had enough of war, but it seems the Percutio Alliance, encouraged by the KimMorii, are about to launch a massive attack on the Liberal Alliance.'

'I value your candid assessment, Ban-Ten, but with respect, this is not news. We are expecting a full attack within 100 light-times. Would I be right in assuming the Percutio Alliance has invited Dicio to pool resources with it, backed by the explicit threat that if Dicio declines, it will be deemed an enemy alliance — along with the Liberal Alliance?'

'Your perception is acute, Lento-Fin. If Percutio should learn of these peace talks we would be attacked within one dark-time. They are treating with the shapeshifters. I suppose they do not have much choice, but no good will come of it, that is a certainty.'

'And has the Dicio Alliance reached a decision?'

'We have. We will not be party to any more war.'

'War is coming, regardless. Invasion is coming.'

'Lento-Fin. We value your frankness. Please answer the next question honestly. We understand an artefact has been discovered which could be exploited for its power. Your dome is in possession of this artefact.'

'I know of no such artefact with this power, Ban-Ten.'

'And yet, I have reliable reports this artefact is the property of an alien who has visited the Liberal Alliance on more than one occasion.'

'Your intelligence network is the envy of us all. Yes, we have been visited - by an Amnian — called Cassièl. Amnians are spirits, but can manifest as avatars in physical universes. He came to warn us the KimMorii will soon invade Lemtor and all will become slaves. Millions will be taken away in skyships to work on mining planets. Cassièl says he has seen many such invasions.'

'Thank you for your candour, Lento-Fin. I suggest, before we move to the final item on the agenda, we all take some rest and reconvene next light time.'

* * *

Bento-Tor stood to attention before Sin-Tun and Sreen-Gar in interrogation room 298-411. Sin-Tun was studying moving pictures on the screen and Sreen-Gar was studying Bento-Tor studying Sin-Tun.

Sin-Tun waved his hand at the screen. The pictures dissolved, leaving it clear. 'Bento-Tor. I appreciate you've just had a major operation. I appreciate drugs can affect people in different ways. And I appreciate that after Sreen-Gar you are our most skilled SF, not to mention signaller. However, this does not give you the right to cut the throat of one of our SFs. In the refectory of all places. And by the way, everyone has the right to sit at any table.'

Sreen-Gar continued to stare at Bento-Tor. Bento-Tor wasn't sure how long the silence had lasted, but when Sin-Tun spoke it startled him.

'Make your case.'

'Right. Everyone has, as you say, the right to sit at any table. Except when Avena has made them aggressive. The SFs were abusive to Tanun. It is not becoming for an SF to imply Tanun and I were about to go back to my den. Even if we were — and we were not — that is not a subject for mockery. SFs should always maintain the highest standards. Due to their excess consumption of Avena, the situation was getting out of hand. There would likely have been more injuries but for my action.'

'From reviewing the pictures,' said Sreen-Gar, 'Bento-

Tor speaks accurately. There was much provocation.'

'We have enough violence outside. I do not want further violence inside,' said Sin-Tun. 'Although I appreciate the circumstances you found yourself in, you will be confined to your den for three light times and three dark-times, without food.'

'Thank you, Sin-Tun. May I ask if the three SFs will receive any punishment?'

'It is not usual to declare other punishments. However, let this be a warning. They have been confined to their dens for five light-times and five dark-times. Without food. And stripped of their rank.'

* * *

The conference tables were arranged to form a square. On one side sat Ban-Ten, flanked by seven Elders each side of him. On the opposite side sat Lento-Fin, and to his left, Joor-Jen with two SFs to her left, and the other two SFs to the right of Lento-Fin.

On the adjacent side to his left sat Ban-Ten's Clerk, with three recorders on either side. On the adjacent side to Lento-Fin's right were five Dicio SFs. Each delegate faced a thin transparent screen which displayed the spoken text, or, when required, illustrative pictures pertinent to the subject under discussion.

Ben-Tan announced the official start of the final session and the last item on the agenda.

'I hope we have convinced you, Lento-Fin, the Dicio Alliance does not want war, and we especially do not want hostilities between our alliances.'

Every delegate's attention was concentrated on Ben-Tan, which generated a tension everyone felt acutely.

'Although cloning was in common use prior to the

religion wars,' Ben-Tan continued, 'member domes of the Dicio Alliance developed and codified the procedures and protocols, which they believed was for the benefit of all on Lemtor. We regret that our skill and good intentions have been corrupted into producing clones with the sole purpose of being expendable fighting personnel.'

'I and the Liberal Alliance regret this also.'

'Then I trust you will see the merit in the proposal that all cloning reverts to the control of the Dicio Alliance.'

Joor-Jen heard the intakes of breath from her SFs and watched every pair of eyes turn towards Lento-Fin. He leant towards her and whispered, 'This was the only point of substance in the whole talks. Ban-Ten has handled the talks well, but I was anticipating this.' He turned to face Ban-Ten. 'Ban-Ten. I understand your reasoning, and there is merit in your proposal. My dome has always adhered to the protocols and we have never produced clones solely for military purposes, although some have acquired the appropriate skills. Unfortunately, as I am sure you expected, I would never be able to persuade a majority of domes in our alliance to accept this proposal.'

'Should we leave the room so you may discuss the details more fully?' said Ben-Tan. 'It would be a pity if the talks foundered on this last point.'

'Thank you. If I believed more time and more discussion would alter the situation, I would gladly accept. Yes, it is the last point, but that is merely because the agenda was structured so.'

'Is there no way we can move forward, Lento-Fin?'

'Not on this point, Ban-Ten. I very much fear we have reached an impasse.'

'So be it. We nevertheless appreciate your visiting us in good faith and thank you for your professionalism over the past light-times. May I suggest, as it is approaching dark-time, we all enjoy a meal together so you can set off refreshed at light-time?'

'You are most generous, Ban-Ten. We accept.'

# TWENTY: The Case

There was little talking during the first part of the trek back apart from the usual observations, warnings, and decisions about where to camp. The disappointment at the failure of the talks hinging on relinquishing control of the cloning program had seeped into everyone and everything like the grey drizzle that had become a permanent companion. During one of the lighter moods, Joor-Jen had floated the possibility that the Dicio Alliance might have offered the talks as a diversion so the Percutio Alliance could launch a pre-emptive attack. Lento-Fin said he didn't believe that was so, more likely Dicio were with good reason concerned they could be subsumed within Percutio. He pointed out that Ban-Ten seemed horrified Percutio were cooperating with the KimMorii, and, although he laughed at the point, the KimMorii probably hadn't offered much of a choice.

Early on the fifth light-time, Joor-Jen heard the footfall of a runner. With no tree or copse to conceal them, Lento-Fin, Joor-Jen, and the four SFs dispersed into the gloom. As the runner neared, Joor-Jen stepped behind, applied a strangle-lock and held her knife against the runner's throat.

'Speak.'

'I've a message for Lento-Fin.'

Joor-Jen released the girl and turned her round. 'How long?'

'Two light-times, Joor-Jen. I'm getting faster, though.'

'Not bad. How old?'

'Fifteen.'

'When we're back, come and find me. Lento-Fin? A message.' Joor-Jen turned the girl again and encouraged her towards Lento-Fin who was emerging from the mist.

'Lento-Fin, I have a message from Sin-Tun.'

He took the roll of cloth and walked away from the group. Not until the others were invisible did he unroll the cloth. After studying the message, he called the runner over. 'Tell Sin-Tun,' he whispered, 'although the talks were not successful, Chyke should inform his handler the talks had been successful and both parties were celebrating a long-term agreement of peace and cooperation. Say Chyke found this out from eavesdropping on Sin-Tun and you, the runner, after leaving the interrogation room. Clear?'

'Clear.'

'Before you set off, though, you must have porridge with us. And some Avena for your efforts. This mist and drizzle are the worst things ever.'

'Thank you, Lento-Fin. On the way, I sensed fighters on the move to the west. So for me the mist and drizzle have been my friends.'

'Well, at least they have one!'

\* \* \*

Tanun was so engrossed in the history of the railway network and the evolution from steam to fusion energy propulsion, he jumped when Chyke put his hand on his shoulder.

'Pod, pause. You startled me. Next time, don't creep up.'

'I didn't creep up. I actually approached from almost in front of you. You were concentrating so hard you didn't notice me.' Chyke looked at the screen Tanun had been studying. 'Was that the last train they developed?'

'Yeah. Can you believe it? Within two hundred years, they'd gone from steam-powered engines to fusion. This one here,' Tanun pointed to the screen, 'could reach 1,250kph.'

'No wheels.'

'Not at that speed, no. Floated on magnetic rails. You Ok, Chyke? You don't usually come and see me in here. Or anywhere.'

Chyke sat down and looked around before bringing his gaze back to Tanun and whispering. 'We're not meant to talk in here, are we? Could we go to our den?'

'Sure. Must be serious. Let me close this down.'

In their den, Chyke flopped onto his bottom bunk and Tanun climbed up to his.

'Funny how it's easier to talk like this,' said Tanun.

'Not that you talk much.'

'Actions speak louder. Come on, you. Out with it. Is it Joor-Jen?'

Chyke let out a long breath. 'No.' He puffed again. 'I'm meant to be professional. Discreet. But I'm scared, Tanun. I am so scared. The whole situation has dawned on me.'

'What? War? Us? Feeling like we'll always be newcomers?'

'No. Not any of that. Well, all of that, but not that.'

'What then? What has got you into this state?'

'My cell. Her. The terror. The terror. You know, the psychological stuff was worse than the physical. And it was definitely physical.' Chyke left a silence. 'I'm a spy, Tanun.'

'What? You sure? How?'

'I'm sure. Long story.'

'Well, we've got all dark-time.'

Chyke went through the process, from XorX being

unconvinced and unwilling to believe he would risk death and escape just to be with his brother, and so to avoid more torture he'd invented a story that he'd been left a note in the library and instructed to escape and follow his brother. Chyke stressed XorX hadn't at first believed him, but after some inquiries, seemed convinced and had offered him the chance to escape – if he'd spy for her. 'I mean, you would have agreed to anything just to get out of that cell. And away from her 'friend'.'

'I get that. You must have played a blinder, Chyke. Nerves of metal.'

'I guess I did. Yet I'm more frightened now.'

'Who knows about all this?'

'This is the crazy part. During my millions of debriefs, Lento-Fin and Sin-Tun had already guessed this might have happened.'

Chyke went on to explain how tough the debriefs had been and how Lento-Fin and Sin-Tun had used him to feed false information to his handler. And on top of all that, his handler didn't seem to care about the risks and the pressure and just demanded more and more information. Chyke got off his bunk and paced around their den, all the time looking at the floor. One piece of information he hadn't volunteered was that when he and Joor-Jen had been together in her den, he could tell she was testing him to see if he'd been turned.

'Do you get why I'm so scared?' Chyke didn't look over to Tanun for an answer.

Tanun said he totally got why he'd agreed to spy for XorX so he could get out of his cell, but emphasised one lie always led to another and you end up in a web you couldn't find a way out of. One piece of information Tanun didn't volunteer was the fact he already knew about Chyke's spying from Bento-Tor. He did, though, reveal he knew where Lento-Fin and Joor-Jen had gone.

Chyke reacted by saying he couldn't believe Joor-Jen would go without telling him, so Tanun warned him Joor-Jen was a law unto herself and he should never make the mistake of thinking his welfare would be her first concern.

'Not that you're bitter or anything — you know, cos she's dumped you for me.'

Tanun jumped down from his bunk. 'I am bitter, and if you weren't my brother I'd beat you to a pulp. However ... Brother ... to dump someone, you'd have to have had a relationship in the first place. Not sure Joor-Jen has ... relationships.

'You got me there. I sometimes wonder if I'm being used.'

'Let's talk about your spying situation. Leave Joor-Jen out of things. She only complicates everything. When are you due to see your handler again?'

'I never know. Should be due. I just find a cloth message somewhere.'

'Can you tell me where you meet?'

'I shouldn't, but what the hell. Level 0, so far. And it really is hell down there.'

'I know. I had to plant signal disrupters and explosives in an enemy dome. Couldn't move. Hot. Noisy. Squashed. Smelly.'

'I didn't know you'd done that. Tell me about it sometime.'

'What would happen if you didn't show up?'

'No idea. But they must have infiltrators, mustn't they? Probably wake up with my throat cut, or worse get kidnapped again.'

'Won't let that happen.'

'Thanks. Don't know how you'd stop it, though. See why I'm scared?'

'Yeah, just a little. Tell you what, I can't help with your spying, or your meetings, but how about next time I come down with you? Wait in the lift, obviously.'

'Risky. I mean, what if he chose the same one?'

'He wouldn't do that, would he? Bad tradecraft. And he wouldn't wait with you for the lift door to open in case he was seen.'

'True. Didn't think of that. He never does, anyway. Afterwards, he just sort of vanishes and leaves me to get my own way out.'

'Deal, then?'

'Deal.'

They punched each other's fists and fell into an embrace.

*　*　*

When the geodesic sphere emerged from the grey, Joor-Jen sighed, 'At last.'

The silver-grey was the perfect camouflage in the mist and rain, but right now, everyone strained to bring the dome closer, clearer, quicker.

'I could do without the climb, Lento Fin.'

'We all could, Joor-Jen. Saved us on many occasions, though. Might do so again. Think of a wet room. And two willing boys.'

'I wish you hadn't said that.'

'Sorry, just teasing. Remember ... this expedition ... secret.'

'You don't need to tell me. Anyhow, I've got a job to finish.' Joor-Jen took hold of Lento-Fin's shoulder and dropped back so they were a hundred metres behind the

SFs. 'Who knows what damage Chyke has done while we've been away? As soon as I can, I'm going to find out for sure.'

'Joor-Jen. Leave it. You have no proof. Let's see what Sin-Tun has found out. If you push him too much, you could actually drive him into their hands.'

'No way. He wouldn't know where to start.'

'I don't want to add to your suspicions, but during the time he spent as a prisoner in his old dome, he must have picked up a lot of tradecraft. He's very sharp. Not that his brother isn't. Tanun just plays the longer game.'

'They're so different.' Joor-Jen closed her eyes as they walked. 'Difficult to think of them as brothers.'

'Oh, I don't know. Bento-Tor and Peeso-Lun? Brother and sister.'

Joor-Jen turned to look at Lento-Fin. 'That was different. They're— '

'So? Regardless, I'm grateful to Cassièl for bringing Tanun and Chyke to our dome rather than one of the others.'

The four SFs had reached the dish at the bottom of the leg and waited for Lento-Fin and Joor-Jen to catch up.

'You first, Joor-Jen,' said Lento-Fin. 'I'll follow behind the SFs.'

'Right,' she said. 'Here we go.'

* * *

Chyke called to Tanun from the bathroom. 'We gotta go now. Look.' Chyke ran out of the bathroom and showed his brother the cloth: "Next light-time".

'So, infiltrators know which is our den? And sneak in?'

'They knew before, didn't they?'

'Yeah. Course they did. So disturbing.'

'Soon as I'm dressed, we must go.'

Neither spoke until they were in the elevator.

'Level 0,' said Chyke, leaning into the corner by the door.

Tanun asked him if he always used the same one.

**Level 200**, said the elevator.

'Absolutely not. That would be bad tradecraft.' Chyke smiled at Tanun. 'In fact, not used this one before.'

**Level 150**

'But how do you know where you have to go in Level 0? It must be a nightmare down there.'

**Level 100**

'I don't. It is. Neither do I know where he's going to be. I just take a guess and move around. You have to be so careful. Some pipes are scalding – look.' Chyke pulled up his sleeves to show Tanun the scabs.

**Level 50**

'I'll be waiting for you. Good luck.'

**Level 0**

Chyke rolled around the edge of the elevator doorway. After the door had slid shut, Tanun let out a long breath. Chyke was definitely a total git, but he was also definitely brave. He hoped his brother knew what he was doing.

Steam pulsed across the narrow walkway from a pipe, and Chyke ducked under, remembering to keep his elbows tucked in. A few metres along, the walkway grid was shiny with grease or some slippery substance and he was reluctant to tread on whatever the gloopy liquid was.

'Don't step on it,' said a disembodied voice. 'You'll have to jump it.'

Chyke took three steps back and stared at the glistening lattice. The grease didn't cover too much length of the grid, but there was no width to the walkway; perhaps a couple of centimetres either side, so he'd have to brake hard the other side in case he slipped or crashed onto a pipe or motor. He swayed back and forth building up momentum for the jump, pushed hard, ran, leapt. He crashed to his knees on the other side, with the toe of his left boot just touching the edge of the oil. Pen-Nan appeared five metres farther on from a walkway on the left and strode towards Chyke. He offered a hand to help Chyke stand up. 'Well jumped. That stuff's corrosive. Leaking from that pump up there.'

Chyke gazed up at the jumble of pipes and machinery, but couldn't identify which pump Pen-Nan meant.

'Cloth?'

Chyke handed over the cloth.

'What have you got for me?'

'What have you got for me, more like? I don't see any girls again.'

'Down here? Wouldn't be the best place. You'd get more than burnt elbows. Next meet, early dark-time, get yourself to the bottom of the rungs and I'll take you to a place in the forest. Part of our prep for an attack. Just as you need food and sleep for fighters, for morale you also need ... other things. You'll be back here before light-time. Exhausted. And educated, I'm willing to bet.'

'That sounds better. I've found out something quite important. You know I said Lento-Fin and Joor-Jen were missing? Well, just as I was leaving yet another debrief, a runner went past me into the interrogation room.'

'Male? Female?'

'Female. Fifteen, I'd say. Smiled at me.'

'Get on with it.'

'Funny thing is, the door didn't quite close, so I could listen. She'd met Lento-Fin and Joor-Jen two light-times ago on their way back. What was that word? Delegation, that was it. They'd had secret talks with the Dicio Alliance. Peace talks, and apparently, they'd reached a deal. I heard the runner say Lento-Fin's group were a bit drunk – they'd been drinking most of the way back.' He shrugged.

'Go on.'

'That's it. The door whizzed shut. No way could I hear anything after that.'

'That's very interesting. Well done. I'll make sure you get the top girls. Cloning program?'

'Not yet, but Tanun said they agree on a schedule every 90 days for around 9000 clones. They plan for a 10% loss.'

'Useful. You're getting good at this. That's when mistakes happen, so watch it.'

'I will. Don't want to miss out on those girls. When Joor-Jen gets back, I'll probably find out more from Tanun. You know, their pillow talk.'

'Don't get too smart, but find out everything you can about the peace deal. I need to go.'

'How am I supposed to find that out?'

'You're the spy. Up the ante. But watch it. Which elevator did you use?'

'How the hell do I know? The one back there. Past the oil.'

'Don't use that one. Go along this way to the next walkway. There's one on the right. You've used it before.'

*Shit, Tanun's waiting for me. What if Pen-Nan uses that one?*

'Did you hear me?'

'Er, yes, thanks. Anything to avoid that jump again.'

\* \* \*

Tanun walked the three paces to the other wall of the elevator. Walked three paces back. Walked the diagonal.

Four and a bit paces. Walked along the wall and the diagonal, along the wall and the other diagonal, describing a crossed square. More than a hundred times. Chyke must be in trouble, he should be back by now No rendezvous would take that long. Too much of a risk. He faced the door. Inertia. Momentum. Equilibrium. 'Door, open.'

The heat sucked his breath away. The maze of pipes drained away his motivation. Left? Right? How could he possibly know? Right. Yes, that felt right. A junction to his left. Another.

Pen-Nan's knife grazed a pipe. Tanun turned. Pen-Nan leapt. *Was it instinct? Or training? Probably both*, Tanun thought afterwards. Despite the narrow space, Tanun pulled Pen-Nan into a perfect sasae tsurikomi ashi. He flew over Tanun's head for several metres, ending up in a crash-landing that flexed pipes, pushed motors out of true, bent joints, and pulled seals as he slid along the slick of oil. Clanging. Rumbling. Steam burst from a join. Tanun scrambled up and ran to the lift.

* * *

The steaming water jetted from every angle. 'Again.' While the fluffy rollers spun and caressed every sinew, pore, and muscle, Joor-Jen closed her arms to pull Chyke in harder. 'Stop.' She opened her eyes, stepped out and lifted two white bath sheets from the pile, and after running a towel once over her hair, threw it in the chute. Imagined where he'd be. Would be rather crass to drag him out of his den if Tanun was there. Then again, if Tanun was on his own … But sensible to eat first. See what was happening in the refectory. Get some Avena and chill.

The refectory was relatively quiet with few queues, and only every other table occupied with SFs and various military. Joor-Jen chose circ soup and oatcakes, accompanied by a large bottle of Avena.

'You going to drink all that?'

Joor-Jen looked up to see Sreen-Gar smiling down at her.

'Yes, but not in one sitting. Want some?'

'No, thanks. Need to talk.'

'Thought you might. What's been happening while I've been away?'

Sreen-Gar told her – that the rumour mill had gone into overdrive, forces had been spotted in the west, and missiles were becoming more and more frequent. Food was getting scarce because of the damage to the land from the missiles. The most disturbing thing, though, Sreen-Gar said, leaning over, was that she had spotted Chyke getting into an elevator a long way from his den and very late in dark-time.

'Chyke's allowed to go where his DD permits. Even in dark-time,' said Joor-Jen.

'That particular elevator was one of the express ones. It goes to only two levels. Level 1240 and level 0. No way was he going to the meeting rooms at that point. I checked, by the way. So, he must have been going to 0. Why would Chyke be going there? He's not an engineer.'

'That is strange, I have to admit. Besides checking about the meeting room, what else did you do?'

'I added another two watchers to the three Sin-Tun had allocated.'

Joor-Jen pushed her plate and bowl to the side and reached for the Avena.

'You were expecting someone,' said Sreen Gar, looking at the two containers. 'I won't get in the way.'

'After being away, I was looking for some company.'

Joor-Jen filled both containers and pushed one across.

'Oh, all right then. Time to bring Chyke in? We ought to find out exactly what he's up to.'

'I'm on the case, Sreen-Gar. Thanks, though, that's useful information.'

'I'll get out your way. Hope you find that company. Company and case wouldn't by any chance be the same, would they?' Sreen-Gar smiled at Joor-Jen as she turned and left.

# TWENTY-ONE: Elevators

No sooner had Sreen-Gar left than Chyke slid onto the chair opposite Joor-Jen.

'Hey, Joor-Jen. Long time, no see. Been avoiding me?'

'Hardly. Fancy some?'

'Avena, d'you mean? You bet.'

Joor-Jen filled her container and pushed the remaining Avena across the table.

'Thanks. You smell all fresh. Been in a wet room?'

'I have been known to use them. More to the point, *you* need one. You stink of oil. What have you been doing?'

Chyke described helping to reseed the land damaged by missiles and cleaning the salvageable tools. He said his espionage training was going well although he'd had further debriefs with Sin-Tun, and moaned about them when they'd come to an end. He frowned. 'Usually,' he said, 'Lento-Fin and Sin-Tun work together, but coincidentally,' – he sent Joor-Jen a knowing smile – 'Lento-Fin hasn't been around for about the same time as you. And,' he went on, 'Tanun is getting to be quite the expert on explosives.'

Joor-Jen poured Avena into the other container. 'Difficult to talk here. Fancy going to my den?'

'You've persuaded me.' Chyke, however, shuffled on his chair and looked down. 'The thing is, Joor-Jen, I need to find Tanun first. Pass on a message. I'll be along straight after. Is that Ok?'

'Sure. I'll help find him if you like.'

'No, it's Ok. He'll either be in our den, or in the knowledge room. I won't be long. Don't forget the bottle.'

'You take it. I'll get another.'

\* \* \*

Pen-Nan waited until a third into dark-time before unscrewing one of the wires to the bottom hatch alarm. A hiss of outside air cooled his face as the bottom hatch door swung down, and for a moment the scent of the forest swept away the oily smell. He watched the narrow ladder extend downwards. When it stopped, he climbed down fast and tapped the penultimate rung before letting go. The ladder began ascending. Pen-Nan dropped two metres to the ground and stayed in a crouching position, surveying. With no sign of being observed, he ran swerving towards the oat fields.

\* \* \*

Chyke ran to his den, but Tanun wasn't there. He hadn't been in the refectory either, so he guessed he must be in the knowledge room. He ran along the corridor and into an open elevator.

He didn't see the roundhouse punch. Tanun picked him up under his arms.

'What was that for?' Chyke rubbed the side of his face.

'How could you leave me there? I've been going nuts.'

'Wasn't my fault. There was some spilt oil or grease on a walkway. He made me go back a different way. What could I do? Tell him my brother was waiting for me in the lift?'

'I nearly got killed. Enforcer git with a knife. Was he your man?'

'How do I know? I wasn't there, was I? Probably. I've been frantically trying to find you. Do you think he knew who you were?'

'I dunno. Everything happened so fast. I threw him before I ran back to the lift. Difficult in all that jumble of pumps and pipes and machinery. Look, sorry about that. Just a reaction.'

'Forget it,' said Chyke, rubbing his cheekbone and trying to end the conversation as soon as possible. He pulled the bottle from his pocket. 'How about some Avena?'

'Where did you get that? I thought you were frantically looking for me?'

'I was, and one of the places would obviously be the refectory. Thought you might need this when I found you. Here.' Chyke tossed the bottle across.

Tanun unscrewed the cap and drank two mouthfuls. 'Yuck. That's a bit rough.' He studied the bottle. 'You've been drinking it while you've been looking for me.'

'Each time I didn't find you, I took a swig, that's all. You look pretty pale, Tanun. Let's go back to our den. You can sleep it off.'

'Yeah. 12 more levels to go. Anyway, how did you get on?'

'Best not talk about that. I find it easier to just push it down and forget about it. Safest way to cope.'

'Like I have to with Joor-Jen.'

'That's unfair. She's fond of both of us.'

'That's why it hurts so much.'

**Level 230**

'Here we are. Have another swig and get a good sleep. I've got to update Lento-Fin. Back later.'

\* \* \*

After Joor-Jen had pushed Chyke into the shower, they each in their own way found the release of tension more like a medical intervention than any expression of warmth or longing.

'That was amazing, Chyke. I couldn't stop thinking about this on the way back.'

'Way back?'

'Oh.' *Shit,* Joor-Jen thought. *And there was me trying to get him to make a slip.* 'Yes. Been reconnoitring. Seems enemy alliance forces are amassing in the west. Secret, but I reckon open war will break out soon. They'll try to take over our dome. Does it hurt?' Joor-Jen looked at Chyke's developing black eye.

'Not much. Just when I lie that side.'

'How did you get it?'

'Argument with Tanun.'

'So, you found him. Must have been some message. You two. I'll never understand brothers.' Joor-Jen studied Chyke. 'Any gossip while I was away?'

Chyke was lying on his front with his arm across Joor-Jen, just below her breasts. He nuzzled her neck. 'All I found out was about Sreen-Gar. Guess you know her? Tanun and I were in the refectory with Bento-Tor. She was pretty forward. Tried to get Tanun and me back to her den. Funny thing is, I saw her again shortly after – she didn't see me – she was surrounded by loads of military. It was well into dark-time. All laughing and joking. Looked like they were well into partying.'

'She certainly knows how to do that. And you should see her den. On second thoughts, perhaps you shouldn't. Sreen-Gar's some fighter too. Where were you going when you saw her coming out of the elevator?'

'Can't remember. Going to the knowledge room, I think ... actually, I didn't mention any elevator. Weird you should know that. Tanun showed me trains that could go 1250kph. What a civilization there must have been before the religion wars.'

Joor-Jen lifted Chyke's arm and began sucking his thumb. She moved to his forefinger and worked her way along, dribbling saliva down each finger. After working back to his thumb, she rubbed his wet hand across her breasts. 'Fancy being a train?'

\* \* \*

Pen-Nan made the run through the oat fields to the forest by halfway through dark-time. He wanted to reach the tunnel before light-time so he could sleep before the final leg to 1279-41130. He went over the ways he could present the information to XorX and the Elders. *What a critical piece of information. Chyke overheard a runner so the information must be reliable. Successful peace talks between the Liberal Alliance and the Dicio Alliance. Typical of that Ban-Ten — he could never be trusted. Always on about how peace could make everyone more prosperous. So, the two alliances had agreed to cooperate on defence and coordinate their cloning programs. All bad news, but invaluable to know ahead of time. XorX will be pleased with me. Earn me some credits — promotion, possibly. Operating in enemy territory and managing a bolshie teenager. Sure, Chyke's smart for his age. Astute, but completely lacking in experience.*

Pen-Nan smiled at the pretence of the girls.

*The only disturbing thing is that other guy in level 0. Who was he? What was he doing there? He was good at close combat, that's for sure. That would be two young spooks. Because of their age, much less likely to arouse suspicion. Have to track him down and the only way to do that will be to go into the dome. That never gets less frightening, no matter how many times I do it. Still, worth the risk to recruit a good close-combat fighter. Would the enticement be girls as it is for Chyke, or something else?*

**Stop. Identify**

'Pen-Nan. I bring urgent information.'

**Ascend**

At the meeting, the Elders informed Pen-Nan that XorX was preparing for the KimMorii invasion and investigating some new information, so in the meantime Pen-Nan should update the Elders. He explained he could not reveal his source, but the information had been verified by another in 1279-41618.

'XorX must hear of this as soon as possible,' he emphasised. 'Any alliance between the Dicio Alliance and the Liberal Alliance will hinder our attacks.'

'Yes, thank you, Pen-Nan. We understand that. XorX will be with us shortly. She has already told us that as soon as we have subjugated all enemy domes, the KimMorii will invade Lemtor and, in recognition of our help, we shall take over the government of all domes. We shall dissolve the alliances. We shall be masters of all mining resources and the provision of slaves as required. The meeting is closed. Please wait in your barracks until XorX is ready for you.'

* * *

Chyke was sure the elevator knew the level before he'd spoken. What were they going to say about him going outside to meet Pen-Nan? Would they let him go into the woods? Should he mention the girls? Why not? He'd earned the right, hadn't he? And he might find out some useful stuff.

**Level 298**

When Chyke stepped out, he paused because the place was manic. People were entering and leaving interrogation rooms, running along the corridor, or pushing people into elevators. He'd never seen everyone so animated before and wondered what had happened to cause such activity. At room 298-103, the door whizzed open and Chyke stepped through to see Lento-Fin and Sin-Tun in their usual places. He'd learnt not to sit down until told.

'Hello, Lento-Fin. Haven't seen you for a while.'

'I had a reconnoitring mission to do. With Joor-Jen. But you know that. Please, sit.'

Chyke was glad of the distraction of moving around the chair and turning it slightly before sitting down, so he could process Lento-Fin's remark.

*Do they watch everything? I hope not.*

'It's Ok, Chyke. You're not in trouble. And we won't ask about the black eye.'

'Thanks.' Chyke rubbed his left eye and cheekbone. 'But I am under surveillance.'

'All agents are under surveillance,' said Sin-Tun. 'For their safety and well-being, and ours too. You know that.'

'Just a bit embarrassing ... you know ... private things.'

'Really, you have no need. The machines process the data. We're interested in words, not groans.'

*Stop, stop. They'll see.* But Chyke couldn't prevent the red from rising through his neck, his cheeks, and forehead. *Oh, well, I've performed better ... and worse.*

'To business,' said Lento-Fin, bringing Chyke from Joor-Jen's floor into the room. He explained they knew when he'd last met Pen-Nan but wanted to ascertain Pen-Nan's reaction to the information about the peace talks. Chyke said Pen-Nan had congratulated him on finding that out and also about the cloning program.

'And next time, I'm going to meet him outside. By the leg. We're going to a prep camp in the forest – I hope you know about that – and I'm gonna get my girls.'

Perhaps no sound had come out and he'd imagined

saying it. Perhaps he had just spoken in an ancient language. Perhaps he was actually on Joor-Jen's floor imagining he was in 298-103. *Why aren't Lento-Fin and Sin-Tun reacting? They're just staring at me.*

'This is serious,' said Lento-Fin, breaking the spell. 'Sorry, but much too dangerous for you, girls or no girls. '

Before Chyke's anguished look had got halfway across the desk and any of his gurgled protest had emerged from his mouth, Sin-Tun spoke. 'We can't let you do that, Chyke. Think about it. You'd be on your own with no backup close enough. What you can do is rendezvous with Pen-Nan at the bottom of the leg. His time's up, and we need to ask him a few questions.'

'But that'll blow my cover!'

'If it isn't already, it would be soon. When XorX discovers the information you've been feeding them is false, you'll need to be in a safe place a long way from detection.'

'I can't go back to that cell. I can't.'

'You won't. We'll make sure of that.'

Chyke stood up and paced round the room. Of course. He saw it now. How ridiculous to think Pen-Nan, or XorX, come to that, would let him see their prep camp and rely on him not to report it. As for the girls, well, one was quite enough to deal with at the moment. He sat down again. 'So, what's the plan?'

\* \* \*

'Please, sit down.'

Why he was in a cell with XorX instead of a meeting room or the Court of Elders, Pen-Nan couldn't resolve.

'So, your little spy has provided you with some crucial — if not critical information.'

'Yes, Commander XorX. It was so important, he

couldn't wait to tell me. Coming from a runner, that's as reliable as it gets. And with the cloning information he's gathered, we have surely gained a serious advantage.'

'That would undoubtedly be the case.'

'Commander XorX, I feel my handling of this teenage spy has been exemplary. Enough to be used in knowledge pods for training future handlers.'

'I can understand how you would think that.'

'I might even have found another potential spy. I'd go so far as to suggest we allow Chyke's promised evening with the girls. Get the Avena flowing. He'll learn a lot and we might too, once his tongue's been loosened.'

'A worthwhile idea. Or, rather ... it would be ... Pen-Nan ... if the information were bona fide.'

'Couldn't be better, could it? Chyke heard it all.'

'Indulge me, Pen-Nan, for a moment. You think you deserve some credits. Let me see. Because you think your case handling should become a case study for teaching future handlers? Because you have managed a sulky teenage spy? And you might have found another potential spy? And you think our young spy has earned an evening with girls? With plenty of Avena. Have I got all that correct?'

'Yes, Commander XorX, you have.'

'Good, good. Stand up. Do you know what this is?'

'I ... I am aware of its reputation.'

Well. This "friend" was a little lonely. Doing all the work itself. So ... I now have two "friends". See? Have a good look. Take your time. Use your imagination.'

Pen-Nan stared from one pointed solid black cylinder to the other. He'd not seen them in use, though he'd heard the screams.

'We have been fed lies, Pen-Nan. A stream of lies. A whole knowledge pod of lies. And you have facilitated the stream.'

'But—'

'Please allow me to finish. One of my faults is that I am rather intolerant of people who have lied to me. Especially those who have betrayed my trust. That stupid boy has been playing games. Treating us like fools. Yet, he is so naïve, he had no conception how high the stakes were, and how dangerous the game would be for the loser.'

'But— '

'Listen. You will bring Chyke to me. Alive and unharmed … because … I wish to be the one to do the harming. Apparently, when my two "friends" work together … from each end, the pain, I'm told, is beyond anything yet contrived. Unless you wish to confirm that yourself, you will bring him here within three dark-times.'

'Yes, Commander XorX. Of course … erm … forgive me, but I will need a large number of enforcers.'

'You may commandeer whatever resources you deem necessary. You have my full authority. I do not want to see you again until you bring me Chyke trussed up like a torky. Now, get to work.'

*  *  *

Tanun jumped down from his bunk and went to the refectory. Although he didn't feel like eating, a full stomach seemed sensible to help him tackle his explosives test. They hadn't told him exactly, but he could guess which subjects they'd concentrate on. Placements and Remotes. No good programming a great remote control if placement was weak. No good having great placement if the remote was unreliable.

The six students made their way across the oat fields and into the forest. Each had been given four explosives, red, blue, green, and yellow, and four colour-coded remotes. After separating, they were to find the colour-matched targets, which could be trees, or huts, or huts in trees, or rock shelters. When they had placed the explosive and programmed the remote, they were to come back to the start and wait for the trigger instruction.

After the last student had returned, the instructors checked each remote. With a nod from an instructor, each student in turn pressed their remote. After twenty-one explosions, the students handed over their devices for assessment.

'Well done, students. Initial assessment: this class has generally achieved a high standard. Some failures though. You can make your way back. Your result will be sent to your DD by light-time.'

Tanun listened to the three girls and two boys joshing and boasting all the way back to the rungs. One girl said she'd had all huts as targets, and another, all shelters. The two boys had had one of each for their targets, and they convinced the two girls and the boy who'd had failures they would definitely fail the assessment.

'What if some were tricks, though?' said Tanun.

The five stopped walking and stared at him.

'How do you mean?' said one of the girls. 'They wouldn't do that in an assessment, would they?'

'He's just winding us up,' said one of the boys.

'I'm not. They'd do it, especially in an assessment. I noticed the coloured strip on my targets was removable. And underneath was a different colour. Can't be because they re-use the targets because, remember, we blew them to pieces.'

'What did you do?'

I always went for the colour underneath and kept a record of which colours were on top and which underneath and the order I'd done them.'

'Smartass.'

'Now I'm totally stuffed. I never thought of that,' said another girl.

'Might be nothing,' said Tanun, 'but why would they do

that unless it was to test us? Perhaps that's why some didn't explode.'

\* \* \*

"Explosives Test Assessment. Score 97.00%"

The voice echoed in Tanun's DD as he punched the air and decided immediately to go to the refectory for a drink. Perhaps the others would be there and they could celebrate. The door whooshed open, though, and Joor-Jen stood in the doorway.

'I've just got 97% in explosives, Joor-Jen!'

She pushed him back inside. 'Well done, you. Never expected anything else.' She held his face and kissed him on the lips. 'Were you going somewhere?'

'The refectory, for a drink. See if the others were there.

'Good idea. Mind if I come along?'

'Don't be silly.'

'Tanun, you don't know where Chyke is, do you?'

'Debrief, I guess. Said he might come to the refectory afterwards.'

\* \* \*

Next light-time, the dome's defences deflected eleven missiles, each exploding in and around the oat fields and forest. Although the dome's defence shield had worked perfectly, the shield couldn't stop collateral damage from the shock waves and debris thrown against the dome. Fortunately, its internal cellular structure mitigated against instability and exposure to the outside environment. The worst effect was the devastation of the seed beds, with the result that crops and rations would have to be reduced further as the stores of oats, circs, and leks declined. Mass communication via DDs told everyone to prepare for a likely attempted invasion of the dome and to follow all instructions when given them by military personnel.

Chyke stepped out of the shower and pulled a towel from the pile. A square of cloth fluttered to the floor.

Early next dark-time. Get ready for some fun. Back before light-time.

He put on a clean boiler suit and stuffed the cloth into the left breast pocket. Lento-Fin's words were still echoing in his head: "As soon as you get the cloth, tell me or Sin-Tun. We have to get people in position to protect you." *At least no more level 0*, he said to himself as he walked to an elevator, He stood in front of the door of room 298-103 and took a deep breath.

* * *

At dusk, Joor-Jen opened the hatch and began descending with Sreen-Gar a few rungs above her. They made their way across the oat fields to the edge of the forest, continually looking back at the leg.

'Should we split up or stay together?' said Sreen-Gar.

Joor-Jen scanned the dome and legs with her binoculars. 'Together. Better decision making.'

'Why didn't we get him in level 0?'

'Because he probably knows down there better than we do. And any aggro would damage the pipework and machinery. What we want to know is who else is helping him here in this dome.' Joor-Jen adjusted her 10/10 to stun. She had wanted to hit Pen-Nan with terminal force, but Lento-Fin had insisted vehemently he be taken alive.

'Action,' said Sreen-Gar.

They studied the figure dropping fast from the bottom hatch in the darkening gloom.

'Must be Pen-Nan,' said Joor-Jen. 'His heat signature gives his nerves away.'

'Will he hang around the dish?'

'Reckon so. Ah. Enforcers. At least ten of them. Why would they be here?'

As Pen-Nan reached the bottom, a further eighteen enforcers emerged from the oat fields, including three who swept by Joor-Jen and Sreen-Gar four metres to their right, and divided into six groups of three, surrounding each leg.

'Something's wrong,' said Joor-Jen. 'Why would you have all those enforcers just to escort Chyke to the prep camp? Too late to warn him.'

'Definitely too late. I can see a figure coming down. Must be him.'

'Please keep him safe. We must keep him safe,' said Joor-Jen.

'We will. The company *was* the case, wasn't it?'

Joor-Jen smiled at Sreen-Gar. 'Better strike before he gets to the ground. You go for the ones to the left. I'll take the ones on the right. Three-two-one.'

Joor-Jen set off towards the dome at full speed with Sreen-Gar a metre behind. 'All bets off!' shouted Joor-Jen. 'Take them all down. Every one of them. Protect Chyke.'

When they were less than a hundred metres from the dome, Sreen-Gar fired and took down five enforcers. Joor-Jen took three down and side-stepped an arrow. Sreen-Gar didn't. The metre-long arrow entered below her sternum and half the length emerged from her back. The force lifted her backwards for two metres.

'Go, Joor-Jen. Get them,' she rasped before collapsing to her knees and falling on her side. Joor-Jen dodged three arrows and set off again, firing at the enforcers.

Chyke was a hundred metres above the dish when he heard the commotion and looked down as fifty more enforcers emerged from the oat field. He started climbing. An enforcer on each side of the bottom of the leg fired a net capsule. When they were above Chyke, two explosive cracks blew the canisters apart and nets descended over him. The enforcers pulled the ropes and Chyke tumbled into a hundred waiting arms.

'Get him into the barrow,' said Pen-Nan.

Chyke wriggled and kicked and swore until a punch made him fall limp.

'There's another SF over there!' shouted an enforcer.

'Forget about him,' said Pen-Nan. 'Let's go.'

The enemy SFs wheeled the barrow away with an unconscious Chyke inside, while Pen-Nan scattered smoke canisters to obscure the area.

# TWENTY-TWO: The Next War

Joor-Jen stood at the long top table in the meeting room. To her left was Lento-Fin and to his left, Sin-Tun. To her right was Bento-Tor and to his right sat Tanun. Every seat along the other three sides of the room had been taken and people were standing behind all except the top table.

'We were completely outnumbered,' said Joor-Jen. 'And outwitted. We should never have let Chyke – or anyone – go into such a precarious situation. Even if everything had gone our way and we hadn't needed to use them, we should have had at least a hundred SFs staking out the area. Why didn't we know the enemy had resorted to bows and arrow and spears? This is reverting to the savagery of the early religion wars.'

Tanun buried his head in his hands, prompting Bento-Tor to put an arm across his shoulders.

Lento-Fin stood up. 'Your synopsis is correct, Joor-Jen. I am at fault for not considering the enemy intended to kidnap Chyke. I thought only of us capturing Pen-Nan. I believed stealth was the better strategy, and in using Chyke as bait I exposed an innocent teenager to unnecessary danger. And incarceration. This grave error of judgement leaves me with no alternative but to resign my position.'

The room erupted with shouts of 'no', and 'this is just hindsight'. When the hubbub died down, Lento-Fin said, 'Until a new leader is elected, Sin-Tun has agreed to act in my place.'

After Lento-Fin had sat down, Sin-Tun stood up and

addressed the room. 'I am sure we all wish to express our gratitude for Lento-Fin's leadership and fervently hope he will continue to contribute his wisdom to the well-being of the dome.'

Sin-Tun waited for the applause to die down, and said, 'You have all heard the missiles increasing in frequency. Other domes in our alliance report the same. We believe the Percutio Alliance will attempt to invade our domes, probably within the next ten light-times. After that, if they succeed, or perhaps even if they don't, the KimMorii intend to take over Lemtor and plunder its resources, such as they are after ten millennia of war. You all have your instructions.' He turned towards Joor-Jen, Bento-Tor, and Tanun. 'I appreciate how you must be feeling. We all do. We understand. And you most likely want to try to rescue Chyke. I must, however, emphasise, even if that were possible, your skills are needed here to protect the dome. I am sorry for having to give this order, but Joor-Jen, Bento-Tor, and you, Tanun ... are forbidden to leave this dome until further notice.'

Tanun crashed his fists on the table and made to speak, but Bento-Tor shook his head and pulled him into an embrace. Joor-Jen left her place and sat down on Tanun's right side.

'Sin-Tun,' Joor-Jen turned towards him, 'Tanun is understandably distraught. Please, may we take him back to his den?'

'Of course. Look after him. Do whatever's necessary.'

Joor-Jen and Bento-Tor helped Tanun up and led him out of the room to the nearest elevator. While the elevator descended, Bento-Tor pointed at Tanun and said, 'I know what you need and I've been saving it for the right time. That time, my friend, is now. Xen-Lin gave it to me for us to celebrate. Well, we never did, but we can now use it to do a better thing than celebrate. Joor-Jen, take Tanun to the refectory. I need to fetch something from my den.'

Returning, Bento-Tor ran into the refectory with a white bottle and two silver containers. Inside one of the containers was another clear container. He ostentatiously plonked one silver container down in front of Tanun and the other in front of Joor-Jen. 'Only two, but that's fine. I'm happy with this one. It was Xen-Lin's.' The stopper made a loud plop as he pulled it from the neck. 'Right, Tanun, I guarantee you won't have had anything like this.'

The viscous white liquid glugged reluctantly from the bottle as Bento-Tor filled the three containers. 'Look at me, Tanun.'

Tanun lifted his face towards Bento-Tor, his bloodshot eyes full of questions. Bento-Tor knew the questions. Why did he pick up that stone? Why did Chyke follow him? Why did Joor-Jen love Chyke more than him? Why didn't Cassièl seem to care?

'You're my best friend. You stood by me after Peeso-Lun and Xen-Lin. You didn't question. You didn't judge. What's better than celebrating? I'll tell you. Comforting. I don't care if Joor-Jen hears this or not. I am not staying in this dome while Chyke needs rescuing. Anyone with me?'

'I'm with you,' said Joor-Jen.

'I'm with you, too' said Tanun.

'Right. Let's toast … to mission … let's see … mission little git.'

Tanun smiled, Joor-Jen downed her drink in one, and Bento-Tor thought of Xen-Lin.

'That is the best ever, ever, ever,' said Joor-Jen. 'Where – how – did Xen-Lin get it?'

'You don't know everything that goes on, Joor-Jen. Top

secret, but the medics down there have been making the best Avena for years and storing the top stuff. They trade it. Shifts. Food. Passes. 10/10s. Occasionally, time in a wet-room– '

'Honestly, Bento-Tor,' said Joor-Jen, 'you're a bad influence on Tanun.'

'And I like it,' Tanun said.

While Bento-Tor kept topping up their containers, the three of them formulated the details of mission little git.

* * *

The wall. Dazzling light. Hard bench. When he turned, there it was. The high-backed chair frame. The room spun this way, that way, up and down. Chyke made the toilet just in time and threw up over and over. He crawled back to the bench and curled up. Although his right cheekbone now throbbed along with his left, he bent his arm over his eyes to shield them from the light.

Whoosh. Eight enforcers. One to a limb, one to strangle, one to strip, and two to move him to the chair frame.

'Nice and tight. Those are the orders. Head against the back – use that strap. That's it. He's not going anywhere. Comfortable, pretty boy? Sleep well.'

The cell went black.

* * *

'Tanun, please, may I enter?'

Cassièl entered and stood by Tanun's bunk. 'I am so sorry about Chyke. You are doing the right thing, trying to rescue him. I give the little git mission my blessing.'

'How do you know about it? Won't you tell Sin-Tun?'

'Long story, but we can see all events in all universes, pasts and futures, although we do not necessarily know which future will come to pass. And it is not for Amnians – including me – to interfere in your interactions with others.'

Tanun raised himself to rest on his left elbow. 'XorX is really gonna hurt Chyke, isn't she?'

'I am afraid she is. All the more reason for you three to have a decent go at rescuing him. Better he dies in the attempt than spends eternity suffering.'

'Please, may I get down?'

Cassièl moved from the bunk so Tanun could jump down and he stood close to Cassièl, mentally challenging him to change the world. *Punish evil, reward good. Put everything right.*

'Even if I could do all those things, Tanun, I would not. Each world has to evolve in its own way. If we interfered, where should we stop? You have been granted the greatest gift of all. Free will. That is an awesome responsibility. The choice to do good, or ill.'

'Seems to be more ill around than good.'

'For evil to flourish, it requires only that good people do nothing.'

'Yeah, Ok. I see that. Actually, I think I've read that somewhere. Must have been in the forbidden section. One of the ancient philosophers.'

'Your memory is accurate. The philosopher was Deauchamp, your favourite.'

'Yes! Thanks. I remember now. Cassièl, can you take Dodecahedron?'

'I fear not, but we can try.'

'What if we are invaded and the KimMorii take it?'

'They would not ask you for it. They would just take it. You would die. The quest would be set back billions of years. More suffering, more illness, more slavery.'

Tanun reached under his pillow and held out Dodecahedron on his palm. Again, Cassièl could not lift the stone away.

'Pity. When I touch the Nucleus, I see many futures where children are involved in retrieving Nuclei in some way, though I cannot fathom the conditions. I also see much suffering. Much blood and death.'

'I so wish I hadn't found it.'

'The choice wasn't yours, Tanun, you know that. Dodecahedron found you. Whatever happens, your name will live long in the memory after your molecules have been recycled into other Essentia.'

'We're going this dark-time. We've worked out a plan and the sooner we set off, the less suffering for Chyke.'

'You will need all your wits. Your skill climbing ropes, and no doubt your incredible judo sacrifice fall, not to mention what you have learnt about explosives. See what you can find up on the weapons level.'

'But that'll be locked and guarded.'

'You might find in all the chaos someone has been remiss in their duty. Be discreet.'

Cassièl stared into Tanun's eyes and smiled. Tanun nodded, words superfluous.

'Good luck.'

\* \* \*

The cell lit up and a jet hose in the ceiling drenched Chyke in freezing water. A pipe lowered from the ceiling and stopped in front of his mouth. Two narrow tubes protruded from the pipe and stared at him. The left tube extended to his mouth. A flow of cold liquid food squirted into his mouth and he struggled to swallow quickly. The tube withdrew and the right tube extended, squirting cold water. Chyke swallowed as much as he could.

Whoosh

An enforcer entered. 'You look ready.' He pulled a blindfold from his pocket and wrapped it around Chyke's head. 'Be patient. She'll be along soon.'

Whoosh

Chyke could tell the blindfold wasn't flat - there was a bulge for each eye which pressed in. He could see only red.

Whoosh.

Silence.

'My dear, dear Chyke. We meet again. I have missed our conversations. Pen-Nan hasn't, of course. He enjoyed your meetings, but then … he was unaware at the time you were feeding him lie upon lie upon lie.'

XorX's hands on his shoulders. Rubbing in little circles.

'I'm so sorry, Chyke. You think you experienced pain before?'

Sliding her hands over his chest to his stomach. Lingering.

'That will be as nothing. You see, I now have two "friends" and they are keen to work together. They can't wait to get started, in fact. You're such a fine young man, Chyke. For now.'

A hand tightened around his throat.

'Seems such a pity to despoil a work of art, though when I've eventually finished, you will hate your body.'

A hand stroked each thigh.

'You will hate its corruption, its distortions, its disfigurements.'

The hands slid down his shins.

'But most of all you will hate the pain.'

Each toe clicked as it was pulled to its maximum.

* * *

Tanun grabbed his rucksack. He had to go now or he'd be late meeting up with the others. Their timing hadn't allowed for one of them to visit the weapons level. *How am I going to talk my way past the guards and get into the* stores? *The moment the elevator door opens there will be two 10/10s pointing at me. But Cassièl had said, got to give it a try. How did he know? Too late now. Have to trust him.* Level 1245.'

**That is Weapons Level**

'I know.'

**Checking your DD. Authorised**

Tanun made a face. *Just how was I authorised? Perhaps the systems are breaking down from all the shockwaves.* The elevator door slid open. Nobody. *Where are the guards?* He stepped out and stared at the registration desk over to the left. When he reached it, he saw six small dischargers on the right, arranged in twos. Just what he needed for opening a hatch. He shrugged off his rucksack and put the dischargers in the back pocket. On the left of the desk, in a line, were four bomb-discs the size of his palm. *Why would someone just leave them on the desk? One on its own could destroy a dome if placed correctly.* Lifting each one with both hands, he laid them along the bottom of the rucksack. When he put the rucksack back on, the weight took him by surprise and he nearly overbalanced. He leant forward and trod with ponderous steps back to the elevator. Level 0.'

**This elevator stops at level 230**

'Fine. Level 230.' Shit. He hadn't noticed that. He'd have to change. With a bit of luck, the next one wouldn't be too far. The rucksack felt like he was carrying a dead weight.

* * *

Bento-Tor was at the bottom hatch when Joor-Jen arrived.

'This place is just awful,' she said.

'Where all the crap gets processed. Nobody saw you?'

'Don't believe so. Great idea of yours to use different elevators and go up before changing and going down. Come on, Tanun. I hope he knows what he's doing with the wiring. We need a decent head start before anyone realises we're missing. An alarm going off would scupper our chances.'

'He knows. He's very methodical.'

Joor-Jen's thoughts drifted back to their encounter on his bunk. So unlike Chyke. Very professional and considerate. Chyke was more ... animalistic. Both approaches had their attractions.

'Joor-Jen? You were far away.'

'Sorry, yes. Worrying about Chyke ... and about being up close with Tanun.'

'You do make things hard for yourself. In battle or arguments you're like a machine – processing logic. With Tanun and Chyke you're all over the place.'

'Don't tell me. Each turns my world upside down. Shh, I heard something.'

Bento-Tor and Joor-Jen followed the steps along the lattice walkway above and down the narrow rungs to the lowest level. They nodded at each other.

'Hey, Tanun. We heard you kilometres away.'

'These walkways. They rattle and move. Nightmare. Apart from the obvious, you won't believe what I've brought.' Tanun swung his rucksack round and had to grab it to stop it from hitting a metal pipe. He opened the pocket. Joor-Jen's mouth dropped. Bento-Tor's mouth dropped.

'And these.' Tanun pulled open the main compartment.

'How?' said Joor-Jen.

'Totally amazing, but Cassièl visited and told me to go up to weapons. Couldn't believe it. Place was empty and these were on the registration desk. We'll have to take it in turns because they're so heavy.'

Joor-Jen leant across and gave Tanun a big kiss on his cheek. 'Genius. But look what I have.' She tipped her rucksack up and out fell a boiler suit and pair of boots. From the pocket she pulled four 10/10s and two curved knives. 'I know you two seem to spend most of your time without clothes, but I expect Chyke'll be glad of these.'

Tanun's face reddened. 'I expect he will.'

'So, we have two 10/10s each and two knives each. What have you got, Bento-Tor?'

'Rope.' He shook the coil across his left shoulder. 'Carbon rope, suckers, tracking-locator, light-sticks, pack of mini-tools.'

Well, it's dark-time,' said Joor-Jen. 'Tanun? Do the alarm?'

Bento-Tor passed him the pack of tools and Tanun laid along the grid floor to reach the bottom hatch alarm box.

'This wire's been undone before.'

'That git Pen-Nan, probably,' said Bento-Tor.

Tanun sent the ladder back up and dropped to the ground. 'We should try to get halfway to the tunnel.'

Although the forest was dense and dark, the trails of missiles and DTGs lit up the tops of trees so that the line of three figures was often silhouetted against flashes to their right and left. When the frequency of booms and flashes had decreased, and the pink glow from the red suns had crawled over the horizon, Joor-Jen suggested they set camp before light-time, and volunteered to do first watch.

\* \* \*

Chyke heard the door, and from the shuffling guessed six enforcers had entered. Not XorX. Blindfold gone. He'd guessed right, but had to keep his eyes closed because of the light. Two undid his straps.

'There you go. No clothes, but you can't have everything.'

'Where's XorX?'

'Listen to him, asking all the questions.'

The enforcers sniggered.

'XorX is busy. Too busy for the likes of you. There's a war on, in case you hadn't noticed. She's commanding the assault on the pathetic domes. I expect yours has already surrendered.

'Doubt it.'

The slap across his face stung.

'Just because you're not strapped down, don't think you've got off lightly, sunshine. Two black eyes? You're a troublemaker.'

'XorX told us we can take you to our games room,' said another. 'Everyone's already excited, but we'll wait until dark-time when the Avena's flowing. Pretty boy like you? We'll have some fun.'

After the enforcers had left, Chyke rubbed his wrists and ankles and curled up on the bench. *So, it's started. Dicio and Percutio. I wonder what Tanun and Joor-Jen are doing. They certainly can't rescue me, they'll be too occupied defending their dome. Anyway, how would they get in here? There must be military everywhere. Funny, I can't hear any missiles or explosions. Just show how well constructed the domes must have been.*

* * *

At the tunnel, the three of them agreed Joor-Jen would lead with just one light-stick in case they needed the others later on.

'I don't think I'll ever get used to this tunnel,' said Tanun.

'Nor me,' said Bento-Tor.

'I think the stick will last until we're out,' said Joor-Jen. 'I know there's this light but we'd best be quiet. Never know who might be listening – above, behind, or in front!'

Despite the rocks and old wood making their footing hazardous, as the oval of light grew their pace increased. Joor-Jen told them they should ease out from the side of the tunnel and not in the middle.

'Seems clear,' said Bento-Tor. 'Now for the last stretch.'

# TWENTY-THREE: Way to Go

At the edge of the woodland, the three of them surveyed the dome but saw no activity.

'I think most have left as part of the attacking forces,' said Joor-Jen. 'Means there'll be mostly elderly, children, and invalids. Mostly.'

'That's good isn't it?' said Tanun.

'They can still fire 10/10s and use spears and bows and arrows,' said Bento-Tor. 'Could you, Tanun?'

'If ... they were attacking me ... I suppose so.'

'Your flesh won't care who an arrow's from.'

'No, it won't. I get it. But how could they use arrows and spears? It's barbaric. Like thousands of years ago.'

'We're regressing, that's for sure.'

'When are we going to run?'

'Soon,' said Joor-Jen. 'Remember. Keep low. Swerve. Go!'

Halfway to the dome they dropped flat as the roar of a missile grew deafeningly loud, passing only a few metres above them before swerving away from the dome and exploding two or three kilometres beyond.

'Activity,' said Bento-Tor.

Through their binoculars they could see two enforcers descending, but no others appeared.

'They'll be assessing the damage,' said Joor-Jen. 'See what recovery resources are needed. We're out of their sight line. Let's get there to give them a welcome. Run.'

When the two enforcers were about 50 rungs from the bottom, Joor-Jen and Bento-Tor fired their 10/10s. One enforcer tumbled to the ground but the other fell awkwardly and hung by her left leg. Bento-Tor took aim and made sure she didn't suffer. When they reached the leg of the dome, Joor-Jen opened the breast pocket of the enforcer on the ground and showed the others the access ring. 'Handy. Here, you have the 10/10, Tanun. Can you manage three?'

'I can if someone takes the rucksack for a bit.'

'I'll take it to start. Ready?'

When they reached the hanging enforcer, Bento-Tor took the access ring out of the breast pocket, put it in his and passed the 10/10 to Joor-Jen. He lifted the trapped knee and lower leg away from the rungs and the three of them watched the body bounce and turn all the way to the bottom. 'Shouldn't leave them there but we can't go back down.'

When they were a few rungs below the hatch, Joor-Jen reached up and inserted the access ring in the slot. Nothing. She half-whispered, half-called to Bento-Tor to pass his access ring to Tanun, who passed it to Joor-Jen. Nothing. She looked down at Tanun and Bento-Tor. 'Neither works. How can that be?'

'Someone's locked it from the inside, that's all,' said Bento-Tor. 'Added security. Wow, look over there.'

While hugging the rungs, they all looked left and saw a long missile cruise past less than 10 metres from the edge of the dome.

'That was close,' said Bento-Tor. 'That's the longest I've ever seen. 'Must have been at least a hundred metres.'

'Why was it going so slowly?' said Tanun.

'It wasn't, really. Just the size gives that impression. Probably doing 200. Dangerous up here.'

Joor-Jen asked Bento-Tor to pass four suckers to Tanun. They reminded him of large circs cut in half, except each was attached to the others by flexiwire. Joor-Jen pressed each sucker onto the hatch door.

'Need your little dischargers now, Tanun. We'll have to swap places.'

As Joor-Jen said this, a missile exploded on the ground about a kilometre distant, and they gripped the rungs tighter while they waited for the shockwave.

'Goodness,' said Tanun, 'they're getting nearer, aren't they?'

'Yes and no,' said Joor-Jen. 'What you're not seeing is the defence shield deflecting more than we know.'

'Not sure that's comforting.'

'I'll go over you. You climb when I'm level.'

Joor-Jen slid down over Tanun's back, making sure she always had one rung in her grip. Tanun climbed the few rungs to the hatch. Joor-Jen secured the flexiwire from the suckers around two rungs while Tanun fixed the dischargers to the suckers.

'Right, we're ready. Listen, Tanun, wait for another explosion and set them off at the same time as the boom. I'll pull the wire. The hatch might stay attached. Might not, so watch it.'

All three leant as flat against the rungs as they could, waiting for the next boom.

Tanun hit the remote. Joor-Jen pulled the wire. The hatch opened and cantilevered upwards, the four little explosions lost in the boom.

Tanun climbed into the hatch room and lowered a hand to help up Joor-Jen and Bento-Tor, who closed the hatch behind him.

'So far, so good,' said Joor-Jen, passing the rucksack back to Tanun.'

The internal door to the hatch room whooshed open.

Within a split second, Joor-Jen had twice fired her 10/10. Two enforcers crumpled and Bento-Tor and Tanun dragged the two bodies into the hatch room.

'That was lightning quick, Joor-Jen,' said Tanun.

'We'd be lightning dead if I wasn't. More on the way, probably.' She turned to Bento-Tor, 'Where does your tracker say?'

Bento-Tor read the screen. 'Left out of here, up five levels and 70 cells north. Here, Tanun, you'd better take it. I'll stay to guard the hatch. Good luck.'

'I'll leave a disc on this wall,' said Tanun.

The three of them embraced before she and Tanun checked the corridor outside and set off.

'I'd have thought this place would be heaving with people,' said Tanun.

'I expect they've clustered on the lower levels in case they're hit. Suits us. Here we are. Stand aside.'

When the elevator door opened, no one emerged.

'Level 735,' said Tanun, staring at the tracker as the elevator rose.

The elevator slowed. Tanun and Joor-Jen gave each other panicked looks.

'Level 735. Priority,' said Tanun.

The elevator sped up.

'I think it was stopping to let someone in.'

'Quick thinking, Tanun. How did you know to say that?'

'I remembered it from my trial and being handcuffed to an enforcer. They used it.'

'Genius.'

**Level 735**

'Stand to the side, in case,' said Joor-Jen.

Four enforcers appeared in the doorway. Joor-Jen and Tanun stepped forward.

'Hey!'

Joor-Jen killed the two on the right and Tanun the two on the left.

'Level 0,' said Tanun to the elevator and watched the door close.

'You get better each time,' said Joor-Jen.

'Aren't you the lucky one, then?' said Tanun with a knowing smile.

'70,' said Joor-Jen, pointedly ignoring Tanun's comment. 'That's a lot of cells. Even if the thing's accurate.'

After they had counted 69 cells, Tanun swiped the tracker screen to increase the granularity. 'It says this one. Try the access ring.'

Joor-Jen pushed the ring from the enforcer on the ground into the slot and the door whooshed open.

'Come on,' said Tanun, 'we can't help him.'

'I hope he was dead.'

'He was. Never seen so many wires. At least it wasn't Chyke. This should be it. Try the ring again.'

Whoosh.

'Hey you, you little git!'

Chyke leapt up from the bench and flung his arms around Tanun. Joor-Jen tossed in a boiler suit and boots from her rucksack and said she could give them one minute, no more.'

'Come on,' said Tanun, 'let me help you get this on. How you doing?'

Chyke pushed Tanun aside and leapt to the toilet to throw up. 'Sorry about that. Been worse. Look, sorry about being kidnapped. Twice. And,' he whispered, 'I'm really sorry about the whole Joor-Jen thing. I never meant to hurt you.'

'I know you didn't. I never meant to hurt you, either.

Can't get rid of the hurt, though. Helps knowing how much you love each other.'

'You're also the biggest git, big brother, for being too kind, too understanding. Know that?'

'Shut up a moment and tie your boots. Look. We might not even make it out. We've killed loads already.'

'Just you and Joor-Jen?'

'Bento-Tor stayed at the hatch.'

'That's brave.'

'We all are, but he's on another level. Right, now you've got something on, give me another hug.'

'Time to go, boys.'

'Here,' said Tanun and gave Chyke a 10/10 and a knife. 'Let's go.'

Tanun stuck a disk to the door wall of Chyke's cell.

Joor-Jen took the ring and made to go back the way they'd come, but Chyke said, 'Not that way. This way's better.'

'How do you know?' she said.

'I'm good at sneaking.'

Chyke ran along the familiar curved corridors with Tanun and Joor-Jen close behind. 'This one, this is the one!' he said, swerving right down a corridor.

'We've got to go down five levels,' said Tanun. 'Here – this elevator.'

'Stop. Not that one. It's an express. They'll all be using it. Use this one. A slower one.'

The three of them stood aside as the door opened. Empty.

'Level 230,' said Tanun. 'It'll be busier down there. Guarantee it.'

**Level 230**

'To the sides,' said Joor-Jen. 'Crouch low.'

When the door whooshed, eight enforcers in two rows of four faced them. None had the chance to fire. Tanun stuck a disc on the elevator side wall before the three of them jumped over the bodies and ran towards the hatch room. Around the curve of the corridor, they saw Bento-Tor, a 10/10 in each hand, firing in all directions.

'Quick! Run to me. I can cover you, I can cover you.'

As they ran towards the hatch room, an arrow lodged through Bento-Tor's left shoulder, causing him to drop the 10/10 from his left hand.

Joor-Jen, Tanun, and Chyke, firing continuously, piled into the hatch room behind Bento-Tor.

'They're gaining. We've gotta get out,' said Bento-Tor.

'Quick, Joor-Jen,' said Tanun, 'the ring.'

But the access ring didn't open the hatch.

'We're out of time,' shouted Bento-Tor.

'I know, I know,' said Joor-Jen. Then memory slapped her. How long ago was it? How could she forget? She reached into her breast pocket and pulled out Chyke's old access ring. 'Dump that one. Try this one.'

Tanun gave her a look, grabbed the ring and placed it in the circular recess. The outer hatch hissed open.

'You'd think they'd have reprogrammed that by now,' said Tanun, ducking a series of pulses. 'Just shows you how arrogant they are.'

'Go, Joor-Jen, hurry.' Bento-Tor pointed at the open hatch.

Joor-Jen climbed onto the rungs.

'What about you?' said Tanun.

'I'll hold them off. Love you, guys. It's Ok, really, I'm only a clone, aren't I?' Bento-Tor smiled from Joor-Jen to Tanun to Chyke. Joor-Jen sniffed, Tanun grimaced, and Chyke made a fist.

'Now you, Chyke,' said Tanun, breaking the spell. 'Fast as you can.'

Joor-Jen had disappeared. Chyke climbed onto the rungs and descended.

Tanun searched for the rungs with his feet. He called to Bento-Tor. 'Love you, man. You've gotta be away from here when those discs go. Get yourself down and we'll come back for you. That's a promise.'

Tanun slid down the rungs while the darkness was lit up by flashes reflected in the dome. A shockwave shook him and he lost his grip with his right hand and swung around the rungs with his left. As he struggled to stop himself from falling, Dodecahedron slid unnoticed from his pocket and tumbled to the waiting ground.

At the bottom, Joor-Jen and Chyke embraced until Chyke looked up at Tanun on the rungs. 'What was that?' Something just fell from the rungs. I saw it in one of the flashes. Landed over there.' He broke away from Joor-Jen and ran.

'Careful,' she called. 'Whatever it was might be a booby-trap.'

After scouring the area, Chyke dropped to his knees and swept the grass with his palms. A flash from an exploding missile lit up the area for a moment and in the darkness after, Chyke caught thin silver rays piercing the black and reaching to the sky. He crawled over and wrapped his fingers around Dodecahedron. "You total, total git of a stone. The trouble you've caused.'

'Did he throw it, or did he drop it?' said Joor-Jen when she'd caught up.

'Dunno. Bit of luck to find it.'

'He should be down any moment. We have to get to the woods. And we must swerve. Must swerve.'

After stabilising, Tanun slid down as fast as the heat of his gloves allowed, and when he hit the ground Joor-Jen pulled his arm and Chyke pushed his back as they set off, swerving for the woodland. Coloured cubes, energy pulses and arrows whizzed past.

'That'll teach you to play spies,' said Tanun as they ran. 'How was it this time?'

'Can't ... tell ... you ... brother,' Chyke said between breaths. 'I owe you. I was in your cell. Saw you'd carved your name. How the hell did you do that? I was just about to be taken to a special room. How can our Elders cooperate with evil things like that? What can the KimMorii have promised them?'

'What did they promise you?'

'You do not want to know.'

'Girls, I expect,' said Joor-Jen, making Chyke smile back at her.

'They're not our Elders anymore,' said Tanun. 'Can't answer it. Can't answer it. There are no answers, but we weren't going to leave you there. Or we'd die trying. We were forbidden from leaving our dome, but Bento-Tor had other ideas. He's something else.'

'He definitely is.'

'We must go back for him,' said Joor-Jen.

'I told him we would. He's got to be away before I blow the discs.'

After they'd run in to the woods for three kilometres, Tanun stopped and said, 'We should be far enough away by now. Get down.'

'But Bento-Tor. What if he's still in there?' said Chyke.

'He won't be. He's too good. Even with an arrow in his shoulder. Probably on his way here.'

The three of them dropped to the ground while Tanun

took a small metal rectangle from his pocket and tapped out a sequence of numbers. They all looked in the direction of the dome. And waited.

'Nothing's happened. Why isn't it working? Something must be wrong. I'll do a reset.'

Tanun punched in the numbers for a second time and the three of them again looked towards the dome.

'I'll wipe the memory. One more go.'

Nothing happened.

'You're the expert,' said Joor-Jen. 'If you can't do it, no one can. The only possible reason is they've disabled the explosives ... which means enforcers are on their way. We'd better run for it.'

'Hold on. Dodecahedron's gone. It was in my pocket'

'It hasn't gone,' said Chyke. 'You dropped it as you were coming down. Here, you'd better have it.'

But as Chyke said this, streams of coloured cubes from enforcers zoomed past their heads. As they scrambled up and ran farther into the wood, coloured cubes hit trees and branches and exploded, sending shrapnel and splinters in all directions. When they emerged from the wood, Tanun pointed and shouted, 'The tunnel's around this hill. Quick.'

But they didn't make it to the tunnel. On their feet. The largest, longest, loudest explosion any of them had ever heard, lifted them up and hurled them through the air and along the twisted railway track. Their bodies scudded along the old sleepers and broken rails in a knot of limbs. The aftershock blew trees above them toward the tunnel and lifted the three of them off the ground again. As each body crashed down, stones, branches, leaves, and debris rained from a hurricane wind. Each drifted in and out of consciousness, unable to tell how long, but in time the wind eased, and only scorched leaves and twigs fell from the stars. Tanun was lying face down around three metres from Chyke and Joor-Jen, who was lying half across Chyke's chest. A shard of rail extended fifteen centimetres from Chyke's lower-right rib.

'That explosion wasn't me,' Tanun spat through the blood and dirt. 'Didn't have those megatons.'

'Must have been the KimMorii,' said Joor-Jen, trying to wipe dirt from her face. 'We don't have anything that powerful. Ironic, it was your dome they blew. So that's the reward everyone got for working for them.'

Once Tanun had pushed himself onto his hands and knees, he saw thin silver rays shining up from a glassy-black oval-shaped stone, two metres away. The rays pierced the leaves and branches and soared towards the sky. He crawled through the debris and knelt as he cupped the stone in his hands.

'My poor Liberii,' said Cassièl, appearing in the space between Tanun and Chyke and Joor-Jen. He knelt close to Tanun. 'So good you rescued Chyke. Better taking his chances with you two than dying in his old dome.'

Tanun grimaced, looked up to Cassièl and held out Dodecahedron on his bloody palm. Through his swollen lips he burbled, 'You'd better have this, Cassièl.'

Cassièl clasped the proffered hand between his own, the sticky stone in the middle. 'Thank you, Tanun. You are an exemplar. Your name will live in eternity.'

'Actually, Cassièl, I dropped it coming down the rungs. Or rather, it slipped from my pocket. An explosion nearly blew me down and I didn't know Dodecahedron had gone. But Chyke found it, though he must have let it go in that last explosion.'

Cassièl pressed Tanun's hand and took the stone. 'Rest, Tanun. You are going to be Ok. Let me see to Chyke.'

Chyke's eyes were closed, but he mumbled, 'I've lost Dodeca– '

'No, Chyke, you have not,' said Cassièl, placing his left hand on Chyke's head. 'Do not worry about that. Must have come loose. Tanun has just offered it to me and for some reason, on this occasion, I could take it. Chyke, you are a remarkable boy. Your name will live in eternity. Cassièl stroked Joor-Jen's bloody crew-cut. Thank you for what you have done for them, Joor-Jen.'

She lifted her head from Chyke's chest, looking from the deadly splinter to Cassièl, her face twisted in anguish.

Cassièl shook his head. 'I will give you both a moment.' Cassièl stood up and walked into the shadows.

Joor-Jen brushed the muck and blood from Chyke's face, stroked his bloody lips with hers, fused into a kiss.

When she broke away, Chyke opened his eyes and smiled up at her, dribbling blood. 'Thanks.'

'Chyke ... hear me out. I want you to know ... I'm so sorry for all the hurt I've caused. I mean it. But, but I loved you both, I really did. Although,' she sobbed, 'I always loved you more than Tanun.'

'I knew that.' Chyke's chest whistled. 'Tanun knew it, too ... and loved you all the more for it.' He grimaced. 'No brother like him.' Tears ran from the corners of his eyes and he coughed more blood but kept his smile. 'Hold me, Joor-Jen. Way to go, you know? If you have to, couldn't be better than this.'

She pushed his matted blond hair from his forehead, caressed his face with her hands and stared into his green eyes until his smile relaxed. A teardrop landed on his mouth before she laid her head once more on his chest.

Tanun crawled over and stroked Chyke's cheek with one hand and Joor-Jen's with the other.

'Tanun and Joor-Jen, listen,' said Cassièl. 'I can take you both to Amnia. We can heal you there.'

'Thanks, Cassièl,' said Tanun, looking up. 'I'll be Ok. Just bruises, I think, and I'm used to those. No matter what, I'm going to make them pay for my brother. I'll not abandon the others. They let me be part of their family and I'll fight with them.'

'I understand. You are a good man, Tanun. Joor-Jen?'

Joor-Jen barely raised her head. 'I'll stay, too. If Tanun,' she reached for his hand, 'after everything I've done, will let me, I'll fight with him.' She gently pushed his head down so they were both lying on Chyke's chest. 'Anyway, we've got to find Bento-Tor. You see,' she looked up to Cassièl and clasped Chyke's and Tanun's hands between hers, 'I rather like collecting boys.'

The End
of
Dodecahedron

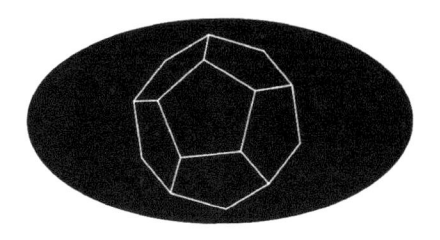

The Story
of the
Second Stone

Printed by: Copytech (UK) Limited trading as
Printondemand-worldwide.com
9 Culley Court, Bakewell Road, Orton Southgate,
Peterborough, PE2 6XD